THE WORLD'S BEST sex WRITING 2005

The World's Best
sex
Writing 2005

EDITED BY MITZI SZERETO

Thunder's Mouth Press
New York

THE WORLD'S BEST SEX WRITING 2005

Published by
Thunder's Mouth Press
An Imprint of Avalon Publishing Group Inc.
245 West 17th St., 11th Floor
New York, NY 10011

First printing December 2005

Library of Congress Cataloging-in-Publication Data is available

ISBN: 1-56025-772-5
ISBN: 978-1-56025-772-1

9 8 7 6 5 4 3 2 1

Book design by Maria Elias
Printed in the United States of America
Distributed by Publishers Group West

Contents

Introduction ix

The Big Ooooooohh!
Jonathan Margolis
The Sunday Herald (Glasgow),
May 2, 2004 1

Andrea Dworkin, 1946–2005
Katha Pollitt
The Nation, May 2, 2005 7

The Sex Files
Ben Ehrenreich
LA Weekly, December 10–16, 2004 11

The Brothel Creeper
Sebastian Horsley
The Observer (London),
September 19, 2004 25

Performance Anxiety
Steven Rinella
Nerve.com, January 31, 2005 31

Focus 19
Alasdair Palmer
The Sunday Telegraph (London),
December 19, 2004 41

Forbidden Science
Barry Yeoman
Discover, August 2004 47

Head Case
Amy Sohn
New York magazine, June 21, 2004 59

Does This Make My Labia Look Fat?
Sarah Klein
Metro Times (Detroit), March 9, 2005 63

The Holy Fuck
Toni Bentley
from *The Surrender: An Erotic Memoir* 77

Exclusive Interview: Harry Reems
Paul Fischer
Moviehole.net, February 11, 2005 81

Sex, Guys, and Fruit Flies
Dave Barry
The Miami Herald, October 3, 2004 91

When Oral Sex Results in a Pregnancy
Sherry F. Colb
FindLaw.com, March 9, 2005 95

Toy Story
Steven Kurutz
Nerve.com, November 1, 2004 105

Deep Gidget
Rabbi Marc Gellman
Newsweek.com, February 25, 2005 117

from *Callgirl*
Jeannette Angell 121

The Invention of Patient Zero
David France
New York magazine, April 22, 2005 143

Tahitillation
Nigel Planer
The Erotic Review, September 2004 161

XXXchurch Wants No More XXX
Julia Scheeres
Wired News, May 20, 2004 167

The Battle Over Birth Control
Gretchen Cook
Salon.com, April 27, 2005 171

Now I Feel Whole Again
Christine Aziz
The Independent (London),
February 15, 2005 179

from ***Blue Days, Black Nights: A Memoir***
Ron Nyswaner 185

Faces of Ecstasy
David Steinberg
Sexuality.org, May 21, 2004 193

Violence in the Garden
Polly Peachum
Submissive Women Speak.net, September 2004 201

Last Rites
Augusten Burroughs
Salon.com, June 28, 2004 239

About the Contributors 243

About the Editor 251

Permissions 253

Introduction

"Sex is the mysticism of materialism and the only possible religion in a materialistic society."

—Malcolm Muggeridge

Human beings have always been interested in sex, which undoubtedly goes some way toward explaining why there's so much written about it. The question remains, however, are we any more enlightened about human sexuality and its impact on contemporary culture than our cave-dwelling ancestors were? Did they sit around the fire engaging in lively discussions on the subject save for uttering the occasional "Ugg"? Probably not. But then, they didn't live in our complex times or deal with the complex issues we face today.

Why so much discourse about sex? There's a hunger at work here—a hunger for knowledge, whether it's presented in an academic fashion or one of prurience. Yet it often seems that the more we learn, the less we know. Too many of us live in a vacuum, unaware of the sexual issues affecting the lives of others, be it disease, exploitation, or subjugation. What happens to a few can impact an entire society. And already has.

As our civilization continues to advance, so too, does the great maze of all things sexual. Nothing is simple anymore, not even the ways in which we choose to have sex. There are so many areas to consider: law, public opinion, even one's own physicality. According to French philosopher Michel Foucault, "Sexuality is a part of our behavior. It's part of our world freedom. Sexuality is something that we ourselves create." Indeed, he certainly has a point. Human beings are multifaceted creatures, and so too, are their belief systems and codes of morality, all of which impact on their sexuality. What outrages one person might be perfectly acceptable to another. The same goes for the legislating of our sex lives by the institutions we know as government and the church. Very often we find ourselves in situations not of our making—as victims of institutions run amuck. There are many such examples included in this anthology, ranging from the ridiculous to the horrific. The same can be said for medicine and technology, and those who either control or seek to control it for financial, religious, or humanitarian gain. Add to this the commercial (and often gonzo) marketing of women as sex objects, and we can see that not a lot has changed since the dawn of the women's liberation movement, thus lending credence to poet, essayist, and feminist Ana Castillo's assertion that "Human sexuality has been regulated and shaped by men to serve men's needs." Then there are the repercussions of our so-called sexual freedom, with more than one article in this collection attesting to the fact that there's no such thing as a free lunch. And let's not forget the simple orgasm. Or maybe not so simple?

Unlike our club-wielding ancestors who were probably more concerned with the day's kill than sexual politics, today we have newspapers, magazines, books, and the Internet—all of which are capable of disseminating information from as near as next door to as far as the outer reaches of Mongolia. Information is what advances us on the evolutionary scale. And an informed individual is one who can offer something substantive to the debate. You may not always like or agree with what's being said, but at the very least it will cause you to think—and perhaps think about it in an entirely new way.

The World's Best Sex Writing 2005 offers journalism, essay, memoir, and opinion from the world's most respected writers and journalists, and even some unexpected voices. It contains work that challenges, provokes, outrages, offends, educates, enlightens, and, yes, entertains. It might even make you laugh. From America's Deep South to the streets of Iran, this anthology presents an engaging critical commentary on the sexual culture of our times—on where we are today, and if we should even be here. Whether we're discussing sex consumerism, reproductive rights, pornography, AIDS, the body perfect, or the suppression of female sexuality, *The World's Best Sex Writing 2005* will force you to look beyond your own bedroom window.

I hope you will agree that this anthology includes the best sex writing the world has to offer for this year.

—Mitzi Szereto
June 2005

SEX

The Big Ooooooohh!

For thousands of years, the orgasm has been the elusive Holy Grail of the bedroom, yet we could never quite put our finger on it. Not satisfied with past investigations, Jonathan Margolis embarked on a two-year quest to get the low-down on sexual climax. His findings make for stimulating reading . . .

By Jonathan Margolis
The Sunday Herald (Glasgow) / May 2, 2004

There can be few subjects surrounded by as many myths as the human orgasm. It was my own belief in a few of them that set me off on a two-year quest to discover the truth about this most sought after, yet elusive, of bodily pleasures.

The specific spur was an article by a celebrated and outspoken female journalist mocking the male obsession with Viagra. What is it with you blokes, she was asking, and your belief that we girls actually want you to be able to hump away for half an hour like a pneumatic broomstick?

When are you going to get it? she went on. Don't you understand that it's quite boring watching you attempt athletic records—especially when we know you're only doing it by reciting football results in your head? And don't you realize we get quite sore down below decks while you think you're impressing us?

I didn't regard myself as sexually naïve at the time—you wouldn't after being married twenty-seven years—but this was news to me. My own performances, I would rate as neither Celtic nor East Stirling, but mid to upper Division One. Please excuse me for imposing my private life on you on a Sunday morning, but for me, I would feel I was giving poor value if I lost the plot within a minute, but was doing quite well at five minutes or so.

As for the Holy Grail of simultaneous, mutual orgasm through straight, penetrative sex with a woman, I had long since suspected that this was strictly for the Champions' League. With a variety of foreplay, during-play, and after-play methods, I'd always muddled through somehow, and received remarkably few complaints, but you couldn't help wondering what it would be like to experience what the media, the movies, and popular mythology strongly suggest is "the real thing."

It was only after burrowing deep into centuries of sexological literature and research, plus initiating my own discreet inquiries with friends and acquaintances (I don't know if people confide in me because I'm seen as harmless or because as a former investigative reporter I'm good at winkling information out of them) that I discovered that "the real thing" is 99 percent the creation of soft pornography and male self-delusion.

Ancient cultures more sexually literate than ours recognized that real, loving sex was far more than a mechanical docking maneuver. Even the Bible recognized the importance of foreplay. To the later embarrassment of both Christian and Jewish religious fundamentalists, the erotic Song of Solomon contains a clear request from a woman to be stimulated manually: *"Let his left hand be under my head and his right hand embrace me."*

In real life, the full house sex we dream of—a mutually perfect period of lithe thrusting followed by perfect orgasm *a deux*—barely exists. Typically, my female friends will have experienced it once or twice, in a variety of propitious circumstances, while my male friends will *suspect* it happened once or twice, but can't be sure because they have wondered for years if the woman in question was faking it.

Even Sting, who made every man in the world feel inadequate (and every woman, I suspect, a bit queasy) with his suggestion that using "Tantric" methods he could keep sex going for eight hours, later confessed that he'd forgotten to mention this included dinner, a movie, and four hours of pleading.

"But don't you long for a guy who can keep it up for hours?" I would ask women friends. "Sometimes," they'd reply, "but if that happens, you suspect he's either incredibly vain, didn't fancy you—or was gay."

There's a serious point here, too. It has long been known, that the best way to avoid premature ejaculation (whatever your definition of that may be) is to have sex with a woman you don't find attractive—or at least to pretend you don't find attractive. Su-nii-ching Fang Nei Chi, author of a seventh century A.D. sex manual, *Secrets of the Bedchamber,* wrote: "Every man who has obtained a beautiful crucible will naturally love her with all his heart. But every time he copulates with her he should force himself to think of her as ugly and hateful."

In many ways, the liberated twentieth century, when we threw off the terrible hypocrisy and misogyny that had afflicted sex in the Western world since Christianity took hold, was as beset by sexual myth as earlier times. One of my other spurs for writing a history of the orgasm was a 1920s sex manual I found in a second hand shop in North Berwick.

It cost 50 pence and was called *Ideal Marriage: Its Physiology and Technique* and was written by a retired Dutch gynecologist named

Theodore van de Velde. It is very probable that readers' parents will have a copy hidden away at home even today, as it remained the most explicit textbook on sex until well into the 1960s.

Van de Velde's was an incredibly brave and outspoken book, as well as being far too explicit for any modern tabloid. But incredibly, its basic premise—that the *only* "valid" sex was penetrative intercourse resulting in mutual simultaneous climax—was the most corrosive form of delusion moonshine. Van de Velde wrote in all seriousness that it was only possible for a women to orgasm when a man ejaculated inside her.

Such piffle probably did as much damage in the twentieth century as Sigmund Freud's bizarre 1905 idea that the clitoral orgasm in women is "infantile" and there was something wrong with any woman who didn't have the "mature" vaginal orgasm in regular penetrative sex.

Today we know that all orgasms are clitoral, even if there are some rather fine ones to be had by stimulating specific points in the vagina such as the G-spot. We also know from countless academic sex surveys that it is extremely rare for women to orgasm by intercourse alone, and that the vast majority never will without a bit of help. Yet Freud's nonsense remained the gold standard of thinking on sex well into the 1970s—and millions of educated people still believe in it.

Even the sex gurus of the modern era got it wrong. The celebrated Masters and Johnson said that a man who couldn't keep thrusting away in sex for more than fifteen minutes was suffering from premature ejaculation. A lot of men, me included, would regard such a feat as Olympian.

Masters and Johnson also said that no woman could or should be satisfied with less than three to five orgasms per sexual encounter. I think it would be fair to say most women in the real world would regard such a marathon as remarkable to say the least.

These influential Americans were, at least, more on the money than a British book of 1953, *Sex In History* by Gordon Rattray Taylor, which does not contain the word *orgasm*. Even its polite alternative, *climax*, only appears twice.

But have we, by contrast, become too orgasm-fixated in today's world, when every women's magazine contains its mandatory monthly article on orgasm and even our cautiously prudish tabloids have started, although only in just the past two years, to run long features on orgasm?

Religions, of course, and clergy in particular, have been unhealthily obsessed with sex for 2,000 years—in their case with stopping anyone from enjoying it. They prefer not to explain how this fails to be a grievous insult to the God who gave us, uniquely among all creatures, organs and mechanisms designed purely for pleasure.

But the modern, democratic cult of orgasmic satisfaction for all has made orgasm something akin to a human right for the first time since the ancient Hebrews (and the early Muslims a couple of thousand years later) wisely made it a religious necessity for a husband to satisfy his wife in bed.

On the whole, I think, this has to be a good thing. One of the downsides of the more equal distribution of sexual pleasure, however, is that we are inclined to overemphasize the importance of orgasm as a life objective, at the expense of the wonderfully pleasurable stuff that could, and should, precede and follow it.

Good sex—and, again, the ancient Indians, Chinese, Greeks, Jews, Arabs, and others (Sting included) knew this—begins hours, or even days, before the much-vaunted act itself.

The soundbite-age compulsion to get to the end of the story

quickly is like watching touchdowns without the football in between—unsatisfying and ultimately a little bit boring. This, in turn, leads to sex being slightly disappointing, frankly, for those of us who are encouraged virtually from childhood to regard it as a principal reason for being cheerful.

The result, to quote a wonderfully named Canadian anthropologist, Professor Lionel Tiger, is that "The gross national pleasure is lower than it ought to be."

The culprit, of course, which didn't exist for the lucky ancients, is time pressure. We are too busy and stressed for good sex. At the kind of Yuppie dinner parties where people used to discuss the G-spot, I have found that in recent years, couples have started talking almost competitively about how much they *don't* have sex any more.

One friend three years ago coined the expression DINS—Double Income, No Sex—and within a few months, it had spread virally all over the Internet. DINS struck a chord with people all over the world who thought they were alone in finding they were "doing it" once a month if they were lucky.

Don't fear for the future of good sex, though. The growth area these days is amongst the over-fifties. Men were always up for it past fifty if they were lucky enough to be unaffected by illness or impotence. But today up to 70 percent of post-menopausal women—women who were young and sexually assertive in the 1960s and '70s—are reporting that their sexual feelings are returning with a vengeance in later life.

Free of the fear of conception, the interruptions of small children and the stresses of worrying about career and finances, they are discovering sex (when, crucially, they can find a like-minded partner) is at last delivering the orgasmic delights they strove for in their youth.

The golden age of the orgasm may yet arrive, but in a way nobody quite foresaw.

sex

Andrea Dworkin, 1946–2005

By Katha Pollitt
The Nation / May 2, 2005

I first heard of Andrea Dworkin in 1968. She had been arrested in an antiwar demonstration and jailed at the old Women's House of Detention in Greenwich Village, where male doctors subjected her to brutal internal exams. Her name was in the news because she had gone public with her story. My good, kind, radical, civil libertarian parents thought this was ridiculous. What did she expect, this privileged white woman, this "Bennington girl"? It wasn't that they didn't believe her, exactly. It was that they didn't see why she was making such a big, princessy fuss. It was like getting arrested and complaining about the food.

Andrea Dworkin died on April 9 at fifty-eight—she of the denim overalls and the wild hair and wilder pronouncements. Although she denied ever uttering the most famous soundbite attributed to her, that all intercourse is rape, she came pretty close: "Fucking is the means by which the male colonizes the female"; "in seduction, the rapist often bothers to buy a bottle of wine." She argued that pornography was an instruction manual for rape, that women had the right to "execute" rapists and pedophiles; toward the end of her life she declared that maybe women, like the Jews, should have their own country. The counsel of despair, and crazy, too—but by then Dworkin was ill, not much in demand as a speaker and several of her major books were out of print. The 1980s were long over: On campus, the militant anti-rape marches and speakouts of Take Back the Night had morphed into cheery V-Day, which marries antiviolence activism to a celebration of women's sexuality.

The antipornography feminism Dworkin did so much to promote seems impossibly quaint today, when Paris Hilton can parlay an embarrassing sex video into mainstream celebrity and the porn star Jenna Jameson rides the *New York Times* bestseller list. But even in its heyday it was a blind alley. Not just because porn, like pot, is here to stay, not just because the Bible and the Koran—to say nothing of fashion, advertising, and Britney Spears—do far more harm to women, not even because of the difficulty of defining such slippery terms as "degrading to women," a phrase that surely did not mean the same thing to Dworkin as it did to the Christian conservatives who helped make the antiporn ordinance she wrote with Catharine MacKinnon briefly law in Indianapolis. Like the temperance movement, antiporn activism mistook a symptom of male dominance for the cause. Nor did it have much to do with actually existing raped and abused women. "For God's sake, take away his Nina Hartley videos" is not a cry often heard in shelters or emergency rooms. If by magic pornography vanished from the land, women would still be the second sex—underpaid, disrespected, lacking in power over their own bodies. Rape, battery, torture, even murder would still be hugely titillating to both sexes, just as in Shakespeare's day, and women would still be blamed, by both sexes, for the violence men inflict on them. What made Dworkin's obsession with pornography so bizarre is that she herself should have known it for a diversion. After all, she frequently pointed out that male dominance is entwined with our very notion of what sex is, with what is arousing, with what feels "right." Like Foucault (who, as Susan Bordo pointed out, usually gets credit for this insight), Dworkin showed how deeply and pervasively power relationships are encoded into our concepts of sexuality and in how many complex ways everyday life normalizes those relationships. "Standards of beauty," she wrote in *Woman-Hating* (1974), "describe in precise terms the relationship that an individual will have to her own body. They prescribe her motility, spontaneity, posture, gait, the uses to which she can put her body. They define precisely the dimensions of her physical freedom. And of course, the relationship between physical freedom and psychological development, intellectual possibility, and creative potential is an umbilical one." Somewhere along the way, she lost interest in the multiplicity and the complexity of the system she did much to lay bare.

Dworkin was an oversimplifier and a demagogue. She wouldn't debate feminists who opposed her stance on porn, just men like Alan Dershowitz, thus reinforcing in the public mind the false impression that hers was the only feminist position and that this was a male-female debate. There is some truth to Laura Miller's quip in *Salon* that "even when she was right, she made the public conversation stupider." But, frankly, the public conversation is usually not very illuminating, and on the subject of women has been notably dim for some time. At least Dworkin put some important hidden bits of reality out there on the table. There *is* a lot of coercion embedded in normal, legal, everyday sexuality: Sometimes the seducer is a rapist with a bottle of wine. A whole world of sexist assumptions lay behind my parents' attitude back in 1968: This is what happens to women who take chances, male brutality is a fact of life, talking about sexual violence is shameful, "Bennington girls" should count their blessings. Polite, liberal, reasonable feminists could never have exploded that belief system.

Andrea Dworkin was a living visual stereotype—the feminist as fat, hairy, makeup-scorning, unkempt lesbian. Perhaps that was one reason she was such a media icon—she "proved" that feminism was for women who couldn't get a man. Women have wrestled with that charge for decades, at considerable psychic cost. These days, feminism is all sexy uplift, a cross between a workout and a makeover. Go for it, girls—breast implants, botox, face-lifts, corsets, knitting, boxing, prostitution. Whatever floats your self-esteem! Meanwhile, the public face of organizational feminism is perched atop a power suit and frozen in a deferential smile. Perhaps some childcare? Insurance coverage for contraception? Legal abortion, tragic though it surely is? Or maybe not so much legal abortion—when I ran into Naomi Wolf the other day, she had just finished an article calling for the banning of abortion after the first trimester. Cream and sugar with that abortion ban, sir?

I never thought I would miss unfair, infuriating, over-the-top Andrea Dworkin. But I do. And even more I miss the movement that had room for her.

The Sex Files

When you find yourself in one and can't get out.

By Ben Ehrenreich
LA Weekly / December 10–16, 2004

The stories of Bill Smith and of a man whom, with all apologies for unoriginality, I will call John Doe, begin not in this bright age of sexual freedom, but beneath the shadow of decades gone by. Back then, from a distance at least, Bill Smith could have passed for a postwar California Everyman. Tall and blue-eyed, he grew up on the East Coast and joined the Air Force not long after the bombing of Pearl Harbor. He returned from Europe in 1944, stopping at home just long enough to meet a girl and marry her before shipping off to a base in Northern California—en route, he thought, to the Pacific. But the war ended, and Smith and his bride found they preferred the West, so he enrolled in an aviation school just outside of Los Angeles. Eventually the pair settled in the suburbs, in Torrance. They had a daughter. Smith got a job in the defense industry. The sun shone almost every day. Smith was neck-deep in the New American Normal, except that he was gay.

This was of course no more unusual in the 1950s than it is today, but it was not something a man could afford to be open about. Social stigma aside, sex between men was not only deemed a sign of madness (the American Psychiatric Association considered homosexuality a pathology until 1973), but it was also a crime. Even just kissing, dancing, or holding hands in sight of a vice cop was enough to get a man dragged off to jail. What gay scene existed in those pre-Stonewall days was completely underground. "They had gay bars," Smith remembers, "but they were raided all the time. Often they would have vice squads in there undercover, and if you even put your arms around or hugged a guy, first thing you know, 'You, you, you and you—you're under arrest.' And that was it." But desires have a way of getting their way. Smith had been involved with men before he married, and even had a lover for two years in the service. For his first few years out of the military, Smith says, "I kind of got away from the gay thing." After several years of marriage, though, Smith found himself cruising the bars. His wife, he now believes, knew all along—"She just didn't want to accept it."

On the night of January 13, 1956, Smith dropped by the Borderline, a gay bar between Compton and South Gate. "I met a fellow there," he recalls, "and we got to talking. We went out to the car and pulled around a corner off the main street, and we were trying to set up a dinner engagement to get together and all that. We weren't there a few minutes when all of a sudden the Sheriff pulled up."

Smith was, he says, "scared to death." Not only his family but his livelihood was in jeopardy—in 1956, homosexuals were little more welcome in the defense industry than communists. The two men were driven to the Sheriff's station in Norwalk, where they were separated and questioned. Smith can laugh about it now: "All they were trying to do is find out if we were performing sexual acts, which we weren't—then. I mean, we were planning on it for later." The police kept him in Norwalk for the night, and then transferred him to county jail, booked on a charge of "suspicion of sexual perversion."

He spent a second night there in a cell reserved for gays. "I had to sleep on the floor there were so many of us," he remembers, but the atmosphere was congenial enough. In the morning his cellmates found him a comb and a razor so he could clean himself up for court, where he would ultimately plead guilty to a reduced charge of vagrancy. (At the time section 647(a) of the California penal code defined a vagrant as "every lewd or dissolute person." The statute was frequently used against gays. Just two slender parentheses differentiated it from section 647a, a now obsolete child-molestation statute.) The judge gave Smith two years of probation and a fine of $500. As part of his probation, he was required to see a psychologist, which he did, Smith says with a chuckle, until "after a few sessions, he started cruising me."

Aside from the residual fear and humiliation, and a further dent in an already troubled marriage, Smith's ordeal, he thought, was over. "I tried to erase it all, like it never happened," Smith says. His wife performed a similar feat of repression. "It was never discussed," Smith says. "Over all those years, I kind of forgot about it." The Smiths stayed together until the late 1970s. They never divorced and, though they now live apart, remain close.

Today Bill Smith lives with a younger man named Dave in an upscale, gated trailer park somewhere in the Southern California desert—he would rather I didn't tell you precisely where. Smith is eighty years old and, despite some recent health troubles, remains fit, sharp and charming. He wears a thin mustache and combs his white hair back with a Clark Kent curl in front. Smith had no cause to think of his arrest outside the Borderline for nearly five decades, until this past February, when he opened his mailbox and, he tells me, sitting in his kitchen, photos of his grandchildren propped on an end table a few feet away, he "just about came unglued."

The first letter was mysterious—a form letter from the city of Torrance, which hinted only that the "Torrance Police Department is currently investigating a case in which the report indicates you have some involvement," and ended with a polite but ominous request that Smith please contact a Detective Keith Thompson "regarding your obligation to register under California Penal Code section 290(a) within five days from the date of this letter, or a WARRANT will be issued for your arrest."

Four days went by before Smith was able to get Thompson on the phone. Thompson explained, Smith says, that Smith was required to register as a sex offender. When he protested, Thompson told him, Smith says, "that it was better for me to register first and then clear up any problem later." The detective promised to mail him the paperwork for his registration.

That envelope arrived two days later. With immaculate bureaucratic logic, Thompson (who did not return calls requesting an interview for this story) instructed Smith in a cover letter to contact him again after he had registered, promising that at that point, "I will obtain copies of your court docket in order to determine if you are required to register." He sent along a transcript of Smith's criminal record. To Smith's horror, the printout identified him as a "convicted sexual offender," and listed his 1956 conviction not as 647(a), the vagrancy charge, but "647a Annoy Molest Children."

Smith was, he says, "completely devastated." He wrote to Thompson, who again responded, Smith says, "You register, then we'll try to clear it up." Smith wrote to the courts requesting his case files. The Compton court wrote back that his records had been destroyed. (Courts generally do not keep records of misdemeanor convictions for longer than ten years.) The county had nothing, and neither did Torrance. Smith wrote to Sacramento, and the state eventually sent him a copy of his arrest report, which recorded that he was charged with "Suspicion/Sex Perversion," but said nothing about the final disposition of his case.

Smith put together a packet of documents to try to plead his case to Thompson. In response, Smith says, Thompson called to tell him that if he didn't register by the next day, a squad car would arrive at his home, and he would be arrested. So on February 23, Bill Smith drove to his local Sheriff's station and reluctantly signed his name to the forms declaring him a successfully registered sex offender.

Though it has not always been strictly enforced, California has had a sex-offender-registration statute in effect since 1944. At the time, very few states had similar laws on the books, and none as harsh as California's, which required anyone convicted of certain sex crimes to register with the police once a year or whenever they changed addresses, for the rest of their lives, because, as the statute had it, "The Legislature deemed them likely to commit similar offenses in the future." Those crimes included not just rape and child molestation, but even the most innocent and consensual touching between adults of the same sex, so long as a vice cop was around to declare it "lewd and dissolute." Child pornographers and those convicted of bestiality, or of raping "a person incapable of giving consent," on the other hand, faced no such restrictions.

So by law, Bill Smith was made to register as a sex offender immediately after pleading guilty to vagrancy. Five workdays after his birthday every year thereafter he should have marched down to the Sheriff's station to re-register. He never did and, he says, never knew he had to. But some things have changed since 1956. In 1975, the California Legislature repealed the laws criminalizing sodomy and oral copulation between consenting adults by a margin of one vote (the lieutenant governor had to be called in to break a tie). The laws stayed on the books—section 288a of the penal code, for instance, today bans oral copulation, but since 1975, it has only applied to nonconsensual oral sex, or oral sex with minors. Four years later, the state Supreme Court ruled that the phrase "lewd and dissolute conduct" in the antivagrancy statute—which was still, twenty-three years after Bill Smith's arrest, being used to arrest gays in stings on public bathrooms and parks, gay bars and adult bookstores—was "unconstitutionally vague."

Attorney Jay Kohorn, who in the 1980s shepherded a number of landmark gay-rights battles through the California courts and is now the assistant director of the California Appellate Project (a nonprofit entity operated by the state bar association), says that the sex-offender registry was nonetheless "clogged with these guys who didn't do anything but engage in consensual acts of brief touching with a vice officer." In 1983, in a case litigated by Kohorn, the California Supreme Court ruled that requiring gays convicted under vagrancy laws to bear the "ignominious badge" of lifetime sex-offender registration constituted cruel and unusual punishment. Earlier this year, in a vastly different political climate, the court, now composed of a majority of Pete Wilson appointees, reversed that ruling. (Registration, the justices determined, is purely "regulatory in nature" and not punishment at all.) In the meantime, though, the Legislature removed the vagrancy offense of which Bill Smith was convicted from the list of crimes requiring registration.

Something happened in the 1990s. Until then, registration appeared to be on its way out, an artifact of a more fearful and repressive age. By the early '80s, California was one of only five states requiring any kind of sex-offender registration. But in July of 1994, seven-year-old Megan Kanka was raped and killed by a convicted sex offender living across the street from her New Jersey home. Within two years, all fifty states and the federal government had adopted some version of what would come to be known as Megan's Law. Just three months after Kanka's murder, California updated its registration law, expanding the list of qualifying crimes and establishing a 900 number which residents could call to find out if a sex offender lived among them. (Later the state would make CD-ROMs of the registry available for the public to search at local police stations.) When the new law took effect in 1995, the state Department of Justice began updating its old files, and local police departments began making efforts to track down everyone who had ever registered, or who they thought should have.

The problem with this approach—enforcing something as potentially catastrophic as the registration mandate based on a database patched together out of old and often incomplete, misleading or entirely missing records—became evident soon enough. In 1997, the *Los Angeles Times* published an article about other men in Smith's situation—some of them married, some as old as ninety, guilty at the most of an ancient, slightly-too-public indiscretion, nonetheless getting letters in the mail lumping them in with pedophiles and rapists, demanding that they show themselves at their local police stations and declare themselves sex offenders. The ACLU got involved, and, in late 1997, the Legislature revised the state's registration laws, establishing a legal process through which gay men could appeal to have their names removed from the registry. The following year, the Department of Justice was also required to comb through the list and weed out anyone who shouldn't be on it. One thousand and nine names were removed, says Hallye Jordan, Attorney General Bill Lockyer's press secretary, "on the basis that evidence in their folder showed that [their offense] was consensual." Another 706 were taken off the list because, it turned out, they were dead. In addition, Jordan says, "We had twenty-two letters from registrants asking to be deleted." Of those, only one was denied.

But in the years after that, the state has done nothing more to solve or even evaluate the problem, and nothing has been fixed. The Justice Department did the bare minimum to comply with the law, and since that 1998 review, has kept no records that would allow it to gauge the present accuracy of the registry. No one knows how many people have been removed from the registry in the meantime, or how many have even applied to be removed, simply because, Jordan admits, "Nobody's counting."

John Doe was not among the lucky 1,009. John Doe is, of course, not his real name, which he has been anxious to protect since early 1996, when he opened his mailbox and was alarmed to encounter a letter from the Attorney General's Office informing him that he was required to register as a sex offender. Ten years younger than Bill Smith, Doe is also blue-eyed if not quite as tall. Slender and tan, he wears jeans and a blue T-shirt and a thin gold chain around his neck. Sitting straight-backed on the plush, floral-patterned couch in the living room of his Hollywood Hills home, Doe recounts the events of September 6, 1973.

That afternoon, as he tells the story, he had just finished shopping at a pottery store on Robertson Boulevard and stopped in the small park wedged between Robertson and San Vicente to use the bathroom. "When I went in, there was a guy standing on one wall and a guy standing on the other wall," Doe says. "Well, I'm not stupid. I figured it's a pickup joint. But I didn't care, I had to really go to the bathroom." The moment he was done, he says, "One guy comes over and touches me. I pushed him away and the other guy arrests me." Another officer entered the bathroom, and Doe says, put both him and the man who touched him in cuffs and drove them to the West Hollywood Sheriff's station.

"I panicked," Doe says. He worked in the entertainment industry in a sufficiently public role that he was terrified of publicity. Doe was in a longterm relationship with another man and was open about his sexuality to his friends, but, he says, "I was raised in a society where you didn't flaunt it. People weren't out like they are now." When a Sheriff's deputy gave him a "release form" to sign, he signed it without reading it. "Not bright," he says now. The man with whom he was arrested called a lawyer who agreed to represent Doe as well. (Doe says he does not remember the attorney's name, and kept no record of it.) When the lawyer arrived, Doe says, he was shocked to find that Doe had been charged with a felony. "I said, 'What's a felony?'"

A few weeks later, Doe met the attorney at the Beverly Hills Courthouse. "He said, 'Just plead guilty and you'll pay a little fine and have a short probation.' I said, 'What am I pleading guilty to?' He said, 'You're pleading guilty that you were looking for sex,' and I said, 'But. . . .' He said, 'Just plead guilty. It'll be fine—it's been reduced to a misdemeanor.'"

Eager to put the arrest behind him, Doe says, he pleaded guilty. He never knew, he claims, exactly what charge he pleaded to. He just wanted it all to be over as quickly as possible. He was fined, he says, "either $140 or $160" and given, he remembers, three months' probation. "I left. I gave the lawyer his money. That was the end of it."

Until 1996, that is, when the envelope from the Attorney General's Office arrived. "I just freaked," he says. Doe wrote to Sacramento for his file. "I got the sheet of paper, and it said 'oral copulation.' I'm positive I was never told I was pleading to that," Doe says. He called the courts to request his records and had the same experience as Smith—nothing had been preserved; no one had anything. He hired another lawyer who had his conviction vacated. He figured he was all right.

He wasn't. Despite the expungement of his conviction, and the Justice Department's 1998 review of its records, John Doe's name was not removed from the list of those required to register, presumably because the state possessed no evidence indicating that his offense was consensual, or, for that matter, any evidence about his case at all. In 1998, he got a phone call from a Hollywood LAPD officer telling him to come down and register. Doe's lawyer brought the expungement paperwork to the station house and, for a little while, everything once again seemed settled. Then in February of this year, another officer from the Hollywood station called to tell Doe he had to come in and register. His lawyer accompanied him to the station and spoke with the police. Afterward, standing outside the station, Doe says, the lawyer told him he shouldn't have to register and that everything would be fine, but that Doe should be sure never to get pulled over. He gave Doe the phone number of a bail bondsman, just in case. Doe was, he says, "a nervous wreck."

Soon thereafter, the police called again. Everything was not fine. The officer, Doe says, told him, "'You've got to do something right away. The charge that is on here goes under the umbrella of child molestation.' I said, 'What are you talking about?'"

The bind in which Doe found himself, ironically, derives from the Legislature's 1975 decriminalization of gay sex. After 1975, oral copulation remained a crime and 288a of the penal code stayed on the books—it just no longer applied to consenting adults. If police officers today see 288a on an arrest record, unless they are extremely well-informed, they have every reason to assume that either a minor or violence was involved. But if the fog of amnesia and naiveté surrounding Doe's story at times strains its credibility, one thing is clear: Had he been convicted of any offense involving either force or a minor, he would have been sentenced to far more than probation and a small fine.

This was precisely the sort of mix-up that the 1997 amendment to the registration law was intended to fix, but no matter. After that, Doe says, "It was always on my mind: How can this be? How can this have happened when . . . nothing happened? It's been very, very, very, very difficult to try to think about—if this isn't resolved, then how do you live with it? Because we live in a witch-hunt world in many ways, and it's frightening."

Late this February, Bill Smith came across an article in the *Desert Sun* about a bill that proposed posting California's sex-offender registry on the Internet. (Governor Schwarzenegger signed the bill into law in late September.) The article quoted an ACLU lobbyist opposed to the law. "My whole worry," Smith says, "was that I should die and leave a legacy of being a child molester with my family." He wrote to the ACLU immediately, and found a sympathetic ear in ACLU staff attorney Ben Wizner. Wizner wrote to the Attorney General's Office, explaining that Smith had been convicted of vagrancy under penal code 647(a), for which registration is no longer required—not, as the state had it, under 647a, the now-obsolete child-molestation statute. Somehow, over the years, the parentheses dropped out.

It worked. Wizner soon heard back from Sacramento: Smith's name had been removed from the registry, and Torrance police had been told to lay off. More than forty-eight years after his arrest, Smith's tribulations were finally over.

Sacramento was somewhat less accommodating with John Doe. Wizner wrote a similar letter to the Attorney General's Office on Doe's behalf in July, and received a perfunctory reply from a low-level official stating that until Doe could provide evidence that he should not be, he would remain on the register. "The penal code is pretty specific," says the Justice Department's Hallye Jordan. "You can be removed from the registry if you prove that the crime was consensual."

In Wizner's view, this unconstitutionally left the burden of proof in Doe's lap. "He was in effect being told he had to produce documents that don't exist, or he's a sex offender." Late in August, the ACLU wrote another letter, this time directly to Lockyer, and incorporating an implicit threat of a lawsuit. At around the same time, Doe heard from the LAPD again. His birthday was approaching, and the officer insisted that he register. Wizner accompanied Doe to the police station, and he registered.

On October 5, Doe got a call from the ACLU. Lockyer's office had backed down. In the absence of any evidence of his guilt, Doe would not be required to prove his innocence. His name would be removed from the registry. "This has been a nightmare for so long," Doe says, "that when I heard it I couldn't believe it."

If the endings of Bill Smith and John Doe's stories are happy enough, innocent gay men are still being lumped in with rapists and child molesters. And despite the 1997 fixes to the registration law, getting your name removed from the registry is still, to use Doe's word, a "nightmare." "Even with a lawyer working on [John Doe's] case," Wizner points out, "it took months to get him off the list—that's one person."

"More and more this is a database society," Wizner observes, "but a database is only as good as the information that's put into it. And once you're in one, it's very hard to get out of it." If the government's reliance on databases—from the sex-offender registry to the No-Fly List to California's ever-growing gang-member database—continues to expand, Wizner warns, "Many people are going to experience some version of what [John Doe] is going through."

sex

The Brothel Creeper

As the debate rages about the pros and cons of legalizing prostitution, Sebastian Horsley—a man who's slept with more than 1,000 prostitutes—gives a controversial and candid account of his experience of paying for sex.

By Sebastian Horsley
The Observer (London) / September 19, 2004

I remember the first time I had sex—I still have the receipt. The girl was alive, as far as I could tell, she was warm and she was better than nothing. She cost me £20.

I was 16 then and I'm forty-one now. I have spent twenty-five years throwing my money and heart at tarts. I have slept with every nationality in every position in every country. From high-class call girls at £1,000 a pop to the meat-rack girls of Soho at £15, I have probably slept with more than 1,000 prostitutes, at a cost of £100,000.

I am a connoisseur of prostitution: I can take its bouquet, taste it, roll it around my mouth, give you the vintage. I have used brothels, saunas, private homes from the Internet and ordered girls to my flat prompt as pizza. While we are on the subject, I have also run a brothel. And I have been a male escort. I wish I was more ashamed. But I'm not. I love prostitutes and everything about them. And I care about them so much I don't want them to be made legal.

In English brothels you shuffle into a seedy room so dim you can only meet the girl by Braille. But in New York last year I sat on a four-poster bed while ten girls paraded in front of me one by one, like bowls of sushi on a carousel. "Hi," they would say, "I'm Tiffany," "I'm Harmony," "I'm Michelle," and I would rise and kiss them. It was so touching, so sweet, so kind. There should always, no matter what, be politeness. It is the way the outside world should work, selfishly but honestly.

The great thing about sex with whores is the excitement and variety. If you say you're enjoying sex with the same person after a couple of years you're either a liar or on something. Of all the sexual perversions, monogamy is the most unnatural. Most of our affairs run the usual course. Fever. Boredom. Trapped. This explains much of the friction in our lives—love being the delusion that one woman differs from another. But with brothels there is always the exhilaration of not knowing what you're going to get.

The problem with normal sex is that it leads to kissing and pretty soon you've got to talk to them. Once you know someone well the last thing you want to do is screw them. I like to give, never to receive; to have the power of the host, not the obligation of the guest. I can stop writing this and within two minutes I can be chained, in the arms of a whore. I know I am going to score and I know they don't really want me. And within ten minutes I am back writing. What I hate are meaningless and heartless one-night stands where you tell all sorts of lies to get into bed with a woman you don't care for.

The worst things in life are free. Value seems to need a price tag. How can we respect a woman who doesn't value herself? When I was young I used to think it wasn't who you wanted to have sex with that was important, but who you were comfortable with socially and spiritually. Now I know that's rubbish. It's who you want to have sex with that's important. In the past I have deceived the women I have been with. You lie to two people in your life; your partner and the police. Everyone else gets the truth.

Part of me used to enjoy the deception. There was something about the poverty of desire with one's girlfriend. Sex without betrayal I found meaningless. Without cruelty there was no banquet. Having a secret life is exhilarating. I also have problems with unpaid-for sex. I am repulsed by the animality of the body, by its dirt and decay. The horror for me is the fact that the sublime, the beautiful and the divine are inextricable from basic animal functions. For some reason money mitigates this. Because it is anonymous.

What I hate with women generally is the intimacy, the invasion of my innermost space, the slow strangulation of my art. The writer chained for life to the routine of a wage slave and the ritual of copulation. When I love somebody, I feel sort of trapped. Three years ago I was saved. I found a girl whom I could fall in love with . . . and sleep with prostitutes with. She sends me to brothels to sleep with women for her. I buy her girls for her birthday and we go to whorehouses together. I am free forever from the damp, dark prison of eternal love.

A prostitute exists outside the establishment. She is either rejected by it or in opposition to it, or both. It takes courage to cross this line. She deserves our respect, not our punishment. And certainly not our pity or prayers.

Of course, the general feeling in this country is that the man is somehow exploiting the woman, but I don't believe this. In fact, the prostitute and the client, like the addict and the dealer, is the most successfully exploitative relationship of all. And the most pure. It is free of ulterior motives. There is no squalid power game. The man is not taking and the woman is not giving. The whore fuck is the purest fuck of all.

Why does a sleazy bastard like me like whores so much? Why pay for it? The problem is that the modern woman is a prostitute who doesn't deliver the goods. Teasers are never pleasers; they greedily accept presents to seal a contract and then break it. At least the whore pays the flesh that's haggled for. The big difference between sex for money and sex for free is that sex for money usually costs a lot less.

But it is more than this. What I want is the sensation of sex without the boredom of its conveyance. Brothels make possible contacts of astounding physical intimacy without the intervention of personality. I love the artificial paradise; the anonymity; using money, the most impersonal instrument of intimacy to buy the most personal act of intimacy. Lust over love, sensation over security, and to fall into a woman's arms without falling into her hands.

Having an instinctive sympathy for those condemned by conventional society, I wanted to cross the line myself. To pay for sex is to strip away the veneer of artifice and civilization and connect with the true animal nature of man. Some men proudly proclaim that they have never paid for it. Are they saying that money is more sacred than sex?

But one of the main reasons I enjoy prostitutes is because I enjoy breaking the law—another reason I don't want brothels made legal. There is a charm about the forbidden that makes it desirable. When I have dinner every evening in Soho I always think: isn't scampi delicious—what a pity it isn't illegal. I'm sure I am not alone in this. Even Adam himself did not want the apple for the apple's sake; he wanted it only because it was forbidden.

As for the girls, the argument is that making it legal will somehow make it safer, but Soho has one of the lowest crime rates in the country. Anyway, crime and risk are part of the texture of life.

Indeed, Freud tells us: "Life loses interest when the highest stake in the game of living, life itself, may not be risked." Risk is what separates the good part of life from the tedium.

I decided to ask my Claudia, my favorite prostitute. I first spotted her in the street in Knightsbridge ten years ago and was so taken by her haunted beauty that I decided to follow her. There was an air of great quality about Claudia. The faces of English girls look as if there are not enough materials to go round. They have thin lips and papery eyelids, box jawbones, prominent Adam's apples and withered hearts. Claudia looks Mediterranean—her lips are full and curly, her nostrils flared, her eyes black and as big as saucers.

She walked and I stalked all the way to Soho and down Brewer Street. No. No way. She couldn't be! She turned, and walked into a brothel. I couldn't believe it. I could fuck Raquel Welch for £25.

When I ask if she wants prostitution legalized, she reacts violently: "No way! I tried to take a regular job a few months ago. After tax and national insurance I was left with practically nothing. So I came back here. On a good day here I can take £500. I don't have a pimp, so after paying the overheads and the maid I've got more than enough." There you are. Income tax has made more liars out of the British people than prostitution.

I know a little bit about the business side. Some years ago I became a madam and a male escort. I turned one of the rooms in my flat in Shepherd Market into a knocking shop and joined an escort agency. I went into prostitution looking for love, not money. That said, I always took cash. The women wanted company, someone willing to please at the midnight hour, and straight sex. It was nerve-wracking wondering if I was going to be able to get it up or get on, but at least I had a valid reason for liking my lovers—they paid me. I didn't care if someone called me a whore and a pimp.

So you see, I have always been a prostitute by sympathy. As for the rest of society, prostitution is the mirror of man, and man has never been in danger of becoming bogged down in beauty. So why don't we leave it alone? Or learn to love it, like me? Sex is one of the most wholesome, spiritual, and natural things money can buy. And like all games, it becomes more interesting when played for money. And even more so when it is illegal.

Hookers and drunks instinctively understand that common sense is the enemy of romance. Will the bureaucrats and politicians please leave us some unreality? I know what you are thinking. That it's all very well for people like me to idealize whores and thieves; to think that the street is somehow noble and picturesque; I have never had to live there. But so what? One day I will. Until such time, I have to pay for it. How else would someone young, rich, and handsome get sex in this city? Yes, yes, I know. Prostitution is obscene, debasing, and disgraceful. The point is, so am I.

sex

Performance Anxiety

There's no right way to watch your friend's wife strip.

By Steven Rinella
Nerve.com / January 31, 2005

There's an old saying: "You can pick your friends, you can pick your nose, but you can't pick your friend's nose." I've never actually tried to pick a friend's nose, but I recently found myself in a situation that brought the saying to mind. Afterwards, I tried to update the saying with a more adult theme, but sadly, my revision lacked the lyrical quality and poetic tidiness of the original. But here goes anyway: "You can pick your friends, you can watch your wife masturbate, but you shouldn't watch your friend's wife masturbate."

If someone had given me that piece of advice a few years ago, I would have said, "Well, that seems perfectly obvious." But when the invitation to watch my friend's wife masturbate came straight from my friend himself, I was lured unwittingly down a treacherous path.

The friend was Bruce. We met because I wanted to work for him. Bruce had long, oily hair, and he lifted weights. His muscular physique contradicted his attire: a really nice leather dress coat and shiny, almost feminine loafers. I often thought that he looked too sleazy to star in an action movie but not sleazy enough to be a hit man. Lucky for him, his job fell somewhere in between.

Bruce was involved, as he described it, in the "pleasure industry." He managed a cadre of strippers whom he'd hire out for bachelor parties. His was the only such business in Bozeman, Montana. My buddy, Matt, worked for Bruce as a security guy. On a job night, Matt would pick up the stripper at her apartment, drive her to the location of the engagement, then stand in the corner of the room and act like a tough guy while she flossed her ass crack with twenty-dollar bills.

Matt informed me that Bruce was looking for other guys to fill in on busy weekends. To be on the business end of the pleasure industry—to be an insider rather than an outsider—sounded like the perfect job to me. When Matt warned me that Bruce would never hire a guy he didn't know personally, I decided that it was high time for Bruce and me to strike up a friendship. So I started hanging out where he hung out, buying him drinks, asking about his business, and acting like a standup guy. Eventually, I scored. He asked me if I wanted to go with him to a strip club the next Saturday, to watch some girl named Twilight do a special weekend-only performance.

"I've got the night off," Bruce said. "It'll just be a good time on the town."

"Right," I said, though I had a hunch that this was actually a sort of audition. He wanted to see how I handled the heat. I tried to express some professional interest.

"Who's Twilight?" I asked. "She work for you?"

"Twilight?" He looked at me with a smug smile. "Twilight's my wife."

The coolness I conveyed upon learning that Bruce and I would be watching his wife perform nude on a stage was completely artificial.

I've never been an avid strip-club patron, but I've been around enough to know that the personal life of a stripper is best left to the stripper herself; there is a distinct separation between the performance and the personality of the performer. This separation doesn't just happen on its own; it requires work on the part of the audience. The work involves *not* wondering about the stripper's private life, and *not* trying to imagine that the stripper would think you were cool if she just got to know you. The fact is: You're not cool, because you're paying to watch a woman take off her clothes. You are even less cool because that woman does not want to fuck you.

Beyond the fact that I was going to violate my own rules about how to behave around strippers—watching a stripper as her husband's guest definitely violates her privacy—I was also violating a much more serious code of ethics, the one that legislates how dudes are supposed to behave toward each other's girlfriends and wives. For example, you should not stare at your friend's girlfriend's breasts, no matter how wonderful they are. When your friend's girlfriend tells a story, you should look her in the eye and listen. When she gets up to go to the bathroom, you shouldn't follow her out with your eyes. And, above all else, you shouldn't tell your friend that his girlfriend is hot, unless she isn't, which makes it okay to say that she is, because you're just trying to make him feel good about himself.

This strip club situation was going to turn the ethical code on its head. If I didn't stare at Bruce's wife's tits, wouldn't that be rude? And if I looked her in the eye, wouldn't that invite a level of intimacy inappropriate to the occasion? And if I didn't tell Bruce that she was hot—which I suspected she would be—wouldn't that be impolite? Following the code in this situation was going to make me look like an asshole.

By the time I got into Bruce's car Saturday night, I had decided that getting into Bruce's car wasn't such a good idea. But on the way to the club, Bruce acted so cool and natural about everything that I started to feel better. I decided that I should just act cool and natural, too.

The doorman at the club shattered our ruse of total coolness.

"No fucking way, guys," he said. "Bruce, you know the rules."

"Dude, come on. Don't embarrass me. I've got a friend standing here."

"It's not my rule, man."

Bruce walked back out across the gravel parking lot. His hair swung angrily against the collar of his leather jacket. We got into the car.

"What was that all about?" I asked.

"Mr. Dickhead there is the only bouncer who actually pays attention to that rule."

"What rule?"

"No dancers' boyfriends or husbands allowed," said Bruce. He fired his car up and revved the gas.

"I guess that makes sense."

"The fuck it does. If I gave a shit about guys paying my wife to take off her clothes, would I be in the business I'm in? I fucking doubt it."

Instead of being upset about our dismissal, I was relieved. The bouncer had a point. In fact, the bouncer had *my* point: Exotic dancing is a sort of private, anonymous act. It's not for the dancers' husbands and the husbands' buddies. I was ashamed we'd even tried to get in. What had I been thinking?

Bruce pulled out of the parking lot. Instead of heading back to the highway, though, he shot his car straight across the road to a bar that looked like a log cabin. We sat in the bar for an hour, drinking, as Bruce grew increasingly agitated. Every minute or two, he got up to look out the window toward the club, checking to see if the bouncer's car was gone.

"They switch shifts at midnight, and I'm friends with the next dude," he assured me.

On his sixth or seventh look, he pumped his fist in the air. "Show-time," he said. We drove back across the road.

The new bouncer gave us a nod and sent us through the door. Bruce made a beeline for two chairs in the center of the front row and we sat down. A dark-haired woman was dancing around on the stage, opening her labia with her fingertips and watching the ceiling. She seemed distracted. She had a big bruise on her hip, pierced nipples and breasts that lay far out to the sides of her chest. Almost telepathically, I just knew this wasn't Twilight. I was reluctant to confirm my suspicion, though, because it wouldn't have looked too cool to be like, "Hey, is that your wife? . . . Well, is *that your* wife?" There was a scattering of bills on the stage when she finished, and she walked around picking them up like she was collecting dirty socks from her bedroom floor. My question about her identity was resolved when Bruce leaned over and whispered in my ear, "Jessica's pretty lame."

The next dancer was looking pretty goddamn good. Wearing thigh-high boots and nothing else, she strutted out like a runway model, one boot placed authoritatively in front of the other. A shiny cylinder of metal dangled from her clit ring on a little chain. She approached the edge of the stage, just inches away from us.

Holy shit, I thought, *it's Twilight.* Suddenly, I didn't know what to do with my hands. I adjusted myself in my chair and tried to prevent any blood from flowing into my penis by pinching it tightly between my legs. From the corner of my eye, I tried to discern whether Bruce was watching her or me. He was watching her, his fingers pressed contemplatively to his chin. Then the DJ's voice rose up over the music. "Say good evening to . . . Fantasia!"

I loosened my legs and let things go their own way. Fantasia folded her arms and gave everyone in the front row a look of dramatic disapproval, as though we were all in a police lineup and had just tried to pass off some ridiculous alibi. Then she shook her head, turned and wiggled her ass in our faces. Bruce tilted his head for a better look; I tilted my head. Bruce laid a few bills on the faux-leather rail; I laid down a few bills. Fantasia reached between her legs and grabbed the little piece of swaying metal. It was a miniature flashlight. She aimed the light from between her legs, to interrogate us all. I found the performance intoxicating, even though the light wasn't turned on. Some guys behind us were screaming, "Your light's not on! Your light's not on!" She pointed the light at herself, verified the complaint, and snapped it to get it working again. When the light lit up, everyone clapped. I thought it was a little funny, but Bruce was miffed. "Fucking assholes," he said.

When Fantasia finished her third song, she slipped back through the curtains. Bruce explained that the club runs three strippers per night. The math was simple: two strippers down, Twilight to go. The music switched to an upbeat, jazzy number as Twilight parted the curtains. She had on thigh-high stockings held in place with garter belts. Her seemingly natural blonde hair was streaked with dark brown highlights. Her breasts were small and firm, with nipples that angled upward.

Unlike the other performers, Twilight was sort of chatty with the audience without actually chatting. She started at the back corner, or stage right. Each guy, in his turn, got a little eye-to-eye contact, and a little eye-to-asshole contact. She interspersed her one-on-one treatments with a brief interludes of pole dancing, but she always came back to where she left off. If a guy slipped her some bills, she did not let the gift go unacknowledged. Discreetly, she would come in nice and close to the man and move her middle finger down in between her legs to give herself a quick oscillation or two.

Twilight was working toward Bruce and me in a counter-clockwise motion. As she drew near, I felt a dreadful, horrible sinking feeling in my stomach. It was a feeling I recognized as guilt. All my apprehensions about this moment peaked in intensity. I felt like standing up and screaming, "This is a man's wife we're all coveting! Go home!" Instead, I dug into my wallet. I wanted to have a bill handy in case Bruce pulled out a bill. All I had was a ten, which was twice the amount I'd given to Jessica and Fantasia. Twilight still seemed pretty far away, and I knew she'd get to Bruce before she got to me. I sat there waiting, like how you wait in your car for a cop to walk up after he pulls you over. I was sweating so bad that the ten in my palm felt like I'd fished it out of a rain gutter.

Then something horrible occurred to me: Bruce wouldn't give Twilight money; they were married! They filed a joint tax return! It wouldn't be practical or reasonable for him to pay his wife for a lap dance.

So I was now entirely without guidance. I had to decide for myself whether I should keep my money and look like an unappreciative tightwad, or pay my buddy's wife to masturbate in my face. Wasn't it enough that I came here? Did I really need to take things to the next level?

I knew I only had about a minute to think. After a second, I came up with a brilliant idea: I'd go take a piss, thereby missing her passage. Then, without warning, there she was. It was as though she had arrived via sci-fi teleporter. She'd skipped Bruce and was smiling down at me. Stupidly, I looked right over at her husband. He looked at me. I gave him the dopey smile that I should have been giving to her. He smiled and nodded his head to the beat of the music. I thought I should probably say something to Bruce. Something like, "Right on, bro." But instead I finally looked at Twilight. Her face was no where to be seen. Instead, I was glaring into the moistened passage where Bruce had undoubtedly found countless pleasures. I assumed the facial expression of someone looking at a painting in a gallery: unequivocal appreciation, but also objectivity.

Within seconds, she was on to the next guy. I felt intense relief. Then I looked down. I was still holding the stupid bill in my hand. Bruce had to see it, curled there in my lap. I felt as though I was clutching his rent money, something that rightfully belonged to him and his wife. Twilight had earned that money. But to fork it over at that point would have been even more awkward than if I had paid in time. I opened and closed my sweaty fist around the bill. Then I plopped it down on the stage. It lay there in a wet, folded clump.

When her set finally ended, Twilight came by to pick up my cash. I almost wished then that she'd just do it, just give herself a delicate, pleasurable touch. Instead, she bent at the knees to pick up the bill, like a polite woman in a skirt. As she rose, she slapped her ass, right in my face.

What the hell does that mean? I wondered. Then she was gone. Bruce led me to a booth against the back wall. Within seconds, Twilight came through a door and took a seat next to me.

Bruce said, "Steve, Twilight. Twilight, Steve."

I sat there uncomfortably. If I had been at a poetry reading, I would have said something like, "I liked that one poem about your mom. You know, the last one." I thought I'd better say something, to show that I would be able to make appropriate small talk with my strippers when driving them to and from engagements. But nothing seemed quite right: "Wow, that dancing was very exotic." Or, "I like the way you apply glitter to the inside of your vagina." Or, "Man, did you see that one guy? He really liked your ass." Instead, I sat there like a bump on a log until Bruce and Twilight decided to go to Denny's for a snack. Then I excused myself and called a cab. On the way home, I speculated that I would not hear from Bruce again. And I was right.

Focus 19

sex

Under Iran's "divinely ordained justice," girls as young as nine are charged with "moral crimes." The best that they can hope for is to die by hanging. As one young woman awaits sentence and another faces death, Alasdair Palmer reveals the Iranian legal system's shocking barbarity toward children. Zhila, thirteen, will not see school or home again. The last thing she will see will be stones hurtling toward her head.

By Alasdair Palmer
The Sunday Telegraph (London) / December 19, 2004

"My mother doesn't visit me in prison. If you see her, tell her she promised to bring me cheese curls and chocolate. And she shouldn't forget to bring my red dress."

Those pathetic words may be among the last utterances of a nineteen-year-old girl, identified only as Leila M., who has been condemned to death in Iran for "acts incompatible with chastity."

According to Amnesty International, Leila has a mental age of eight. What evidence there is of her life so far records an existence of unrelieved misery and brutality. She was sold into prostitution at the age of eight by her parents. She recalls the experience of when her mother "first took me to a man's house" as "a horrible night. I cried a lot . . . but then my mum came the next day and took me home. She brought me chocolate and cheese curls." Forced by beatings and threats to continue "visiting men" from that night onward, she became pregnant and had twins when she was fourteen. She was punished with 100 lashes by the Iranian courts for giving birth to illegitimate children.

Leila was bullied back into her degrading and demeaning work. Earlier this year, she confessed to the authorities that she had been working as a prostitute since she was a child—perhaps because she thought that they might help her escape her miserable existence.

The courts did respond by pulling Leila out of prostitution, but they also imprisoned her and used her confession to convict her of "moral crimes," for which the judges have decided the appropriate penalty is death. They dismissed evidence from doctors and social workers that she has a severe mental handicap. This week, Iran's Supreme Court, which by law must confirm every death sentence imposed by the lower courts, will rule on whether to uphold her execution.

There is every indication that the Supreme Court will decide that Leila must die. Earlier this year, they upheld a sentence of death on sixteen-year-old Atefeh Rajabi. Atefeh had also been convicted of "acts incompatible with chastity." In her defense, she said she had been sexually assaulted by an older man. The judges did not care. So, on August 16, at 6 A.M., Atefeh was taken from her cell and hanged from a crane in the main square of the town of Neka.

Witnesses report that she begged for her life as she was dragged kicking and screaming to the makeshift gallows. She shouted "repentance" over and over again—a gesture which, according to Islamic law, is supposed to grant the accused the right to an immediate stay of execution while an appeal is heard.

Atefeh's cries were in vain. Haji Rezaie, the judge who presided over her trial, put the noose around her neck himself. He said he was pleased to do it. "Society has to be kept safe from acts against public morality," he insisted. He ordered that her body be left hanging from the crane for several hours so people could see what happened to teenagers who "committed acts incompatible with chastity."

In the case of Hajieh Esmailvand, a young woman found guilty of adultery with an unnamed seventeen-year-old boy, the Supreme Court has not only confirmed the death sentence imposed by the lower court, but changed the means of death from hanging to execution by stoning. Hajieh's original sentence had been for five years' imprisonment followed by death by hanging. A month ago, the Supreme Court annulled her jail sentence—but only so that Hajieh could be stoned before December 21, and with the recommendation that she should be.

In the next two days, it seems likely that Hajieh will die from wounds caused by stones thrown by "executioners." The Iranian Penal Code states that women should be buried up to their breasts before being stoned. Article 104 is specific about the type of stones that should be used when a woman is to be punished for adultery. They "should not be large enough to kill the woman by one or two strikes, nor should they be so small that they could not be defined as stones." Hajieh will die slowly, in agony, buried in sand, as officials lob correctly sized stones at her head.

It is a fate that also awaits Zhila Izadyar, a thirteen-year-old girl from the northern province of Mazandaran. She has been sentenced to be stoned to death after her parents reported that she had had an incestuous relationship with her fifteen-year-old brother and had become pregnant by him.

Zhila has already received a "preliminary punishment" of fifty-three lashes. A representative from Iran's Society for the Protection of Children's Rights has managed to visit Zhila in prison. She found the thirteen-year-old in a desperate state, in solitary confinement and unable to keep down food. She has not been allowed to see her child.

"I am scared. I want to go home," said Zhila. "I want to go back to school like the other children." But if Iran's judges have their way, Zhila will see neither her school nor her home again. She will be buried up to her neck and the last thing she will see will be stones hurtling toward her head.

The barbarity toward children of the Iranian legal system is all the more surprising in that it contradicts the international legal obligations on the treatment of children, which the Iranian government has adopted. Iran is a signatory both to the International Convention on Human Rights and the Convention on the Rights of the Child, both of which explicitly forbid the execution of minors—let alone their killing by stoning.

Even Iran's chief justice has seemed to recognize that, although stoning is prescribed by Sharia law as the punishment for women who have sexual relations with men to whom they are not married, pelting a woman to death with rocks counts as excessively cruel. Two years ago, he ruled that, while stonings should still be the nominal punishment for adultery and premarital sex, that sentence should be routinely commuted to execution by hanging.

It appears from the fate in store for Zhila Izadyar, however, that his commitment to the de facto abolition of stoning was about as sincere as the Iranian government's commitment to the Convention on the Rights of the Child. There are no plans to change any of the provisions of the Penal Code that relate to children, and which state that girls as young as nine can be executed (boys have to reach the age of fourteen before they can be killed).

Many Iranians are revolted by the brutality and injustice of their judges' attitude to children. Shadi Sadr, an extremely brave lawyer who represents Atefeh Rajabi's family, has filed a suit against the judiciary for wrongful execution, and is preparing a murder charge against the judge who hanged her.

While fundamentalist mullahs still hold on to power in Iran, her suit is unlikely to succeed. Indeed, those who are disgusted by judicial decisions cannot even safely express their condemnation of a system that not only hangs children, but beats them to death in public: Kaveh Habibi-Nejad, a fourteen-year-old boy, suffered this fate on November 12 for eating on the streets during Ramadan. Witnesses said that they thought he died because "the metal cable being used to flog him hit his head."

Mahbobeh Abbasgholizadeh, an Iranian academic, was arrested on November 1 after having queried some aspects of Iranian justice in a speech she made at a conference. She was held for a month before being released and charged with "acting against the security of the country." If she is convicted, it could mean an indefinite prison sentence.

The European Union has said that it is ready to "intensify" political and economic ties with Iran if the Iranian government takes steps to allay international concerns over its involvement in terrorism and the abuse of human rights. But the Islamic administration seems to care more about protecting what many of the religious hierarchy regard as "divinely ordained justice" than achieving fresh political and economic concessions from the EU. Britain, France, and Germany, acting on behalf of the EU, have already agreed to further trade links with Iran, after Tehran agreed to suspend its uranium-enrichment process, which could yield material suitable for nuclear bombs.

For Hajieh Esmailvand and Zhila Izadyar, the prospects are bleak. The best they can hope for is to die by hanging rather than being stoned. As for the mentally retarded Leila M.—she seems likely to hang in public before Christmas.

sex

Forbidden Science

What can studies of pornography, prostitutes, and seedy truck stops contribute to society?

By Barry Yeoman
Discover / August 2004

Yorghos Apostolopoulos was at his office at the Emory University School of Medicine in Atlanta last October when his red voice-mail light started glowing. When he picked up the phone, he heard a somber voice. "We need to speak," said the caller, a program officer at the National Institutes of Health, which funds Apostolopoulos's research on infectious disease. Her voice was drained of its usual casualness. "Don't have any of your assistants call," she said. "I want to speak with you personally."

Apostolopoulos is a confident Athenian with a mop of salt-and-pepper hair and an intensity that belies his compact frame. With the NIH's help, he has been pursuing a cutting-edge question about human behavior: How do networks of people—in particular, long-haul truck drivers—work together to accelerate the spread of an epidemic, even when some of them don't know one another? Epidemiologists have long connected the spread of HIV in sub-Saharan Africa with truckers who get infected on the road and bring the virus home to their wives and girlfriends. But does the same hold true in the United States?

Working with a team of ethnographers, who study different cultures, Apostolopoulos and his partner Sevil Sönmez burrowed into the hidden world of truck stops, first in Arizona, then in Georgia. They began mapping the overlapping groups of people who come into contact with drivers: prostitutes (sometimes called lot lizards), drug suppliers, cargo unloaders, and male "truck chasers," who fetishize drivers. The researchers conducted extensive interviews to understand how truckers' occupational stresses led to depression, drug abuse, and unprotected sex. And they have collected blood, urine, and vaginal swabs from drivers and members of their social network to map how infection travels from state to state.

Apostolopoulos considered his work essential, but not everyone agreed. That's why the NIH officer was calling: Apostolopoulos's name had topped an alphabetical listing of more than 150 scientists whose research was being challenged by conservative political activists. An eleven-page list of NIH-funded grants was circulating around Capitol Hill and had been sent by a congressional staffer to NIH's Maryland campus. Now the Emory research was being targeted by a group called the Traditional Values Coalition. "Wait until you see how angry the American people get when they discover . . . NIH [has] been using federal tax dollars to study 'lot lizards,'" coalition director Andrea Lafferty declared in an open letter. "What plausible defense can be constructed for 'investigating' the sexual practices of prostitutes who service truckers?"

Many, though not all, of the grants on the hit list involved research into human sexuality. Each had been funded after rigorous peer review. But Lafferty raised a provocative question: Why *do* we study truck-stop prostitutes? Or American Indians who consider themselves both male and female? Why survey the sexual practices of Mexican immigrants? Or hook women to monitors to quantify how their genitals respond to erotic movies? In short, what is the scientific value of delving into the forbidden?

As almost anyone who has followed the exploits of Bill Clinton or Pee Wee Herman knows, humans will place themselves at tremendous peril to satisfy themselves sexually. From an evolutionary standpoint, this makes sense. To pass our genes on to the next generation, we must engage in an activity that puts us at risk for disease and injury. Natural selection has endowed us with a hormonal system that sends us urgent psychological messages to have sex. It has also created considerable redundancy in how we receive sexual cues, making it hard for any single mechanism to shut down our libidos. "This is a very complex system, where the complexity is part of its evolution," says Kim Wallen, an Emory University neuroendocrinologist.

Because it is intricate, there is much about sexuality that we don't know, and we have few answers for many practical health questions. Why do people have unprotected intercourse, knowing they could become infected with a lethal virus? Why does female dysfunction remain resistant to treatments like Viagra? Trying to untangle these questions has required sophisticated research tools, and over the past decade a two-tiered approach has emerged.

The first involves probing the brain to understand the nature of sexuality. At Northwestern University in Evanston, Illinois, for instance, psychologist J. Michael Bailey and his former graduate student, Meredith Chivers, have discovered that men and women are fundamentally different in their arousal patterns. Bailey and Chivers fitted their research subjects with instruments designed to measure blood flow to their genitals, then showed them explicit two-minute video clips. The male participants responded predictably: Heterosexuals were aroused when they watched women having sex with women; gay men responded to watching men having sex with men. But women had a different reaction: All the film clips aroused them equally. "Their sexual arousal doesn't seem to map onto their stated sexual preference," says Chivers, who is now a fellow at Toronto's Centre for Addiction and Mental Health.

The implications of the Northwestern studies are enormous. For one, they start to explain why Viagra doesn't work for women, even though it stimulates blood flow to the genitals: The relationship between physiological arousal and sexual function is complicated. The results also offer important information to psychotherapists whose clients are struggling with sexual issues. "Because we have a male model of sexuality, women who don't fit that model feel they're different or weird," says University of Utah psychologist Lisa Diamond. The new findings may help clinicians whose female patients are confused by their erotic reactions to the "wrong" sex, for example.

The other research tier involves looking at networks of people rather than individuals. "Nothing occurs in a vacuum," says Alan Leshner, head of the American Association for the Advancement of Science. "The more we learn about the context of risky behavior, the more we can develop strategies for dealing with its consequences." Epidemiologists now talk about syndemics—sets of interlocking afflictions (such as AIDS, violence, and substance abuse) that affect entire communities. By studying the social forces that bind these ills together, "you can really push the boundaries of public health," says Dale Stratford, a medical anthropologist at the Centers for Disease Control and Prevention in Atlanta.

NIH is funding researchers to look at risk behavior in many communities: Hispanic immigrant men who live thousands of miles from their wives, teens who cruise the Internet for pornography,

Thai and Vietnamese women who work in San Francisco brothels. Each group presents specific health challenges. At the University of Washington, Karina Walters, an associate professor of social work, is studying American Indian "two-spirits," who consider themselves a blend of male and female. (Many are gay or bisexual.) HIV is spreading through American Indian communities "on the scale of some small African countries," she says, and men who have sex with other men are at particularly high risk. Walters has uncovered a syndemic of violence, substance abuse, and psychiatric problems among two-spirits and is now conducting extensive interviews to determine the underlying causes. She's also exploring whether those with a stronger sense of their indigenous identities are less likely to participate in unprotected sex, drinking, and gangs.

Because much of this work involves interviews and observation rather than microscopes and Petri dishes, it's not always recognizable as hard science. It is science nonetheless. "Science is a way of obtaining knowledge through a systematic collection of data and testing of hypotheses," says Christine Bachrach, chief of the demographics and behavioral sciences branch at the NIH's National Institute of Child Health and Human Development. "In some studies, you draw blood and hook people up to machines. In other studies, you might need to map out the sexual ties that person A has with person B and that person B has with person C."

Precisely this connect-the-dots method led to one of the most significant public-health breakthroughs of the past quarter century: In the early 1980s, epidemiologists studied the sexual and social connections among a group of gay men on both U.S. coasts who were developing fatal cases of *Pneumocystis carinii* pneumonia and Kaposi's sarcoma. Their diagrams led them to realize that the cases were manifestations of an infectious disease spread by sexual contact—what we now call AIDS. Since then, network mapping has helped public-health officials control disease outbreaks throughout the United States. They learned, for instance, that tuberculosis was being spread in Kansas when crack cocaine users blew smoke (along with water droplets containing the TB bacterium) into one another's mouths. This allowed TB-control experts to better identify people for screening and prevention. By identifying and targeting social networks, health researchers have also designed education campaigns that reduced needle sharing in Baltimore and unprotected anal sex in Louisiana and Mississippi and increased the use of modern contraceptives in Bangladesh.

"It's not rocket science," NIH's Bachrach says. "It's *harder* than rocket science, because what we see in the real world is the result of very complex forces. One of the challenges in observational science is sorting out what leads people to behave in the way they do."

NIH officials were delighted when Apostolopoulos's grant proposal arrived in January 2002. Except for a small project in the 1990s by Dale Stratford, little research had been done on American long-haul drivers and sexual health. "We knew from studies in Africa that truckers have played a role in the spread of HIV," Bachrach says. "In the United States, the epidemic started on a different foot, so we never paid attention to the role of truckers. Yet truckers can bridge from one risk group to another, as well as bridging to the folks they've left at home."

Apostolopoulos had come recently to health research. He earned his Ph.D. in sociology, studying the economic impact of tourism in his native Greece. That work spawned an interest in other mobile populations. Reviewing the literature, he discovered that few scientists had explored migration and health in any depth. This perplexed him. "Over a billion people are moving constantly in the world," he says. "How can we study disease if we don't study those people who are connecting high-prevalence and low-prevalence regions?"

Apostolopoulos teamed up with the Turkish-born Sönmez, whose own doctoral work explored the social psychology of travel. Over the past five years, the two have become intellectual migrants themselves, studying mobile populations on three continents. They've looked at how sexual networks of semi-nomadic Ethiopians disseminate HIV in a country where famine and poverty have already weakened people's immune systems. They've examined how sexually transmitted diseases spread among an estimated two million U.S. college students who travel to beach resorts during spring break. They're now gearing up to study Eastern European women (and some men) who migrate throughout the more affluent European Union, engaging in what Apostolopoulos calls survival sex.

In 2001, while teaching at Arizona State University, Apostolopoulos and Sönmez turned their attentions to the 3.6 million long-haul truckers crisscrossing North America. For their preliminary fieldwork, they zeroed in on two truck stops. One was a hulking complex rising from a barren patch of desert fifty miles south of Phoenix. Across the road, prostitutes came and went from two budget motels with peeling paint and weedy entranceways. The other, smaller and more urban, sat on a forlorn stretch of dust-covered road pocked by squat houses and occasional palm trees on Phoenix's south side. There, women in short skirts solicited drivers, and homeless men slept in cardboard boxes at the side of a convenience store.

For a while, the researchers and their students observed quietly, eating french fries, conversing casually, and watching the hustle and bustle of the truck stops. "When you spend a lot of time, you kind of blend into the wallpaper," Sönmez says. Over time, they began to parse out different populations. There were "polishers," who earn $50 to $100 for shining the chrome on a truck. (Drivers are very proud of their rigs.) And "lumpers," who load and unload freight. Truck-stop waitresses, who sometimes have sex with drivers. Drug dealers. Prostitutes. Pimps. "Then we began to realize that they're not existing in a vacuum," Sönmez says. "Rather, they are constantly interacting among themselves. A sex worker may also run drugs. A polisher may do pimping. A polisher may also provide sexual services in certain circumstances, if his economic situation is desperate enough."

By the time they finished their initial research, Apostolopoulos and Sönmez had mapped out twenty different populations that interact with truckers. "No one had ever described or even spoken about these networks before," Apostolopoulos says. What's more, the truck stops were not closed systems: A driver could carry infection from one way station to another, then home to his family. With only an initial study under their belts, though, the researchers couldn't even start to quantify the potential consequences.

Apostolopoulos and Sönmez moved to Emory in 2002. By then, they had secured $1.1 million from NIH to expand the study. They chose two truck stops in Atlanta, along with a gritty urban corridor where drivers congregate. All are located in depressed semi-industrial areas where government housing mingles with liquor stores and adult video stores, and where prostitutes loiter near phone booths waiting for customers' calls. At one site, a windowless gray nightclub—its parking lot perfumed by roasting meat from a nearby barbecue shack—features exotic dancers who sometimes sell sexual services on the side. At another, a patch of tall deciduous trees known as "the jungle" provides cover for covert sexual coupling.

Since September 2002, the Emory team has conducted extensive interviews—not just with truckers but with the entire network—to make sense of the social and sexual landscape. They have also tested drivers, prostitutes, and other truck-stop denizens for HIV, syphilis, gonorrhea, and Chlamydia to see if the risky behavior in these sexual networks actually spreads disease.

So far, what they've uncovered is a syndemic that includes not only sexually transmitted infection but also drug abuse, violence, psychological distress, and depression. Some of the factors are relatively obvious: When truckers are away from home for twenty-six days a month, they get lonely and anxious and seek out sexual companionship. Other factors are buried more deeply in the social fabric. As the drivers came to trust the Emory researchers, some confessed that their dispatchers provide them with amphetamines to help them stick to their superhuman delivery deadlines. Amphetamines increase sexual arousal and lower inhibitions, so users were more willing to have unprotected sex. Truck-stop prostitutes, desperate for cash, often permitted the behavior. "What do you do when someone refuses to use a condom?" one researcher asked a sex worker. "Well, I make sure I use baby wipes," she replied.

Apostolopoulos and Sönmez also focused on another phenomenon ignored by scientific journals: male truckers who have sex with other men. There are Web sites and even conventions for truck chasers, who are drawn to the cowboy mystique of long-distance drivers. But their liaisons—often arranged over the Internet—look nothing like those in urban gay communities. "Many of these truckers identify as straight," says Donna Smith, a researcher with the Emory team. "Because they define risk as being associated with identity—and because they are not gay—they believe they are not at risk. We've collected ethnographies in which truck chasers are asked by truckers, 'Are you married?' They perceive safety in a sexual encounter with another married man."

When he began his research, Apostolopoulos had no idea his work would be held up for ridicule. In the summer of 2003, when a colleague sent him an e-mail message that four NIH-funded projects had barely survived a congressional defunding vote, he deleted it without much concern. "I assumed it was just a few unconventional studies," he now says. "I didn't pay attention till last fall."

The political storm had actually started gathering force at the tail end of 2002, when a reporter for the conservative *Washington Times* called Michael Bailey of Northwestern at his small office overlooking Lake Michigan. The two men chatted for a while about the psychologist's sexual-arousal study. Then the journalist blurted out his real reason for calling: "Isn't that a little strange, that the National Institute for Child Health and Human Development is funding a study that uses porn?" On December 23, the *Washington Times* published an article questioning Bailey's work, kicking off its crusade against NIH-funded sex research. (The psychologist sardonically calls the article "an early Christmas present.") By New Year's Eve, the Northwestern study had been ridiculed on two television talk shows, and soon Congress had joined in. "This flagrant frittering away of federal funds is borderline criminal," declared Representative John Doolittle, a California Republican, the next summer. In July 2003, an effort to strip funding from four projects, including Karina Walters's two-spirit study, failed on the House floor by a 212–210 vote.

Rather than settling the controversy, the close vote cranked it up. Last fall, the Traditional Values Coalition publicly challenged grants worth more than $100 million. "Some people may think it's worthy to wire up female genitalia as they watch erotic video," says Lafferty, the coalition director. "But dollars are scarce, and juvenile diabetes and heart disease need the funding."

By most accounts, including Apostolopoulos's, NIH has stood by its scientists, helping them draft explanations of their work's scientific value. In January 2004, after ordering a comprehensive review of the institutes' sexuality research, NIH director Elias Zerhouni sent his own letter to Congress. Biological research has done a great deal to improve the nation's health, he wrote. But with half the country's disease burden stemming from lifestyle, "the constant battle against illness and disease . . . has to include behavioral and social factors as well." Critics, unconvinced, plan to press on. "The National Institutes of Health has been treated as a sacred cow," Lafferty says. "No one is allowed to question it, and now we are. Researchers are freaking out because they realize the trough may dry up."

Of course, this isn't the first time science has collided with politics. Government-funded research is political by nature and designed to be accountable to taxpayers. Public pressure has sometimes helped refine science over the years, forcing researchers to treat women and minorities fairly during clinical trials, for instance, and improving the treatment of laboratory animals. Stem cell research and human cloning are legitimate topics of debate. "Science is stronger and more able to meet societal needs as a result of these conflicts," says Daniel Sarewitz, managing director of the Consortium for Science, Policy, and Outcomes at Arizona State University in Tempe.

The incivility of the NIH debate, however, has promoted neither good dialogue nor good science. And it has had ugly ripple effects.

"We have had scientists who have received death threats," says Simon Rosser, director of the University of Minnesota's Center for HIV/STI Intervention and Prevention Studies. "Some have been professionally slandered. Some have been mocked by colleagues. Some have received calls at 2 A.M. saying, 'Do you know where your children are?' We've got enough of a problem trying to fight HIV without also having to fight threats, fear, and intimidation."

Others worry that the current political battles might keep potential sex researchers from entering the field. Apostolopoulos, for one, acknowledges he has considered lying low until the political climate changes, though he continues to write proposals dealing with sexual behavior and disease transmission. He believes his submissions are strong enough to survive the meticulous peer-review process. "But in the back of your mind you think, 'Are the reviewers going to be influenced by what has happened?'"

If that chill descends, Apostolopoulos hesitates to envision the consequences. "We could have a skyrocketing of disease," he says after a long pause. "The ramifications could be explosive."

Head Case

How one man's enduring obsession with pleasing women orally led to a mind-numbingly thorough how-to guide.

By Amy Sohn
New York magazine / June 21, 2004

In a town where everyone wants go down in history remembered for something, Ian Kerner wants to go down as the champion of going down. Thirty-seven and diminutive, but boyishly handsome, he's a sex therapist who has written *She Comes First: The Thinking Man's Guide to Pleasuring a Woman,* a Chilton's manual for cunnilingus. Kerner is so committed to teaching new skills that he names his licks—the Elvis Presley snarl (gum against clitoris, lip up), the Jackson Pollock lick ("broad strokes with pinpoint targeted precision"), even the Rope a Dope, in honor of the Thrilla in Manila (let her push and grind and then spring back with a strong stroke). If it sounds too theoretical, Kerner says that what's important is the overall message: Sex doesn't make women come and oral sex does, so men need to put the tongue before the sword.

Kerner grew up in Chelsea, went to Dwight and Walden, and spent his teenage years like most of the guys I dated in high school: making out with girls, not making them come, reading a lot of porn, and struggling with premature ejaculation. "It was my Achilles' penis," he says over afternoon tea at Thé Adoré. "Men train themselves by masturbating furtively, quickly, and in private, and build a neuropath between their brain and body."

He lost his virginity at seventeen, went off to Brandeis, and, in hopes of helping himself overcome his problem, read *The Kinsey Report* and Masters and Johnson. Feeling like a sexual cripple, à la Jon Voight in *Coming Home*, he resisted sex and instead spent all his dates dining at the Y. As a result, he became known for his talents: "I got really skilled at turning oral sex from an arbitrary aspect of foreplay into something that I codified. I became deeply aware of how to satisfy a woman." He began worrying less about his own orgasm and eventually learned to slow down his response time when he did have sex.

After college, he had stints as a playwright and a creative-writing professor, got married, and worked for a start-up. When the dot-com bubble burst ("a big premature ejaculation"), he decided to get his doctorate in clinical sexology. As he began seeing patients, mainly married couples, he became convinced that most men were too focused on intercourse, and that couples needed to find a way to, as he puts it, "turn foreplay into coreplay."

"The average man can maintain genital thrusting for two and a half minutes before ejaculation, but the average woman requires fifteen to eighteen minutes of persistent clitoral stimulation to have her first orgasm," Kerner says. "That twelve-and-a-half-minute difference is a gaping maw of frustration on the part of women."

Anyone with half a brain could tell you this, but his book is detailed to the point of exhaustion—with a section on anatomy, a step-by-step guide to going down, and a mere seven pages (out of 228) on the old in-and-out. It's almost too thorough. Isn't it overoptimistic to think a guy can do the perineum clasp while moving the woman into a semi-split, alternating with vertical and horizontal tongue strokes? "I wanted to be more extensive and rigorous on this subject than anyone had heretofore been," Kerner says.

There's certainly a nobility to the book; any guy who picks it up in a store, even if he doesn't buy it, will come away learning something new. But if women out there aren't getting what they want from men, it may not be entirely the fault of the men. I have many female friends who shrug when the subject of cunnilingus comes up—they say they can take it or leave it, or it takes too long, or even, dismissively, "I prefer sex." On *Sex and the City,* the Mr. Pussy character was portrayed as a laughingstock because of his obsession—and Charlotte ultimately realized she couldn't have a relationship with him.

Kerner thinks women are part of the problem: "They have just as many hang-ups about receiving as men do about giving." He blames Freud, who scarred generations of women by defining "vaginal" orgasms as more mature than childish little clitoral ones. Seventies feminists refuted much of this, but in the eighties, the debate was renewed again with the publication of *The G Spot.* In more recent years, the vagina has enjoyed a comeback as sex shops have begun selling G-spot vibrators and videos on female ejaculation through G-spot stimulation. Kerner is skeptical about all this. He believes the G-spot is part of the clitoris and that a G-spot orgasm is a kind of clitoral orgasm. As for all those squirters, he points out that some say ejaculating has no positive effect on their pleasure.

For most women, he says, it's cunnilingus that does the trick—but most men just don't know how to do it. "One of the biggest complaints I hear from women is, 'I love it when my guy goes down on me, but it's like the running of the bulls in Pamplona. It's like a stampede for the clitoris, and I just want to get out of the way.'"

This is why so many men say they don't have the energy for long sessions. "The men are too aggressive, and that leads to a lot of guys saying, 'After three minutes, my tongue hurts. My neck hurts.' But that's because they're approaching it in the wrong way." Furthermore, Kerner points out, the more you do it, the less time it takes—something I have discovered with the help of my own personal Clitoral Conqueror, my husband, Jake.

Kerner believes a book on muff-diving is all the more necessary in the phallocentric era of Viagra, Levitra, and Cialis. Before pills, men would get creative—something no longer required. "A lot of women say these days that Viagra's the worst thing that ever happened to them," he says. "It brings everything back to the penis and back to intercourse."

But in case anyone accuses him of eliminating the penis's role in male sexual contentment, he's quick to say, "I wrote the cunnilinguist manifesto, but I'm not proposing a Stalinist purge of the penis. I love my penis as much as the next guy. In many ways, though, my tongue was the mentor to my penis, and taught it to behave like a gentleman."

sex

Does This Make My Labia Look Fat?

Medicine and marketing collide below the belt with designer vaginal surgery.

By Sarah Klein
Metro Times (Detroit) / March 9, 2005

The names of the patients interviewed for this story have been changed.

Kim is a twenty-seven-year-old woman with a shy face and perfectly shaped pink acrylic nails. She's naked from the waist down, wrapped in a flimsy paper gown, perched on the edge of an examining table. Looking nervous and uncomfortable, she wraps her arms protectively around her stomach as she fidgets. Kim has had three children, and no longer enjoys sex. Her husband doesn't either, and the couple thinks Kim's vagina has been stretched out by the births and damaged by her last episiotomy, the incision made to enlarge the vaginal opening during delivery.

So today Kim is here to consult with Dr. Joseph Berenholz, an OB/GYN who recently founded the Laser Vaginal Institute of Michigan. If she qualifies for the outpatient surgery, Berenholz will use a ballpoint pen-sized laser to cut Kim's vagina and suture it, restoring the tightness she experienced before the childbirth. And Kim is willing to pay out-of-pocket for the procedure—which isn't covered by medical insurance, and has an average cost of $7,000.

Berenholz's office offers several other elective female genital surgeries, the primary selling points being enhanced sexual gratification for the woman, and aesthetically pleasing results. Starting at $4,500, a woman can have a labioplasty, in which her inner labia are cut and reshaped if she thinks they're too large or asymmetrical. Or she can become "revirginized" and have an approximation of her hymen restored. (This is particularly popular among Middle Eastern women who need to "fake" their virginity before marriage.) And if she wants to combine more than one surgery, she can end up paying more than $10,000 for newer, tighter, prettier genitals.

This is the latest facet of cosmetic surgery—designer vaginas. Women have already nipped, tucked, implanted and vacuumed every other part of their bodies, and are now turning their perfection-obsessed eyes to their own genitals. Elective surgeries that promise a better sex life or more aesthetically pleasing private parts are rapidly gaining popularity, but both the medical community and cultural observers are divided over whether these are valid, beneficial surgeries—or just a case of personal vanity gone too far.

Though relatively new, these elective surgeries have already drawn a torrent of publicity and controversy. The technique was born in the country's capital of plastic surgery—Los Angeles—but has now arrived in metro Detroit with Berenholz's new venture, established at the end of 2004.

Everyone from medical professionals to feminists has weighed in on the topic. Some say it's simply a way for greedy doctors to capitalize on women's insecurities; but some patients who've undergone the procedure say it has changed their lives for the better.

The term laser vaginal rejuvenation (LVR) was coined by Los Angeles OB/GYN and plastic surgeon Dr. David Matlock, who says he has performed the procedure for ten years now. Both

Matlock and his work have been extensively profiled in glossy magazines and national media since the late '90s.

The surgeries straddle the line between traditional OB/GYN surgery and elective cosmetic procedures. LVR is based on a long-established procedure for incontinence or weakened vaginal walls—called anterior and posterior repair. Several conditions can result from childbirth: stress incontinence (losing urine when laughing, coughing, sneezing, etc.), the wall between the vagina and bladder is weakened (cystocele), or the wall between the rectum and the vagina is weakened (rectocele)—which is what anterior (bladder) and posterior (rectum) repair addresses. While these repairs are intended for medical purposes, they also may—or may not—result in a vagina that feels "tighter."

Matlock adapted the surgery to focus on tightening the vagina, and swapped the traditional scalpel for a laser, which he says accounts for less blood loss and faster healing. He repackaged and marketed the surgery as a cure for women who've given birth and no longer enjoy sex.

Unlike Matlock, Berenholz is not a plastic surgeon, but an OB/GYN with twenty years of experience. He also has a private OB/GYN practice and says he's delivered hundreds of healthy babies in his career. With a rounded face and salt-and-pepper hair, Berenholz has the tranquil voice and soothing demeanor of someone who's accustomed to making nervous or frightened people feel at ease.

Berenholz says that over the years in his career, he's had many patients complain they could no longer enjoy sex after childbirth.

"You're trained in residency to reassure a woman, to let her know this is normal, and to simply go home and live with it," he says.

Traditionally, women who complain of these symptoms are

advised to do Kegel exercises, a simple muscle training regimen women can perform either with or without instruments.

But Berenholz says the Kegel regimen doesn't always work.

"The people we see have done millions of Kegel exercises," he says. "There is no exercise that can help women recover from torn muscle and damage."

Berenholz says to meet this demand, he began performing a surgery to tighten and strengthen the vaginal muscles. Then, six months ago, he flew out to Los Angeles to take a training course with Matlock, and founded the Laser Vaginal Rejuvenation Institute of Michigan a month later. Business is already booming.

The institute is actually a small cosmetic surgery office in the suburb of Southfield, where Berenholz usually works two to three days a week. The rest of his time is spent in surgery at area hospitals, or at his private practice.

The doctor says he performs an average of two to three surgeries a day at the LVRI office, and receives as many as twenty email inquiries on any given day via his Web site, lvriofmich.com. He even has a PR rep, and has aggressively advertised his institute with press releases on the Internet and in local print (including *Metro Times*).

LVR is an outpatient procedure, usually finished in about an hour. Patients can expect discomfort for the first two to three days, which Berenholz says is roughly equivalent to healing from an episiotomy. Sex can be resumed within six weeks. Berenholz says pricing depends on the needs of the patient, but can range from $6,500 to $8,500.

Besides LVR, he also offers several forms of Designer Laser Vaginoplasty (DLV). These include labioplasty, hymenoplasty, augmentation labioplasty (removing fat from the patient and transferring it to the labia majora, providing an "aesthetically enhanced and youthful" look) and vulvar lipoplasty (removing unwanted fat from the mons pubis or labia majora, which can "alleviate unsightly fatty bulges of this area and produce an aesthetically pleasing contour"). Prices range from $3,800 to $6,000. Berenholz says the two major risks of the surgery are infection and bleeding.

Although he says he's yet to personally receive criticism from his local colleagues, Berenholz recalls a departmental OB/GYN meeting he attended, where he got some ribbing from his fellow physicians.

"I was being teased by several of them, being called 'The Revirginator,'" he says. "I silently laughed it off, but afterwards, two physicians came up to me and asked where they could learn the techniques."

And he believes this interest will only grow.

"I think this will become the fastest growing area of elective surgery in the U.S. over the next five years."

Many pundits and talk radio hosts who've discussed cosmetic vaginal surgeries rejoice in mocking it, pointing out that most men who encounter labia are simply happy to be there, and couldn't care less about perceived size abnormalities or unevenness. After all, have you ever heard a man utter the phrase "Yeah, she's really a great catch, but those labia? Man, that's a deal-breaker." Ironically, many LVR doctors claim they are empowering women, while their practice caters to perhaps the most sexist of all notions—that, to be desirable, women should have a youthful, pert, tight vagina.

Labioplasty is nothing new, an established medical procedure used to treat women with labia hypertrophy—enlarged inner labia that protrude beyond the outer labia and cause discomfort. Again, Matlock revamped the surgery by swapping the traditional scalpel for a laser, and marketed the procedure for aesthetic purposes.

"It's being driven primarily by what the woman wants," Berenholz says of labioplasty reshaping, "but there has to be some anatomical problem to correct."

But what entails a problem, or, for that matter, normal? The procedure has sparked a firestorm of criticism in some feminist camps, who say this is yet another manner in which women are being pressured to conform to a homogenized, physical ideal. After all, Berenholz's site says many of his prospective labioplasty patients come in with a copy of *Playboy* in hand, with the centerfold serving as their aesthetic model.

"Nobody thought about that until someone said, 'Hey, here's a body part nobody's hit with the lasers yet. Let's make a little money here,'" says Detroiter-turned-New Yorker Ophira Edut, editor of *Body Outlaws,* an anthology examining women's body image issues. "Like there's a right way for a woman's private parts to look? I believe the majority of men don't expect women to go out and surgically alter their bodies to look like a *Playboy* centerfold.

"It's a tricky subject," Edut says. "I respect a woman's choice, and she should be the ultimate authority on her body and what to do with it. But at the same time, if a labioplasty is what you really think it will take to make you happy, it might be time to re-examine your idea of happiness."

Berenholz says the majority of his patients who choose labioplasty do so for physical comfort, not just aesthetics.

"It's, 'Doc, I ride my bike five miles a day and it hurts,' or, 'I want to wear blue jeans. I can't wear tight clothes.' Not one of these patients has been vain," he says.

But Susan Hendrix, professor of OB/GYN at Detroit's Wayne State University and director of the Women's Health Initiative, says the occurrence of true labia hypertrophy is rare.

"Labioplasty is only done in very unusual or rare cases," Hendrix says. "I've been in practice for over sixteen years and I've maybe done two or three." She says she only performs the procedure "when medically indicated" because possible complications are serious, including chronic pain, and, in a worst case scenario, the inability to have sex.

"It's really somewhat repulsive to me," Hendrix says of aesthetically driven labioplasty, "because it implies this is a cosmetic surgery somehow, and women should worry about how their vagina looks.

"There's a right and wrong in what you practice in medicine, and patients really rely on their doctors. To go out and establish something just for money? That's disgusting that a physician would do that."

Despite the fact that the clitoris is the woman's primary source of pleasure, doctors who perform LVR claim it will improve sex for both partners, not just the man. Matlock's literature (titled, "As a sexual biological organism, women are superior to men") states that LVR will result in increased friction, which will in turn increase pleasure for the woman.

Isabella is a trim, forty-four-year-old blonde from the Detroit area, mother to three children. Her last child weighed nine pounds at birth, resulting in a pronounced episiotomy for the 105-pound, small-framed woman. Though her youngest is now nineteen, she says she began to experience problems within the last five years. In addition to some stress incontinence, sex with her partner was no longer enjoyable. "I couldn't feel anything. And I knew if I couldn't, he couldn't."

Isabella was certain the problem was coming from her end, not her mate's. Her gynecologist advised her to do Kegels, which she says didn't work. Isabella then turned to the Internet to research alternatives. She learned of LVR and was convinced the procedure was right for her—so convinced that she was ready to fly to Los Angeles to undergo it. Then she found Berenholz's Web site, just after it launched.

"He never made me feel like a freak of nature. He's very compassionate," she says.

After undergoing the procedure, Isabella was back to work within a few days, and says the pain and healing process was on par with her last episiotomy. She's thrilled with the results.

"Any kind of surgery has risk, but I would do it again in a second," she says. "It's definitely been an incredible experience for me." She's even inspired some of her girlfriends to get the surgery.

"This problem is more widespread than people think," she says. "Honestly, I think if more women knew about this procedure, it would save marriages. Men are men. If a man's going to stray from marriage it's for sex."

With her experience completely satisfactory, Isabella brushes off opponents of the surgery.

"I think criticism comes from people who don't have this problem and don't understand how it can affect you emotionally and physically," she says.

Happy patients like Isabella serve as Berenholz's response to criticism from others within the medical field. He offers the following response to those who object to the procedure:

"I'd pose this question: What have they offered their patients who come to the same complaints? To deny these women an alternative or choice is absurd."

What options are available for women who feel the need for a tighter vagina? And at what cost?

The traditional surgery LVR is based on, anterior and posterior repair, is covered by most insurance when medically necessary to treat cystocele, rectocele, or incontinence. But it may or may not result in a tighter vagina. And because LVR is elective surgery, it doesn't qualify for insurance (which Berenholz doesn't accept anyway).

The price tag was daunting for Jane, thirty-four, of Indianapolis, who has two kids and traveled to Michigan to undergo LVR from Berenholz.

"Price was an issue for me," Jane says. "I financed part of this. My guess is a lot of women who do this have a lot of money. I would consider it a luxury. Not to say that I don't think it should be covered by insurance, because I think it should be."

Dr. Laura Berman is director of the Berman Center in Chicago, a clinic for women's sexual issues. She says many women who complain that Kegels don't work simply aren't performing the exercise correctly, an error that can be monitored by an over-the-counter device.

"And it's not just strengthening the muscles, it's learning how to use them during sex," she says. "A lot of times women have these surgeries because some jerk told them they were too loose, when in fact he may have been too small."

Berman says that when a woman learns to strengthen and control her pelvic floor muscles, "she can squeeze around any size she wanted to, even the size of a pinky."

Dr. Hope Haefner is director of University of Michigan's Center for Vulvar Diseases. "I see a lot of women who have vestibulodynia—they're having pain because their vaginas are too tight. So there's the issue of overcorrection."

Haefner remains undecided on the value of these surgeries.

"I'd really like to see the studies that show this really makes a difference in the long-term outcome of relationships," she says. "I'd like to see studies that *prove* this is beneficial."

The marketing of the procedure is of concern to registered nurse and sex therapist Casey Wilhelm. "I think the public has the idea that this laser means it's less invasive of a procedure, and it's not," says Wilhelm, who works with Haefner. "The laser cauterizes while it cuts, but it cuts nonetheless."

On the other hand, Wilhelm says patients should have the right to choose whether or not to undergo such surgery. "I support the idea of a woman being able to do whatever she wants to with her body, and that goes along with cosmetic surgery or other body work," she says. "While having something medically indicated is important for certain kinds of surgery, it shouldn't be contraindicated because there isn't a medical basis for it.

"There's no one answer for everybody. There's no absolute line, and that's why this is controversial. A one-size-fits-all answer to the problem is highly unlikely."

There's no certification required to perform LVR, other than a medical license. Berenholz says after researching online, he's found many plastic surgeons who offer the procedure but have no background in OB/GYN. "For this kind of surgery, I firmly believe it should only be done by a board-certified OB/GYN," he says.

Plastic surgeons agree—for the most part.

Dr. V. Leroy Young chairs the committee for emerging trends for the American Society of Plastic Surgeons (ASPS). He says the trend of elective female genital surgery is growing rapidly, "but we don't have any hard statistics." He says lots of plastic surgeons perform labioplasty procedures, and have done so for some time—without the laser, which he describes as "a gimmick"—but that LVR is better left up to those in the OB/GYN field.

"Labial reduction is reasonably common among plastic surgeries," he says. "This new interest seems to be affected by the mainstreaming of pornography, and the lack of understanding of what is normal versus what represents a perceived ideal. The thing that surprises me is how little understanding there is of what normal is."

Young says the ASPS has seen an influx of inquiries about these elective surgeries. "We've been waiting to see, is this real, and is there enough demand for it that we need to collect stats? And that's a decision I think we'll have to make this year," he says. "If the numbers are there, then we'll develop some guidelines."

Young thinks that unless a woman has prolapse of the rectum or bladder, "it's meddlesome surgery. It also poses the risk that you can end up with loss of sensation or a painful scar. But if you've got a real problem, then, sure, there's nothing wrong with the procedures, but they ought to be performed for a legitimate reason." When told of Isabella's scenario, Young says he feels the surgery was justified in her case.

Berman, on the other hand, thinks there's never justifiable cause for LVR, and that the procedure can actually cause damage.

"Over the years I've treated many women who've had these surgeries because their partner told them to, and they end up with some sexual dysfunction," Berman says. "Our genitals and pelvic region in general is rich in nerves and vascular bundles, so any kind of vaginal surgery runs the risk of affecting sexual response because of nerve damage."

Dr. Stanley Zinberg of the American College of Obstetricians and Gynecologists issued a letter in June of 2004 expressing concern over the surgeries. The following is an excerpt:

"The Committees on Gynecologic Practice and Ethics are continuing to monitor this issue and expressed several concerns. First, it is difficult to determine exactly what procedures are being performed, as the nomenclature used for procedures such as 'vaginal rejuvenation' and 'revirginification' does not describe standard gynecologic surgical procedures.

"Of concern to the Committee on Ethics is the way in which

these procedures are being marketed and promoted. The use of a business model that aims to control the dissemination of scientific knowledge is troubling. For physicians who perform these procedures, obtaining a patient's informed consent will be challenging, given the absence of medical literature about these procedures."

Some physicians charge that these surgeries are simply a way for doctors to cash in on women's insecurities. For his part, Matlock does little to counter that notion.

About five years ago, Matlock decided to expand his ventures. He trademarked the term "LVRI" and "vaginal rejuvenation," and actually patented some of the procedures. Then he started a franchise operation.

"We don't want to term it franchise," Matlock objects hastily by phone, in between surgery and international phone calls. "The doctors are *associates* of LVRI. We taught and trained them in all techniques, and offered them a business model. We also offer support to these *associates.*"

And for that support, those associates pay Matlock a monthly fee. Doctors who wish to enroll in his four-day course pay an initial fee of $8,900, followed by a program participation fee: $2,500 per month over the next twenty-four months. That's a total of nearly $70,000. Matlock says he has about a dozen such associates in this country (Berenholz is one of them), and about thirty internationally, including doctors in Canada, Sweden, France, Indonesia, and Australia. That all adds up to nearly to $3 million.

He's already sent cease-and-desist letters to other doctors who are using any variant on "vaginal rejuvenation" in their advertising, citing trademark infringement. Although others in the medical community have expressed chagrin over Matlock's attempts to corner the market, Matlock, who also has a master's degree in business administration, sees it differently.

"If this is intellectual property, why should I give it away?" he asks. "Medicine is a business too. Doctors want in because it's a cash business. Insurance, you might get paid nine months, six months, three months at best. But here, they're coming in and they're paying cash."

One breath later, he offers the following pledge:

"Our whole mission is to empower women with knowledge, choice, and alternatives."

"I think that's wrong," Jane says after learning of Matlock's trademark and patent. "That troubles me. It makes it seem like it's just a cosmetic procedure. It's going to make it expensive and unavailable. They're covering Viagra with Medicare; I don't get it."

In contrast to Matlock's bluntness, Berenholz says he's providing women with a choice, when, in the past, they were told they simply had to live with vaginal looseness or aesthetically displeasing labia. "This is being driven by women, not doctors," he says.

And he isn't afraid to turn patients away. He tells of a woman in her twenties who came in complaining of long labia. "But there was virtually no hypertrophy. We saw nothing wrong," he says. They sent her on her way.

Another woman flew all the way from California for an LVR consultation, because her husband said he could no longer feel her. But after examining her, Berenholz found no relaxation in her vagina, and, as it turns out, the woman's husband had erectile dysfunction. She got on the next plane back to California.

"She told us she didn't know if she should laugh or cry," Berenholz says.

During Kim's consultation, Berenholz asks her a number of frank questions about her ability to orgasm, before and after childbirth.

"I'm just really loose down there," she says with a shrug. Having finished with his questions, Berenholz begins conducting his exam, speaking gently and telling Kim exactly what he's doing as he probes her vagina with a speculum and conducts a rectal exam. A flash of surprise emerges on his face.

After finishing the exam, he tells Kim that if he had to classify her on a scale from normal to slightly relaxed to very relaxed, he'd classify her as normal.

Kim looks shocked. "You think so?" she asks, unconvinced. "I know so," Berenholz assures her.

He then gently suggests that the problem may lie with her husband. He refers Kim to urodynamic testing, to treat her issue of stress incontinence, but says she has no need for LVR.

"You really don't think so?" she asks again, looking perplexed and rather disappointed. After a moment, she wonders, "Well, maybe *he's* got a problem."

Despite the fact that she's just learned she's normal, and won't have to pay nearly $7,000 to have her vagina surgically altered, Kim looks almost crestfallen.

"It happens a lot," Berenholz's assistant assures her. "Because we're women, we'll see a doctor when we think something is wrong, but men are very prideful . . ."

"There are many women who've had more than three or four children who have a very fine sex life," Wilhelm says. "It doesn't mean because your sex life is no longer enjoyable it's because you've had three kids and your vagina is stretching. That's a lot easier to fix than looking to yourself or your relationships."

sex

The Holy Fuck

By Toni Bentley
from *The Surrender: An Erotic Memoir*

> *"This pleasure is such that nothing can interfere with it, and the object that serves it cannot, in savoring it, fail to be transported to the third heaven. No other is as good, no other can satisfy as fully both of the individuals who indulge in it, and those who have experienced it can revert to other things only with difficulty."*
>
> *—Donatien de Sade*

His was first. In my ass.

I don't know the exact length, but it's definitely too big—just right. Of medium width, neither too slender nor too thick. Beautiful. My ass, tiny, a teenage boy's, tight, and tightly wound. Twenty-five years of winding as a ballet dancer. Since age four, the age when I first declared war on my daddy. Turning out the legs from the hips just winds up that pelvic floor like a corkscrew. I worked my gut all my life standing at that ballet barre. Now it is being unworked.

His cock, my ass, unwinding. Divine.

As he enters me I let go, millimeter by millimeter, of the tensing, pulling, tightening, gripping. I am addicted to extreme physical endurance, the marathon of uncoiling intensity. I release my muscles, my tendons, my flesh, my anger, my ego, my rules, my censors, my parents, my cells, my life. At the same time I pull and suck and draw him inward. Opening out and sucking in, one thing.

Bliss, I learned from being sodomized, is an experience of eternity in a moment of real time. Sodomy is the ultimate sexual act of trust. I mean you could really get hurt—if you resist. But pushing past that fear, by passing through it, literally, ah the joy that lies on the other side of convention. The peace that is past the pain. Going past the pain is key. Once absorbed, it is neutralized and allows for transformation. Pleasure alone is mere temporary indulgence, a subtle distraction, an anesthetization while on the path to something higher, deeper, lower. Eternity lies far, far beyond pleasure. And beyond pain. The edge of my ass is the sexual event horizon, the boundary to that beyond from which there is no escape. Not for me, anyway.

I am an atheist, by inheritance. I came to know God experientially, from being fucked in the ass—over and over and over again. I am a slow learner—and a gluttonous hedonist. I am serious. Very serious. And I was even more surprised than you are now by this curiously rude awakening to a mystic state. There it was: God's big surprise, His subtle humor and potent presence, manifested in my ass—well, it sure is one way to get a skeptic's attention.

Anal sex is about cooperation. Cooperation in an endeavor of aristocratic politics, involving rigid hierarchies, feudal positions, and monarchist attitudes. One is in charge, the other obedient. Entirely in charge, entirely obedient. There is no democratic, affirmative-action safety net swinging below ass-fuckers. But they'd best be of firm action, very firm. You can't half-ass butt-fuck. It would be a travesty. There are no understudies, no backups, for anal Cirque du Soleil. It's a high-wire act—all the way up.

The truth always shows itself with the ass. A cock in an ass operates like the arrow on a lie-detector test. The ass doesn't know how to lie, it can't lie: it hurts, physically, if you lie. The pussy, on the other hand, can lie at the mere entry of a dick in the room—does so all the time. Pussies are designed to fool men with their beckoning waters, ready opening, and angry owners.

I've learned so much, maybe the thing of most importance, from getting fucked in the ass—how to surrender. All I learned from the other hole was how to feel used and abandoned.

My pussy proposes the question; my ass answers. Ass-fucking is the event in which Rainer Maria Rilke's hallowed dictum to "live the question" is, in fact, finally embodied. Anal penetration resolves the dilemma of duality that is introduced and magnified by vaginal penetration. Ass-fucking transcends all opposites, all conflicts—positive and negative, good and bad, high and low, shallow and deep, pleasure and pain, love and death—and unifies them, renders all one. This, for me, is therefore The Act. Butt-fucking offers spiritual resolution. Who knew?

If I were asked to choose for the rest of my life only one place of penetration, I would choose my ass. My pussy has been too wounded by false expectations and uninvited entries, by movements too selfish, too shallow, too fast, or too unconscious. My ass, knowing only him, knows only bliss. The penetration is deeper, more profound; it rides the edge of sanity. The direct path through my bowels to God has become clear, has been cleared.

Norman Mailer sees the sexual routes in reverse: "So that was how I finally made love to her, a minute for one, a minute for the other, a raid on the Devil and a trip back to the Lord." But Mailer is a man, a perpetrator, a penetrator, not a recipient, not a submissive. He hasn't been, I assume, in my compromising position.

My yearning is so large, so gaping, so cavernous, so deep, so long, so wide, so old and so young, so very young, that only a big cock buried deep in my ass has ever filled it. He is that cock. The cock who saved me. He is my answer to every man who came before him. My revenge.

I see his cock as a therapeutic instrument. Surely only God could have thought of such a cure for my bottomless wound—the wound of the woman whose daddy didn't love her enough. Perhaps the wound is not psychological in source at all, but truly the space inside that yearns for God. Perhaps it is merely the yearning of a woman who thinks she cannot have Him. A woman whose daddy told her long ago that there is no God.

But I want God.

Getting fucked in the ass gives me hope. Despair hasn't got a chance when his cock is in my ass, making room for God. He opened up my ass and with that first thrust he broke my denial of God, broke my shame, and exposed it to the light. The yearning is no longer hidden; now it has a name.

sex

Exclusive Interview: Harry Reems

By Paul Fischer
Moviehole.net / February 11, 2005

Thirty-three years ago Harry Reems became an unwilling legend of an era that reinforced sexual liberalization. The most famous male porn star of all time, Reems became the darling of a new sexual and cultural revolution, but when push came to shove, Reems, after being arrested and used as a pawn in the conservative 1970s political arena, was eventually abandoned by Hollywood's establishment. For almost two decades, Reems would be forgotten, an alcoholic and homeless. Now, as *Deep Throat* has taken on a whole new meaning, Reems is alcohol-free, married, and a highly successful real estate broker in, of all places, Park City, Utah, home of the annual Sundance Film Festival.

Interest in Reems has resurfaced, thanks to the much acclaimed documentary *Inside Deep Throat,* which chronicles the highs and lows of a film and industry that changed the course of sexuality and American politics. Avoiding the spotlight for over twenty years, Reems spent some time detailing a life that is at times funny, tragic, and ultimately uplifting, as Paul Fischer discovered when he spent some time chatting to the once infamous actor about a life less ordinary.

The trademark mustache is gone, and Harry Reems, now fifty-six, is at the Sundance Film Festival to reflect on a life marred with alcohol, sex, and renewed faith and optimism. He was at Sundance to attend the world premiere of *Inside Deep Throat,* marking the first time in over twenty years that Reems, star of over a hundred porn films, would talk openly about the film that made him an unlikely celebrity. Sitting in a small hotel room in Park City, Reems, who was starting to lose his voice at this point, recalled a youth defined by religion and repression. "My grandparents were orthodox Jews from the old country, but my parents kind of broke that barrier and ate ham, fish, and lobster as well as played golf on the Sabbath," Reems recalls, smilingly. "They never really taught us very much about Judaism, although my brother and I were bar-mitzvahed, but after that we never even went to synagogue."

Harry was born Herbert Streicher in New York City "and lived my first five years in the Bronx. Then we moved up to Westchester County to a town called Harrison," Reems recalls. Reems joined the military and left the Marine Corps in 1967. Initially intent on being an actor, Harry studied acting with Lee Strasberg and was a founding member of the experimental theatre company, Café La Mama. From such lofty beginnings, Harry Reems was surprisingly born. "I needed to supplement the income, because this was off, off Broadway and so a fellow actor said: I know where you can make a hundred bucks and get laid at the same time," he says, laughingly.

It was the late '60s and the adult world of porn was still in its infancy and not an industry. Reems recalls when he first started making adult films, it was all very much under the counter, and "little eight millimeter, ten-minute epics, which would be shown in private homes." With changes in the obscenity laws in 1968, Reems says that "these little filmmakers who were doing the small films started to do bigger films, all with the pretense that there was an educational value and social redeeming value." It was during this period, that Reems donned a white coat, and played various versions of the doctor that audiences would see in *Deep Throat.* "I wore that white coat in hundreds of films before *Deep Throat,* and stayed very anonymous, as a very small group of people frequented adult films."

By 1972, Harry had already appeared in close to a dozen underground films and was already getting bored with acting. Then in 1972, Harry was asked to fly to Florida as a lighting cameraman for what he assumed was going to be another small, anonymous film. The movie was *Deep Throat,* its director, Gerard Damiano. "I had acted for this director before, so when the actor that was supposed to play this doctor couldn't act, he threw the white coat on me and said, 'One more time, and have fun with it. Go crazy.' I think there was a six-page script." Nobody thought they were making history, but Reems was ready to act one last time. He remembers the fun times he had on that set, and scowls when we come to the inevitable mention of star Linda Lovelace. Reems says he had "made movies with Linda prior to *Deep Throat,* and Linda was never forced at gunpoint to do anything," remerging, angrily, that Lovelace had willingly appeared in "some films that I would never even think of being in," including early bestiality movies. "The name Linda Lovelace was invented, as was the name Harry Reems, and then she tried to catch a train to fame and it didn't work." Reems recalls that Lovelace "wasn't articulate, couldn't act, and so she went to all the Hollywood parties. So eventually to make money she joined the women's movement, antiporn—'I was forced at gunpoint'—and of course that lasted for a while, but when she couldn't make money doing that anymore, or when she wasn't a good interview anymore, she went right back to porn, or back to nudity. She was doing nude photographs at the end of her life and films with nudity." As for Lovelace's literary account of that period in her now infamous book, *Ordeal*, "it was a total lie. But, she was a nice enough woman and sexually she was fun and when you look at the film you see this big smile, and I was on every set because I was the lighting director, not just the scenes I did, and nobody ever forced her to do anything."

Deep Throat would emerge as more than just a porn film, a theme explored in the *Inside Deep Throat* documentary. Reems says that nothing could have prepared him for the effect that little film would have on America's burgeoning sexual revolution. "I was totally shocked, and I think I now know the reason," says Reems. "*Deep Throat* was the first film to say that it held no social redeeming value; we are going for straight out burlesque comedy, and just have fun. Of course it caught the attention of a few celebrities, the word of mouth spread and the government started to prosecute it because it was becoming famous, which only led to more people going to the theatres. So, the Justice Department basically made the film succeed."

And succeed it did, raking in the money and turning pornography into a virtually legitimate and almost respectable art form. While *Deep Throat* would emerge as the most profitable film of all time, life for Harry Reems would also undergo a dramatic change. Initially, the world post–*Deep Throat* was still his oyster. "After *Deep Throat*'s fame I did a few more porno movies, but instead of getting a hundred bucks like all of the others I was getting three, four, five thousand a day. They just wanted my name on the poster and theater marquees." Reems even got offered adult films in Europe, "so I made several films in Germany which were shoot-'em-ups or gangster movies." Then, Reems's world began to slowly unravel. "I came home for a couple of weeks to do my laundry, say hello to friends, before I started another movie in Rome and I got arrested for *Deep Throat.*

The FBI came to my door in the middle of the night, handcuffed me, and took me to the New York courts."

While much of this is discussed in the documentary, hearing the actor's recounting of this entire incident remains an eye-opener, with the whole *Deep Throat* case emerging as one of the most damaging trials of the 1980s. "They told me to waive extradition, that I'm going to Memphis, Tennessee, to stand trial for distributing a movie," recalls an emotional Reems, who understands why he was going on trial for distributing the movie, referring to it as a conspiracy. "If you have knowledge of a crime in the United States and you don't legally disavow and destroy that crime you're held responsible for it. So, I knew the film was in distribution, but what I didn't know was that there was going to be eight members of the Columbo organized crime family that I was on trial with. I think the prosecutor was trying to do nothing more than get some press and bring his trial to the attention of the public and maybe build up his name. What he didn't realize was I went and got more press. This was the first time an artist acting—first time an artist of any kind—was being prosecuted by the federal government. There were new laws and new obscenity statutes in 1981 and they went back to the '76 statutes, and then the broadest use of the conspiracy laws in the history of the United States." Tearfully, Reems recounts going through this trial, every day listening about murders, "about money going in suitcases and the street fights between two families over the proceeds." It was then, that Reems began drinking heavily, as the trial began to bear its toll.

"I was told by Alan Dershowitz, who is a law professor up at Harvard, that if the Republicans were re-elected I'm going to jail but if the Democrats get into office I'd be Scot-free. Of course, Dershowitz knows a lot of people in Washington so I got calls from

Ramsey Clark, who is a past attorney general from the '60s, during the Kennedy era. I got calls from Eugene McCarthy saying, 'Harry, don't worry, if we take the White House we're letting you go,' because I'd be crying to Dershowitz because I was scared. I mean, I didn't commit any of those murders. I didn't steal that money. I didn't do those things to those people. I didn't even know it was obscene. It was nothing more than to try to take attention away from his Watergate fiasco."

Reems did not go to jail, but his life was a shambles. "I became a real low-bottom drunk and stopped doing movies." He tried to segue into straight acting, was offered the role of the coach in *Grease,* but the stigma associated with his past put a stop to that weeks prior to filming. Reems's old Hollywood pals Nicholson and Beatty had deserted him, and all he had was the solace of the bottle. "I was getting worse and worse as a drunk and was in a hospital in New York City for thirty-two days, and over the thirty-two days some friends came by to visit and all of them said 'I don't want to see you again. You look like you're ninety years old and you look like you're going to die, and that's a shame, Harry, you're too nice a person, too good a person. You need to stop drinking.' When they released me from the hospital, I had asked for quarters for the telephone from my friends, but I went and bought a bottle of vodka. I woke up six or seven days later in Los Angeles County Jail with excrement in my pants and sleeping in my vomit, and had no idea how I got from New York to L.A. I had no money, I was panhandling in the streets and so I went to a meeting, a program of recovery. I went to a twelve-step meeting where I'm told other alcoholics learn how not to drink."

Reems pauses, sighing at the memory. "I walked in the building and got arrested by the police officers. It was in City Hall where the police department was, and the meeting was taking place in the same building and I got arrested. It seems I had three or four warrants out for me. I got to Park City in '86 and I didn't get sober until '89. I guess there was vagrancy and lewdness, breaking and entering, you know I'd walk into somebody's door and sleep on their living room couch. I didn't know who they were. They'd wake up and see this person and they'd call the police. So, the police officer very kindly said, 'Go to that meeting, you need it, but come out of that meeting and come right back here because I've got four warrants out for your arrest. Do you promise me you'll come back here?', and I said 'Yes, I just wanna go see what these people do, how this thing works.' And, I walked back out after the meeting and he put the handcuffs on me and we . . . our jail is up at the county seat about twenty minutes away, and this officer said to me, 'Harry, if you could only get sober, if you could only fix this problem, you have no idea how many people you could help, how many lives you can save, how valuable your life could become,' and nobody had ever told me I could be of any value. I spent that week in the jail, I paid my fines. I got sober. I went to twenty or thirty meetings a week in Park City and Salt Lake."

Reems was finally determined to put the past behind him. "It took a long time for me to learn how to sleep again, have bowel movements, to keep food down, because I was the kind of alcoholic that seizured and had DT's, and eventually it went away. Eventually that program taught me how to love myself, how to be a help to others, how to find God in my life, and I found God in those rooms. Today I live a very honest and loving life." The former Jewish kid from Manhattan is now a born-again Christian, living a quiet, but successful life in Park City. "I have a wonderful marriage, a beautiful home, a very successful business, and I still go to those rooms and still go to those meetings."

Reems would have been more than happy to go about his business and let the past take care of itself. Until recently, Harry had never discussed his past, declined all interview requests and preferred to live the life of an entrepreneur in this ski resort. Then he was contacted about a new film being made, a documentary on a time that he would rather forget. "I was ready to say no. Over the twenty years since I had done my last film, and living here in Park City, I have three, four, five times a week somebody wanting to do an interview with me, or would I come out and do this talk show, or you know, let's do your life story as a movie of the week—lots of comedy, sex, drugs, rock and roll—and I had been through this horrible experience, so I never wanted to tell that story. When I met directors Fenton Bailey and Randy Barbato and they were out here at Sundance three or four years ago, we sat down and we met and they said 'what's your fix.' I mean, I had refused to do interviews. I had refused to do anything. But, when he mentioned Brian Grazer's name it perked my ears and I wanted to know what direction the film is going in." The directors' response was "we won't know until we get the footage shot." But, they saw it as taking *Deep Throat* and using it as a thread to show the social and cultural change in America that took place in the late '60s and the '70s and '80s, and they were going to tie that all together. "I said 'well, do you know about me being a drunk' and they said 'it's a wonderful story of redemption.' I said *that's* the story I'd be willing to tell, and so I agreed to be cooperative, to be in the film, and I'm very impressed with the final product."

Surprisingly, Reems insists, watching the documentary for the first time at Sundance, did not bring back any unwanted memories. "I have a new life now. They flew my wife and I out to L.A. about two weeks ago to see a rough cut and to ask if I would participate in a promotion and I said, well, let me see the film and, I was quite pleased. I mean, they had things in the movie that I didn't even know about." Reems says the film didn't touch the surface of what it set out to do. "I mean, they didn't go into any great depth about the mafia, they didn't go into great depth about my journey, but they did go into depth about the sexual revolution that took place in America in the '60s, and I was right in the middle of it all—in the East Village, a hippie, in the late '60s, Mama Cass, Jimi Hendrix, all of them, Janis Joplin, the bell-bottoms and the crazy hair and the free love, and I came from such a repressed Jewish background. You bet I became a hippie—even though I got caught up in it and the next thing you know I'm a voice. But this movie is factual, accurate, in-depth, and it really captures the world as it was, that world as it really was, and I'm proud to be a part of it, I really am. I never thought I'd come out the hero, or that they would use me as the redemptive sort of angle in the movie."

For Reems, *Inside Deep Throat* remains but a memory, the glare of the spotlight has once again dimmed, and Harry Reems says that he looks forward to returning to reality. "On Tuesday morning I have a listing appointment to list a house." Reems is more than happy being a real estate broker, finally saying, laughingly, "if you love your work you're not working."

Charles Dickens once wrote, "They were the best of times, they were the worst of times." It's a fitting prologue to the life and times of Harry Reems, actor, porn star, alcoholic, and gentleman capitalist. He hopes the documentary and the recently announced re-release of that original porn classic, will remind us of an era that forged a revolution and the beginning of one of the more unique film industries in Hollywood history.

Sex, Guys, and Fruit Flies

By Dave Barry
The Miami Herald / October 3, 2004

Over the years I have been harshly critical of the scientific community for wasting time researching things nobody cares about, such as the universe. I don't know about you, but I'm tired of reading newspaper stories like this:

> Using a giant telescope, astronomers at the prestigious Crudwinkle Observatory have observed a teensy light smudge that they say is a humongous galaxy cluster 17 jillion light years away, which would make it the farthest-away thing that astronomers have discovered this week. However, astronomers at the rival Fendleman Observatory charged that what the Crudwinkle scientists discovered is actually mayonnaise on the lens. Both groups of astronomers say they plan to use these new findings to obtain even larger telescopes.

With all due respect to astronomers: We don't *need* to find any more stuff in the universe. We already have more stuff than we could ever use, right here in our garages. We need the scientific community to focus on a topic that is of far greater importance, yet remains a baffling mystery to humanity, or at least guys: sex.

Guys think about sex a *lot.* You know the painting of Washington crossing the Delaware, where the guys in the boat have facial expressions of grim resolve as they approach a battle that will determine their fates, and the fate of the revolution? Those guys are thinking: "Maybe there will be women in New Jersey."

But despite several million years of thinking virtually nonstop about sex, guys have made very little progress toward answering such basic questions about human sexuality as: How can you obtain more of it? How much talking is required? What is the role of jewelry? How important is the size of a guy's, um, car?

For guys, these are uncharted waters. That's why I am so pleased by a recent Reuters article, sent to me by alert reader Jorge Gomez, concerning research being done by scientists at Stanford University into the sex life of fruit flies. This research is significant because fruit flies have many biological similarities to humans. For example, both species eat fruit. The list goes on and on.

According to this article, when a male fruit fly wants to have sex with a female fruit fly, he goes through a series of specific steps, the first one being to pound down approximately eight martinis.

No, wait, that's what a human guy would do if he were going to attempt to mate with a female who had six legs and 17,000 eyeballs, which, trust me, is not out of the question for some guys, and you know who you are. What male fruit flies do is engage in a courtship ritual, which according to the Reuters article includes "tapping the female, extending and vibrating a wing and singing." (The article doesn't say what they sing, but I assume it's "Can't Get Enough of Your Love, Babe," by the late Barry White).

The Stanford scientists found that these ritual mating actions are controlled by a sector of the fly's brain consisting of sixty cells—about twice the number of brain cells required to cast a vote on *American Idol*. According to the article, when scientists mess up these cells, the male flies rush through the mating steps—"essentially try to do everything at once"—which causes the females to become turned off and develop little fly headaches.

This, of course, is exactly the mistake that male humans make: We're always trying to rush through the mating steps. Stand next to any construction site, and when an attractive woman walks past, you'll hear guy construction workers suggesting that she go directly to, like, Step 74. This approach *never* works. Construction workers have been trying it since they built the pyramids, and not once in all that time has a woman ever said: "That's a great idea! Let's have carnal relations right now on this pile of dirt!"

And yet guys keep trying. Why? Because we're dumber than fruit flies. Fruit flies at least have some clue what their mating ritual is supposed to consist of, whereas human guys get most of their information from letters written by imaginary people to *Penthouse* magazine.

That's why we need scientists to determine exactly what steps are required for successful human mating. And I don't mean some vague psychobabble about "listening" or being "sensitive." I mean specific written instructions that we guys can understand, like "caress the target region in a clockwise pattern, applying 1.8 foot-pounds of torque." Wouldn't that be great?

No, because we guys don't read directions. So I guess we're stuck with blundering around, learning what "turns women on" through trial and error.

Tonight, I will vibrate my wings.

sex

When Oral Sex Results in a Pregnancy: Can Men Ever Escape Paternity Obligations?

By Sherry F. Colb
FindLaw.com / March 9, 2005

In a lawsuit against his ex-girlfriend, Richard O. Phillips has alleged that about six years ago, he engaged in oral sex with her. Unbeknownst to Phillips, he says, his girlfriend, Sharon Irons, allegedly saved the resulting semen and used it to inseminate herself. A pregnancy resulted, Irons gave birth to a baby, and DNA tests proved Phillips to be the genetic father.

Though Phillips allegedly did not learn of either the pregnancy or the birth until some time later, a court nonetheless ordered him to pay approximately $800 a month in child support.

Irons disputes Phillips's claims and asserts that she conceived her child in the ordinary way. For purposes of this column only, however, I will assume the truth of Phillips's allegations.

Phillips's suit originally contained allegations of theft, fraud, and intentional infliction of emotional distress. An Illinois appellate court, however, dismissed the theft and fraud claims a few weeks ago, allowing only the emotional distress action to go forward.

The facts of this case raise significant questions about the contours of a man's right—if any—to avoid paternity.

A WOMAN'S RIGHT TO CONTROL PATERNITY

When a woman becomes pregnant, the man who impregnated her has few legal rights with respect to that pregnancy. He cannot, for example, require the woman to remain pregnant if she chooses to have an abortion. Conversely, he cannot force her to have an abortion if she wants to remain pregnant and give birth.

Whether it is the right to become a parent or to avoid becoming a parent, then, the pregnant woman's choice trumps that of the father of the pregnancy. Furthermore, if the woman chooses to go to term with the pregnancy, the father is legally liable for child support.

All of this may seem quite unfair. If a man has no control over paternity, then why should he have to pay for the resulting child? Don't responsibilities ordinarily come with rights, and vice versa?

One reason for the inequity between women and men surrounding pregnancy is the disparate physical circumstances in which a pregnant woman and the man who impregnated her, respectively, find themselves. To grant a man a legal say in whether or not a woman stays pregnant and bears his and her child is effectively to give him dominion over his partner.

As the crucial three-Justice plurality opinion stated in *Planned Parenthood of Southeastern Pennsylvania v. Casey,* the case in which the Supreme Court declined to overrule *Roe v. Wade* and accordingly struck down the husband-notification provision of a Pennsylvania statute, "it is an inescapable biological fact that state regulation with respect to the child a woman is carrying will have a far greater impact on the mother's liberty than on the father's. The effect of state regulation on a woman's protected liberty is doubly deserving of scrutiny in such a case, as the State has touched not only upon the private sphere of the family, but upon the very bodily integrity of the pregnant woman."

Providing otherwise would give a man not simply a voice in whether or not he acquires the status of parent. It would authorize him to order the invasion of a woman's body, whether to destroy a pregnancy that she wants to continue, or to force her to sustain a pregnancy she wishes to terminate.

As the Justices also said in *Casey,* "the Court today recognizes that, in the case of abortion, the liberty of the woman is at stake in a sense unique to the human condition and so unique to the law. The mother who carries a child to full term is subject to anxieties, to physical constraints, to pain that only she must bear." The law accordingly gives her the right unilaterally to override the wishes of the man who impregnated her.

THE FINANCIAL IMPLICATIONS OF PATERNITY

Even accepting the unequal distribution of rights over a pregnancy, however, some argue that if a woman has complete control over whether or not to have a baby, then she should also bear the financial consequences if she chooses to remain pregnant.

In other words, if a woman can impose biological paternity on a man against his wishes, then that power should simultaneously relieve the man of his obligation to support the child that results, shouldn't it?

The answer that the law gives is no. When a baby comes into the world, both the man and the woman whose genes led up to the child's existence are ordinarily responsible for the care of that baby, regardless of whether the child was "wanted" by both parents. Unless the two genetic parents decide to give up their baby for adoption, that responsibility continues until the child reaches the age of majority.

Men, in other words, can seemingly be conscripted into fatherhood against their will and then forced to take care of the child whom they never agreed to have.

Some say, in response, that the man, in effect, agreed to have the child when he had sex with a woman and thus risked such an outcome. On this view, a man who engages in sexual intercourse assumes the risk of becoming a father. If he wants to avoid paternity, he must abstain from sex or undergo sterilization. Because pregnancy as well as its termination have such physically intimate consequences for a woman, the man—physically separate from these experiences—loses control over paternity once he consents to having intercourse.

This argument, of course, is in some tension with the notion that a woman does not consent to maternity when she engages in intercourse. Such tension is surely not lost on disgruntled fathers.

But even if one accepts that intercourse equals consent to paternity, what happens when a man does not consent to intercourse? Does he still bear the risk of becoming a father? The case of Phillips and Irons—as described in Phillips's complaint—tests our intuitions about that very question.

INVOLUNTARY PATERNITY: EXAMPLES

When Phillips—according to his version of the facts—engaged in oral sex with Irons, did he truly assume the risk that he would have a child?

Let us examine a series of hypothetical examples and attempt, through them, to answer this question.

First, consider the case of Adam and Eve. Eve gives Adam the date rape drug GHB, and he becomes unconscious. She then uses a needle to extract sperm cells from his body. Eve promptly goes to a doctor with the sperm, and the doctor uses it to fertilize her egg, implanting the resulting zygote in her body.

If Eve gives birth, is the resulting child Adam's? Genetically yes, but it would nonetheless appear grossly unfair to require Adam to pay child support. He has done nothing, after all, to surrender his childless status.

Now take the case of Onan and Eve. Onan masturbates in his home and deposits the resulting semen in the garbage, located in his kitchen. Eve visits Onan's home shortly after his encounter with himself. When Onan leaves the room for a few minutes, Eve takes the opportunity to rummage through his garbage and finds the discarded semen. She makes a quick exit and proceeds to inseminate herself.

If Eve becomes pregnant and gives birth, should Onan have to pay her child support? Again, as in the case of Adam and Eve, it would seem unjust to impose financial obligations on Onan. Though less violently than in Adam's case, Eve has stolen semen that did not belong to her and has used it to make children that Onan had no way of predicting would come into being.

The case of Phillips and Irons, as narrated by Phillips, falls somewhat further down the line toward consensual fatherhood than these two cases do. As Irons asserted, and as the Illinois appellate court agreed, "when plaintiff 'delivered' his sperm, it was a gift—an absolute and irrevocable transfer of title to property from a donor to a donee. . . . There was no agreement that the original deposit would be returned upon request."

Unlike Eve, Phillips—even on his own version of the relevant events—did consensually surrender his sperm to Irons. Should this fact make a difference?

DOES ORAL SEX ASSUME THE RISK OF PATERNITY?

In the earlier examples, it was only through nonconsensual wrongdoing that Eve came into possession of Adam's and Onan's sperm cells in the first place. That is, if Eve had respected Adam's bodily integrity and the privacy of Onan's garbage, then she would not have been able to become pregnant through these men.

In our real-life scenario too, Irons allegedly crossed a line that Phillips did not anticipate, but that crossing occurred *after* she legitimately (and with his consent) came into possession of his sperm cells. In other words, Phillips may have expected and hoped that Irons would discard his sperm rather than keeping and using it, but—unlike Adam and Onan—he did give it to her of his own free will.

IS SECRETLY OMITTING BIRTH CONTROL DIFFERENT FROM SECRETLY USING SPERM?

Is there a distinction, however, between Phillips (on his version of the facts) and a man who has consensual intercourse with a woman he (mistakenly) believes is using birth control?

If so, the distinction would seem to turn on a vision of "natural" versus "artificial" conception. When a man has intercourse with a woman, however "protected" from pregnancy he believes himself and her to be, he initiates a process that—left to its own devices—will sometimes yield a pregnancy. As a result, we hold him to have assumed the risk of such a pregnancy occurring, even when the man thinks that he and/or his partner have taken adequate precautions.

When a man does not engage in intercourse at all, however, then "nature," left to its devices, will never yield a pregnancy. It is only with the intervention of a third party (here, the woman with whom he allegedly engaged in oral sex) that the sperm will have the opportunity to fertilize an egg. In our real-life case, then, "but for" Irons's alleged intervention, the sperm cells were destined to die. In the language of torts and the criminal law, Irons's alleged actions rather than those of Phillips were therefore the "proximate cause" of the child's existence.

Though a man may have no right to expect nature to go as planned, he does perhaps have the right to expect that a human being will not affirmatively intervene and deliberately turn an act of "safe sex" into a pregnancy. Seen in this light, Irons's alleged use of artificial means to convert discarded semen into a pregnancy and ultimately a live birth appears to take Phillips out of the equation and to turn him into an unwilling sperm donor, just as Adam and Onan were.

But is the fact that Phillips surrendered his sperm voluntarily irrelevant? I would argue that it is. To understand why, consider an analogy.

TRANSFORMING A GIFT INTO SOMETHING ELSE

Suppose John Doe invites a police officer to visit his home. The officer comes over and brings John a gift: a pottery vase. Without telling John, the policeman has placed a listening device into the vase. After leaving John's home, the officer is able secretly to monitor the conversations and other activities that go on in John's apartment.

It is clear that on these facts, John—by inviting the officer to his home—has not assumed the risk of the police listening to his conversations and the activities in his home. Indeed, the officer's behavior represents a violation of John's Fourth Amendment right against unreasonable searches and seizures.

The fact that John accepted the vase from the police officer has no Fourth Amendment significance, because what he accepted was a piece of pottery, a gift that in no way entails the assumption of audio-monitoring. The vase-as-vase, in other words, is an entirely different entity from the vase-as-listening device.

Similarly, when Phillips surrendered his sperm to Irons, allegedly through oral sex, he agreed only to her gaining custody of the sperm-as-sperm. Absent preservation and fertilization, moreover, sperm cells die and become garbage. Phillips thus consensually surrendered nothing more than waste products to Irons, on his version of the story, and Phillips legitimately relied upon Irons to leave the status of that waste alone.

Instead, through insemination and pregnancy, Irons purportedly converted the surrendered sperm into something else entirely—a child.

WHAT ABOUT THE CHILD'S NEEDS?

In examining these issues, one last concern deserves our attention. Child support, as its name suggests, is not simply a monetary payment by a noncustodial parent to a custodial parent. It is—primarily, in fact—the fulfillment of an obligation by a parent to his child, the latter of whom is an innocent bystander in his or her own conception.

Though, on his account of the facts, Phillips did not consent to the creation of his child, the child may still feel entitled—like other children—to have two parents that share financial responsibility. The child, in other words, did nothing wrong to Phillips and seems to deserve no less than another child of a "surprised" father.

One response to this point is that every child deserves to have everything that he or she needs, and to have people called "parents" take care of him or her for the duration of childhood. But when a man does nothing that foreseeably risks a pregnancy, the genetic link between him and the resulting baby is of no greater significance than that of two siblings who are wide apart in age. Yet the law does not demand child support of the older sibling, precisely because he or she did nothing to create the biological relationship with the younger one.

Even when he avoids intercourse and does nothing to donate sperm to a reproductive endeavor, a man can still be forced into factual biological parenthood. Irons's alleged actions demonstrate as much. Further, that reality may lead to great suffering, as the Illinois appellate court recognized by allowing Phillips's emotional distress claim to go forward. That reality should not, however, necessarily carry financial ramifications along with the emotional ones.

At some point, a man's lack of actual responsibility for the creation of a child must absolve him of financial responsibility as well. The circumstances of Phillips and Irons—as claimed by Phillips—seem a sensible place to start.

sex

Toy Story

The accidental Alabama sex-toy ban.

By Steven Kurutz
Nerve.com / November 1, 2004

Sherri Williams, the woman who has spent the past six years suing the state of Alabama in an effort to overturn its ban on adult toys, didn't set out to be a constitutional crusader for vibrators and dildos. Initially, she simply wanted to sell them. Williams is the owner of Pleasures, a small chain of adult stores in Alabama in Huntsville and Decatur. The stores are noticeably less seedy than typical adult emporiums, which tend to resemble windowless bunkers cemented into the highway. The Pleasures branch in Huntsville is in a busy shopping plaza, a few doors down from a Chili's restaurant. Couples in jeans and button-downs browse through zebra-print panties and more inventive products like the "Ten-Inch Quivering Cock." The manager, a friendly man named Wayne Tribble, likens the Pleasures experience to "walking into a Wal-Mart. But an adult Wal-Mart." Williams calls the stores "upscale adult boutiques," a retail concept she claims to have invented.

If there's such a thing as an upscale-adult-boutique look, Sherri Williams has it. Tall with dark blonde hair, a pixieish face and skin the color of a Coppertone bottle, she's fond of boxy jackets and shiny blouses that accentuate her bust. When I met her for dinner in New York recently (she was in town for an adult-industry convention), Williams, who is forty and single, passed her business card around to the waiters, suggesting both a practical business sense and an up-for-anything attitude. "Anyone who knows Sherri," she said in a woozy Southern drawl between sips of a martini, "knows that I live to live."

Until the state of Alabama intervened, Williams was living pretty well. She opened her first store in Huntsville in 1993 and quickly expanded into her current space, then a second location. Women whose sex lives had been dormant for years flocked to her stores, weighing the pros and cons of the "Silver Bullet" vibrator and the "Wascally Wabbit" as if they were shopping for washing machines. One seventy-year-old widow sent Williams a thank-you card after getting her new vibrator home. Then in June of 1998, Williams got a call from a reporter at the *Decatur Daily*. The reporter wanted to know what she thought of the new law banning the sale of adult toys.

Williams responded, "What law?"

On the last day of the 1998 summer session, the Alabama legislature passed Senate Bill 607, which was intended to update the state's obscenity laws with an eye toward banning nude dancing in strip clubs. But buried within language about protecting children from moral corruption was a clause that made it unlawful to distribute "any device designed or marketed as useful primarily for the stimulation of human genital organs." In other words, the bill made it illegal to sell vibrators and dildos in Alabama. Although the legislature stopped short of outlawing their possession and use, if residents wanted to buy a sex toy, they'd have to travel out of state or order one online.

In its attempt to govern the sex lives of its citizens, Alabama is not alone. Several states, including Georgia, Mississippi, and Texas, have similar laws; others have tried unsuccessfully to institute them. What makes Alabama different, though, is the formidable presence of Sherri Williams.

With the help of a lawyer and support from the ACLU, Williams brought a suit against the state, charging that the ban violated a constitutional right to privacy. Twice a federal court judge has ruled in her favor. Each time, however, the decision has been reversed in appellate court. Last summer, the 11th District Appeals Court voted 2-to-1 to uphold the ban, ruling that the U.S. Constitution doesn't guarantee a right to sexual privacy.

Despite her recent defeat and dwindling legal options, Williams has continued to pursue the suit, fighting not only for her own livelihood (roughly 60 percent of her sales are derived from sex toys) but for the unalienable right to battery-assisted masturbation. "Our nation was born because we revolted against politicians legislating morality," she said, sounding like the Norma Rae of dildos. "This case is not just to repeal the ban on toys. It's to kick the government out of our bedroom."

With its pickup-driving populace and abundance of fundamentalist church congregations, Alabama is a red state in all the stereotypical ways. Indeed, the attorney general who first defended the ban, Bill Pryor, is now a federal judge, appointed by the Bush White House for his conservatism.

Huntsville, a sleepy city of 158,000 near the Tennessee border, is the most progressive in the state, home to NASA's rocket program, whose engineers and scientists ensure an educated and socially liberal mix. But drive twenty minutes outside of town, and rusty cars junk the grassy lawns like a scene from *Deliverance.* "This is the buckle of the Bible belt," one Huntsville resident told me. "People here aren't even sure if they should be having sex with the lights on."

Still, there is no real support within the state for a ban on sex toys, either before the ruling passed through the legislature or after. There's also no moral engine driving the ban—no conservative political group or heavily perspiring, holy-rolling preacher. Williams's lawyer, Mike Fees, says there has never been a concerted effort in Alabama to ban sex toys. "I have not run into a single soul that has approached me in six years and said they think I'm wrong," said Fees. "In a worst-case scenario, I think you could say people are ambivalent."

A big, genial man with a graying beard, Fees is a seasoned trial lawyer who was raised in Huntsville and now represents the city in civil lawsuits. Until the Williams case, he had never had any contact with the ACLU. "I agree with them in many ways," Fees told me while we sat in his wood-paneled office downtown, "but I'm something of a gun enthusiast, and in my opinion, they forgot the second amendment." Fees said he took the case because he sympathized with Williams, and because no other lawyer in town would. Since then, many people have wrongly assumed he's a lawyer for the adult industry. "I started getting calls from dancers in town, saying, 'We're getting arrested for wearing T-backs. Can you represent us?'" Fees said, chuckling at the notion of being considered an expert on thongs.

In its own way, the history of *Williams vs. Alabama* is also a comedy of errors. According to several people involved in the case, the ban on sex toys was passed by mistake. The details vary depending on who's telling the story, but the general outline is as follows: several years ago, a Huntsville preacher built a church next to a topless bar and promptly decided that his new neighbor was a negative influence on the community. The preacher approached a state senator named Tom Butler, who then approached a local prosecutor and asked him to find a law that would prohibit nude dancing in Madison County. Legislation was borrowed from a nearby state (some say Georgia, others Indiana) and offered as SB 607.

In what proved to be a crucial oversight, none of the legislators, including the bill's sponsor, Tom Butler, read the bill thoroughly before voting unanimously to pass it. When the portion banning sex toys was later brought to Butler's attention, he sheepishly responded that he had nothing, per se, against sex toys. Accused of governing bedroom activities, he countered that Alabamians were free to skip over the state line to Tennessee to buy vibrators. (He now refers all questions to the Madison County district attorney's office).

The result is that the citizens and lawmakers of Alabama have been left with a dubious law for which there is no real support. "The city attorney and county prosecutor have far more problems to worry about than the sale of adult toys," says Fees, who works closely with both parties. Even the state attorney general seems to be defending the ban more out of prosecutorial duty than belief in its validity. Asked to be interviewed for this article, a representative for the attorney general's office issued this reply: "The Alabama Legislature passed this Act and Alabama law requires the office of attorney general to defend it in court. This office will do its duty."

But while no one is actively campaigning against the sale of adult toys, no one is exactly rushing to overturn the ban, either. There has been no pamphleteering; no pro-vibrator rallies. During the early stages of the lawsuit, a California adult-toy company called Good Vibrations offered to airdrop vibrators over the populace. In a more serious gesture, several adult-toy distributors hired a lobbyist to appeal to the Alabama legislature, but a bill to void the ban failed to pass in 2002. And although Pleasures customers are sympathetic, most would never state so publicly. Masturbation, it seems, remains too personal an issue to become a cause celebre.

While the number of people in Alabama who use sex toys is greater than some would like to believe, those willing to testify about it in court are a select group. For her part, Williams has always possessed a rebel streak. Raised in Kentucky, at eighteen she loaded her belongings into a 1973 Nova, borrowed $250 from her grandfather and moved to Chicago, where she found a job at a shady adult store on the South Side. "I was so naive. I lasted three weeks," Williams recalled. "I quit right after I found out what the holes in the walls were for. The manager called them glory holes, which is what I called the place: the Glory Hole."

Years later, Williams opened her own stores with a similar mix of southern charm and pluck. "I asked the mayor in Decatur, did he mind if I open a store like that in his town?" Williams said. "He said he did mind. I said, 'Well, I'm opening the store anyway. I just wanted to be considerate and let you know my intentions.'" After she opened, Williams said, "I was nearly zoned out of existence." She then hired a renowned lawyer from Tampa who represents strip-clubs to zone her back in. As Williams put it, "I'm not a lay-down-and-die kind of person."

In addition to Sherri Williams, a small group of sexually liberated co-plaintiffs are named in the ACLU suit. In February of 2002, they gathered at the Huntsville courthouse to give sworn depositions to a lawyer for the attorney general. Among those present were

Williams; B. J. Bailey, a middle-aged woman who throws in-home sex toy parties; Deb and Benny Cooper, a married couple who believe sex toys saved their relationship; and a thirty-three-year-old woman named Alice Jean Cope who has difficulty achieving orgasm without sex toys.

A lawyer named Tom Campbell conducted the deposition for the state. Later described by several of the co-plaintiffs as a mild, balding man in his mid-forties who resembled Mr. Magoo, he was visibly embarrassed by the line of questioning his job required. Several times during the proceedings his face became flushed. The co-plaintiffs, meanwhile, seemed to delight in detailing their sex lives. At one point in the deposition, Campbell asked Deb Cooper, an oversexed prenatal nurse, what kind of adult toys she used.

"Well," said Cooper, "I currently have a little briefcase full. But we have I guess it's like a little red vibrator cock. And there's the Jack Rabbit, which vibrates and swirls around like this," Cooper said, rotating her hand before going on. "And then we have the Cyberskin, which you can put on your husband's penis to make it longer. Then we have it's kind of like a Silver Bullet, but it's not; it's a little bit longer and it has little attachments that you can put on."

"Do you have any other sexual devices?" Campbell asked.

"I think that's about all of them," Cooper replied. Reading the deposition, you can almost see the relief pass over Campbell's face as the line of discussion ends. Later, the lawyer asks Cooper's husband, Benny, about his own use of sex toys. "Ever use them alone?" Benny Cooper was asked.

"Sometimes."

"And do these devices serve any kind of medical purpose?"

"I don't know what would be medical," said Cooper. "It's a stress reliever."

"Does it serve any kind of psychological purpose for you?"

"I guess it does, yeah," replied Cooper. "It's like a crutch or something, you know. It helps to achieve maximum pleasure."

A brief pause followed, as if to allow the lawyer a moment to contemplate the concept of maximum pleasure. "Let me shift gears . . ." Campbell said.

Since the lawsuit was originally filed, Williams has distanced herself from the other co-plaintiffs, particularly B. J. Bailey, whom she considers something of a "loose cannon." There's a noticeable undercurrent of competition between the two women, as if Huntsville isn't big enough for two vibrator vendors. Yet their belief that the ban is ridiculous remains mutual, and, surprisingly, something the state has never refuted.

Although Alabama's attorney general has fought two successful battles to overturn rulings that would have lifted the ban, the office has never championed the law itself. In fact, officials have candidly admitted to Fees during proceedings that it's absurd. Their principal concern isn't whether it's a good law, but whether it's unconstitutional. "In some respects, it comes down to how you define the issue," Fees explained. "Is there a constitutional right of privacy to sell and use adult toys? When you narrowly define the issue that way, you can easily come to the conclusion that, no, there is not. Our argument is that the right of privacy protects intimate relationships between consenting adults. Adult toys would be protected under that broader umbrella."

So far, the 11th Circuit Court has disagreed.

B. J. Bailey and her husband, Dan, live about twenty miles north of Huntsville in a two-story, peach-colored house the couple describes as their "dream home." It was built with the proceeds from Saucy Lady, the company by which Bailey throws parties to sell sex toys, Tupperware-style. (To date, Bailey has thrown 2,196 in-home parties).

Bailey is perhaps the person who's been most affected by the ban. Her target customers are women who are too intimidated to shop for sex toys in a store like Pleasures—women who have, no doubt, been further shamed by the ban—and her business model relies on a network of distributors who host their own parties and kick a percentage back to Saucy Lady. Since the ban, many of those distributors have quit, and Bailey has had trouble attracting new ones.

A trim, anxious woman of fifty-one with pale skin and ginger hair, Bailey has a tendency to grow agitated when talking about the ban, her voice becoming louder, louder, louder until she breaks the tension with a nervous laugh. She seems most upset by the hypocrisy behind the ban, which permits a sexual aid like Viagra to be championed by the same lawmakers who deem products geared to women obscene. "I bet there's not one Baptist church I could go into and not see one of my customers," she said, sitting in her family room cheerfully decorated with *Gone with the Wind* memorabilia. "The lawmakers don't understand women's sexuality."

While Sherri Williams is a businesswoman first and a cultural crusader second, Bailey views herself as an intimacy educator liberating the boudoirs of the South. In discussing sex, she is frank to the point of inappropriateness. "Men want a tight vagina," she told me shortly after we met. "If men have a choice between the Grand Canyon and tight, they want tight." In discussing her own coital history, she said, "Oh, honey, I faked orgasms until I was twenty-eight. My mother didn't tell me anything about sex. I tell the women, 'Do your Kegel exercises. If you don't do Kegels, your vagina can fall right out.'"

Neatly organized on steel shelves in Bailey's garage are the various products that she promises will unlock the door to sexual satisfaction: Coochy shave cream; the Flexi-Pleaser; the E.T. Finger. "This is the No. 1 seller," Bailey said, pointing to a product called Silky Sheets Spray, a bed-and-body talc that comes in flavors like Mystical Musk. "It has pheromones. Anything with pheromones is big." Bailey said southern women are in particular need of sex education. "A lot of women don't even know to use a water-soluble lubricant," she said, shocked. "They use Vaseline, Crisco. One woman says her husband wanted to know if he could use gun-cleaning oil. Gun-cleaning oil!"

Said Williams: "Women in the South are raised to think their primary goal is to get married and have kids. They've been held sexually subservient to men for so long. These women have a need, and they used to be chastised for having the need, but society is finally starting to be comfortable with women's sexuality." The adult-toy ban, says Williams, "sets women back twenty years."

One of the more noticeable ironies in the case is that vibrators have been in existence since the 1880s. According to historian Rachel P. Maines, they were the fifth household device to be electrified, right after the sewing machine, tea kettle, toaster, and fan (and before the vacuum cleaner). Following suit, both Bailey and the Pleasures staff approach selling sex toys as if it were just another product designed to rescue women from numbing routine. Holding up a pocket-sized vibrator with a small cord attached, Bailey said, "I tell women to strap one of these under their dress. Takes the drudgery out of housework."

Since their most recent defeat in July, Williams and her legal team have filed a motion asking the entire 11th Circuit to review the case and overrule the 2-1 decision. The motion was denied, but the court left an opening for the plaintiffs to pursue the issue again in the lower court. "We are suing for a fundamental right," Williams said. "We're not giving up."

Williams, in fact, still sells sex toys at her stores, and has since the ban was passed. Both sides seem to have an understanding that until a final legal decision is made, it's business as usual. This doesn't seem to bother the local police, who apparently don't relish the task of arresting a woman for selling dildos or encountering someone they know buying one.

Meanwhile, in case the final decision doesn't go her way, Williams is opening another shop in Huntsville next to Pleasures. A combination hookah bar and adult video store, it will carry a wide selection of the graphic XXX movies her romance boutiques have shied away from. "I don't believe in exploiting women," says Williams of her decision to carry traditional porn, "but because of the adult-toy ban, I may have to now." Taking inspiration from her legal battle, she has named the store Hipocratease.

SEX

Deep Gidget

Sandra Dee's death has our columnist yearning for the days when sex and love were actually related.

By Rabbi Marc Gellman
Newsweek.com / February 25, 2005

The recent death of Sandra Dee and the new release of a high-tone documentary about the porn flick *Deep Throat* got me thinking about spiritually significant movies, and both *A Summer Place* and *Deep Throat* are high on my list. In 1959, the Sandra Dee film marked the end of the era when sex and love were still connected, and in 1972 the Linda Lovelace film marked the beginning of an era where they were not. I also believe that the relationship between sex and love is, unquestionably, one of the great spiritual issues of our time.

The Sandra Dee movies—or if you prefer the Doris Day movies, or if you prefer the Annette Funicello movies—all showed us the American version of a 400-year-old romantic cultural tradition in which sex and love were inextricably linked and then also linked to marriage and then also to procreation. At the heart of this linkage was a fundamental cultural, personal, and religious belief that sex was not just another bodily function akin to burping, urinating, passing gas, or scratching an itch but rather was something really special (for the secularists) or something sacred (for us religious folk). Sex was not just a way to self-pleasuring sensations but a way to self-transcending love and to an enduring cultural and religious context for that love—which is marriage, which builds society, children, and the best parts of ourselves.

All these movies told essentially the same story with different blondes (except for Annette). They told tales of young love blossoming into physical attraction—or was it the other way around? Then the epic, sexually infused dance commenced between the predatory but always respectful and well-dressed suitor and the demure but always respectful and well-dressed blonde (except for Annette). That was the entire story line, plus some surfing and really bad music. But buried in the heart of these '50s morality plays was an unspoken conflict within the body and soul of these blonde virgins (except for Annette): part of them really wanted to do it with Troy Donahue. That suppressed part of them is what made *Deep Throat* possible just thirteen years later.

The new willingness of Sandra Dee and the others (except Annette) to say yes to sex with men promising neither love nor marriage encountered not a scintilla of resistance from the predatory males who were the recipients of this sexual largesse. So the uncoupling of love and sex was complete by the early '70s. The only things needed to complete the greatest cultural and spiritual revolution we have seen in our lifetime were provided by the courts and the culture. We suddenly had birth-control pills, drugs like marijuana that, unlike booze, put you in the mood without putting you to sleep and liberal abortion laws to make certain that nobody had to be inconvenienced by unwanted pregnancies. Maybe most important was the spiritual con job that got women to believe that their liberation was linked to their willingness to provide acrobatic and unlimited sex to a long line of men who did not really care about them, did not want to marry them, would probably dump them for a younger perkier version when they got bored and, most callously of all, would let them struggle alone and unsupported with the immense ethical conflict of killing their own fetus if they blundered into an unwanted pregnancy.

To my mind, the death of the highest possibilities of the feminist movement happened at precisely the moment when Linda Lovelace did her thing and women in the elite centers of our culture thought that this was all just a riot of fun and frolic. What they did not get is that the linking of love and sex is not just a misguided doctrine of ignorant southern Bible thumpers but quite the contrary, a natural and basic and true protection of women from the sexual predations of men and also a true and necessary tempering and taming of the promiscuous urges of men so that they could aspire to be more than humping dogs. Connecting love and sex is not just a religious belief endorsed by Gidget. It is a necessary cultural belief for any society seeking to inculcate the values of respect, sacrifice, bonding, self-transcendence, strong marriages, and strong societies. Disconnecting love and sex, on the other hand, only builds Studio 54, MTV, STDs, and a porn culture that allows teenage girls to go to school dressed like hookers. What a choice!

SEX

from *Callgirl*

By Jeannette Angell

September in Boston is nothing short of glorious. It's usually still too hot, of course, but the leaves know what's happening and are starting their slow demise into a fiery spectacular death. Mornings are chilly and evenings cold. There is at least the promise of something more than heat, heat, and more heat.

It's special here for a lot of other reasons. Boston and Cambridge are educational meccas; they lie low during the summer months, but suddenly come alive with the influx of students in the fall. The sidewalk in front of the Berklee School of Music—known as the Berklee Beach, for obvious reasons—fills with young uncovered bodies. Dreadlocks and tattoos and piercings and cases containing esoteric musical instruments.

The coffeehouses, bars, and Irish pubs are suddenly so full that they have people trickling out the doors. The venerable old trains of the Green Line are inundated with freshmen away from home for the very first time, and making that fact known to the world, sitting on the steps while people try to enter the trains around them, world-weary and arrogant from their extraordinary experiences in high school in Hudson, New Hampshire; or Seekonk, Massachusetts; or Sanborn, Maine.

Even the air feels different.

They say that January first marks the new year, but that isn't true here: for us, it's the third of September, when there is nothing behind to mourn and nothing ahead but promise. U-Haul trucks are everywhere. Hardware stores fill with earnest young customers. Anything can happen. People smile at one another. For a few charmed weeks, it feels as though anyone could make a new beginning, anyone could start a new life, anyone could become what he or she is destined to become.

There's an indefinable air about the whole city, a sense of expectation, of eagerness. Yes: the real new year is in September, when notebooks are still pure and white, when textbooks and course syllabi look exciting, and when foreign films suddenly start making sense for the first time.

That September, however, was hotter than any one I could remember. It was also, fatefully, the month that my car had to be inspected. Please understand this: I loved my Civic. This isn't a commercial, or anything, but honestly, I had 140,000 miles on it—and I ride the clutch, mind you—and I hadn't had to replace anything major, ever. It started up every morning, no matter how cold it was.

I can't really blame the car for not passing inspection; I never paid much attention to it between inspections. If I had been a better owner, this wouldn't have happened. The guy in the shop said he could have it ready by Monday noontime. The problem was, of course, that in the escort business, Saturday and Sunday nights aren't good nights not to work. Friday was the best night to take off; most of the girls did their personal dating on Fridays. It was a bad night for work, because guys had just gotten paid and thought they could go down to the bar and flash the cash around and get laid for nothing. They didn't admit defeat and call the service until after midnight, by which time I personally was way too tired to go out on a call.

Saturdays were good for regulars and for guys who planned their weekend around the agency. A lot of them wanted to see an escort and then afterward go out to the clubs, or on a real date, or meet their wives somewhere for dinner. So there were always a lot of early calls, the ones I liked the best. I loved calls that had me home and curled up with Scuzzy by ten-thirty.

Sundays were always good for business: it was the last hurrah of the weekend, when Monday started staring people in the face and they didn't like how it looked.

So I called Peach that Friday around four and told her that I was without wheels for the duration. She wasn't happy. That was understandable. I'm reasonably sure that at least some of my regulars stayed faithful to me because I had my own transportation. It's a lot less ostentatious than pulling up to a suburban house in a brightly lit taxi—or having one beep the horn outside when the hour is up. It's also a lot cheaper for the client, because he gets charged extra to help cover paying the driver. The cost of transportation to and from the client's place was generally shared by the callgirl and the client, with Peach negotiating as much as she could from the client. None of it ever came out of her fee. Nothing ever did.

So, for the first time, I was without my own car. Peach, however, was nothing if not positive. "Not a problem," she assured me. "I'll get you a driver."

Probably at least half to three-quarters of the girls who work for the service used a driver. A lot of them were college students living in dorm rooms; and the first advice that any school in Boston gives to prospective students is: Get rid of your car. The T—the public transportation system—is efficient and inexpensive; Boston traffic sucks; and the city employs (or so I am convinced) ex-Gestapo guards as meter police. I once met a woman whose son, who happened to be a police officer, ticketed her car in front of the house that they shared. True story. And it's a fact that I have personally paid enough parking tickets to deserve having a small building—at the very least—named after me.

So the girls used drivers. I had already met one of them, Luis, who worked part time for Peach while he went to business school. During my first week, back before she trusted me to hold cash for her, I'd meet him in Kenmore Square to give him Peach's take from the money I'd received from the client. I'd seen him once or twice after that at social gatherings—Peach had singled me out from among the women who worked for her as being worthy of her friendship, and occasionally invited me over to her house for late night soirées. Luis had been there, seemed to always be there. He and I looked at each other in a way that said we were both interested, but not yet.

I don't know where Peach got her drivers. She was usually having some sort of trouble with one or another of them at any given time, but I had never asked her about any of it.

That Saturday I showered and put on a clean pair of shorts and T-shirt (no sense in getting dressed yet when you don't know who you're going to be seeing, and what they're going to want you to wear) and flipped on the television. Nothing. So I put a tape of old *Frasier* episodes in the VCR and was just settling in nicely, with Scuzzy purring next to me, to watch Niles have a telephonic tiff with Maris. And then my own telephone rang.

It's funny, you *want* the phone to ring because you want to make money, and at the same time you are disappointed when it does because you know how annoying the next couple of hours could potentially be.

"Jen? Got work for you."

I pulled a pad of paper across the coffee table and flipped the lid off the felt tipped pen. "Go ahead."

"It's a regular." She always told me that when it was somebody I didn't know. Trying to reassure me, I expect. "Jake. Number is 508-555-5467. You'll have to get directions from him, it's in Marblehead."

"Okay. What did you tell him about me?" This was the most crucial information, from my point of view; it determined my persona for the evening.

"You're twenty-eight, 36-25-35, new to the business. You can be in graduate school or something. I told him you're getting a friend to drive you up there, your car is in the shop."

So that meant she was charging him extra without telling him where it was going. That wasn't unusual. Some clients didn't like the feel of a "professional" driver, it took away from the fantasy that the girl really wanted to be there. If this guy was in Marblehead—way up on the North Shore—it was really going to cost him.

None of my business; that was how Peach earned her fee. All I had to say was that my car was in the shop. Stick to the truth whenever possible—the liar's greatest secret.

"Okay."

"Call John on his cell phone. It's 555-3948. He's been there already. He'll cost you sixty dollars round trip. You'll be getting three-twenty from the client. Give John directions to your place and an ETA, and talk to the client, and call me back."

"Okay."

I put down the phone, feeling both satisfied that I had a call and was going to make some money, and at the same time wishing that I could just stay home and hang out with Scuzzy and Frasier at the Café Nervosa. A double mocha latte here, please.

Scuzzy was glaring at me. He always knew when I was about to leave, presumably deliberately ruining his evening. I sighed and picked up the phone again. "Hello, may I please speak with Jake?"

"Yeah." Scintillating conversationalist, I could tell right off the bat. I'm perceptive that way.

"Oh, hi, Jake. This is Tia, I'm a friend of Peach's. She asked me to call you."

"Uh-huh." He wasn't going to make this easy.

I took a breath. Why the hell do you think I'm calling, asshole? "Peach thought you might like me to spend some time with you this evening. Would you like me to come over?"

"Well, that depends. Tell me a little about yourself."

I was getting good at this. When a potential client asks this question, take it from me, he isn't interested in learning about my favorite author or my thoughts on the political situation in Yemen. "Well, I'm twenty-eight years old. I'm five feet seven, I weigh 126 pounds, I measure 36-25-35 and wear a C-cup bra. I have medium-length wavy brown hair and green eyes." Slight hesitation, slightly more breathless voice. "I'm very pretty. You won't be disappointed." On the television screen, Niles was jumping up and down. Hard to tell if it was frustration or glee. I wished I could turn the sound back on.

"Uh-huh." There was a pause. Great. This was apparently one of the ones who wanted to get off on the phone—on my time. A control freak, usually. Or maybe it was just his version of foreplay.

"Gee, Tia, I don't know. What are you wearing?"

Oh, for heaven's sake. You're going to say you want me, you already told Peach that you did, based on the identical information you just asked me to run through. This is a really stupid game. "Right now I just got out of the shower, so I'm just wearing a towel. How would you like me to dress?"

"Hmm." Jake had all the time in the world, apparently. Well, he could: it wasn't his dime. "How do you like to dress?"

In baggy sweats and woolen socks and my old Rykas, if you want the truth. "I always feel best in black lingerie," I said into the phone, as sweetly as I could manage. Remember, Jen: the car payment is due next Friday. This asshole is your car payment. "A lacy bra and panties, and of course a garter belt and stockings." I giggled, a little breathlessly. "With seams up the back. I don't understand why women don't wear stockings anymore. They're so . . . feminine. . . ." I let my voice drift off just enough so his imagination could take hold. Either I had him now or he was gay.

"Umm, yeah, that sounds great." Ten to one he has his dick in his hand. "Um . . . okay, uh-huh. Uh . . . That's okay. When can you be here?"

Finally. Once we got down to specifics, I could relax. Thank God.

I took another breath. "My car isn't working, so I'm getting my friend to drive me. I need to call him, and I need to get directions from you. I'll be there as soon as I can." To soften the blow, I added, "I can't wait. I like your voice. It's so warm and . . . and intimate. I wish that I could be with you . . . now."

"You like how I sound?" Later, he'll tell people that I was crazy about him from the beginning. If I give him any compliments at all, he'll say that *he* should have charged *me* for sex. "She was so hot for me, I'm telling you, she was getting off on my voice on the telephone . . . "

Can you spell projection?

I rolled my eyes for Scuzzy's benefit (I wanted, after all, to retain at least *his* respect) and did the husky sex voice thing again. "Yes. You sound . . . nice. Warm. Sensuous." Again the sexy *sous-entendre.* No subtleties here. "So, Jake . . . where do you live?"

Long set of directions. I repeated them back, then gave him an hour and a half estimated time of arrival, to be on the safe side. He grumbled, but he had already known it would take that long, he knew that I was coming from the city. He just wanted some leverage, something he could use to make me feel bad. It was amazing, the number of clients who liked that kind of control, who liked to put you at a disadvantage, make you feel from the onset that you needed to work even harder to please them, to make up to them for something. I was already tired of him by the time I hung up the phone. It had taken me ten minutes just to confirm the call. He was a pro at this.

John answered his cell phone on the second ring. British accent. "John here!"

"Jen here," I answered, bemused. "Peach says you can take me to Marblehead."

"Right you are. Where do you live?"

"Allston, just off Brighton Ave. I need a few minutes to get dressed."

"Be there in twenty minutes, then."

Final call to Peach. "It's all set."

"Of course it is," she said calmly. Peach always expects the world to conform to her plans. "Call me when you get there, and tell John to give me a call, too. I want him to pick up some cigarettes for me while you're seeing the client."

I turned my attention to my closet. Great. One of the hottest nights of the year, and I've just committed myself to Full Hooker Jacket. Such is life.

I made it in the twenty minutes, putting a reasonable slightly short but not too cheap print dress on over the much-discussed lingerie, brushing out my hair and putting on makeup, earrings, bracelets, and perfume while trying to watch the end of *Frasier.*

Honestly, that Maris. What a bitch.

I hovered uncertainly in front of the entrance to my building until a Corolla pulled up and the driver leaned across to open the passenger door. "Jen, right?"

"Right." I slid into the seat and shut the door, thanking all the gods within hearing that the man had air conditioning. My brief wait outside had been enough for sweat to start clinging to my neck and trickle down my upper thighs. The stockings weren't helping.

I pulled out my set of directions. "Not him," John protested as soon as I started reading them. I glanced up sharply. "What? Why? What's the matter?"

"Gives different directions every time. The girl's always late and he always uses it against her, and when she says it was his directions, he says she's stupid and is the one who got it wrong."

Wasn't that special? And I was going to have to have some form of sex with this idiot in the near future. That's why they pay me the big bucks. "Don't tell me this," I protested.

John was cheerful. "Don't you worry," he said, taking the entrance ramp to the Pike inbound. "Been there enough, haven't I, I'll get you there in no time, surprise the hell out of him."

I smiled. "You're my hero," I said. Obviously still in flattery mode.

"No problem," he said. "Just remember when it's time for my tip."

Sixty dollars, and I was supposed to tip him on top of that? I managed to keep my surprise silent, but just barely. Thank God, I thought, for my Civic. I was loving every rust spot and frayed bumper sticker on it. This Driving Miss Daisy stuff was way too expensive.

He didn't ask about my musical tastes, just flipped on WFNX, and so we listened to alternative rock all the way to the North Shore. It was an educational experience. I am here to tell you, yes, there *is* a band called the Butthole Surfers. Frightening. I spent quite a few miles wondering how I could reference the group in one of my classes, give the students the impression that I was cool. Not a chance. So after that I just relaxed and listened.

After that, I figured, *he* could tip *me*.

We made it to the oddly pillared colonial (who said that rich people have taste?) nestled above the harbor behind a mile of grass, trees, and driveway, in thirty-five minutes flat.

"The poor fellow will be disappointed," commented John.

"I'll help him work through his pain," I said flippantly. "Don't forget to call Peach. I'll see you in an hour."

He waited, his headlights on the door, until Jake answered the doorbell and I walked in. Gallant. Or maybe just practical. If there were a problem, he didn't want to have to turn around and come right back for me.

If I didn't get paid, he didn't get paid.

I went through the motions with Jake. For all his posturing, for all his selectiveness on the telephone, he himself was five foot three, had to weigh two hundred and fifty pounds, and was one of the most unattractive men I've ever seen in my entire life. Thus was justified what I liked to think of as my Second Law of Prostitution: *The least attractive are always the most demanding.*

And even as I played the slut for Jake, I wondered what it must be like for someone like John to drop a woman off at a house, knowing that he's leaving her off in order to have sex. Possibly unpleasant sex. What does he think about while he's waiting?

Does he imagine what we might be doing? When he picks the girl up, later, does he smell the sex on her? Does he think about it? Does he see her as more desirable, or less desirable, because of what she's been doing?

All in all, an odd occupation, it seemed to me.

He was right on time to pick me up, which was a relief, since Jake and I had run out of things to say to each other within the first five minutes. "Everything all right?" John asked. "Yes, thanks," I said, a little surprised. It was nice of him to ask, almost a comfort. Like someone knew that it *was* an act, a game, an occupation. After an hour with Jake, I needed that. Clever man, John.

"God, you try finding a place to buy cigs in Marblehead at night," he said. "Place closes up tighter than—" He thought better of continuing that thought. "Anyway, Peach says I'm to take you home, she'll call you if anything else comes up."

"Fine." I recognized the code. That was Peach-talk for this is probably it for the night. That was perfectly all right with me, to tell the truth. Jake had not had air-conditioning, and sea breezes had been notably absent during our brief bout of gymnastics on his bed. "Wife's at her mother's house," he smirked, making a production of dramatically turning her picture facedown on the dresser. "Can't have her watching us, can we, now?" A little late to show feelings for her, asshole.

"I'll call her when I get home," I said noncommittally to John. I had been running numbers in my head, not as easy as it sounds, arithmetic had never been my strong point. The call was $320: $60 for Peach, $60 for John, that left a total of $200 for me. That probably meant that Jake hadn't been able to find any other service willing to send someone all the way to Marblehead for him, and that Peach had had no problem asking (and getting) whatever she wanted.

I thought about him turning over his wife's picture with such drama, and wondered briefly why he hated her so much, to intentionally and deliberately make her so much the center of what we did there. And then I dismissed the thought. If I started thinking about the wives, I wouldn't be able to work again.

The money was okay and John had been nice. I slipped him an extra twenty, wondering if I was being a total idiot in doing so.

There were no more calls that night. I pulled off the dress, stockings, garter belt, and fuck-me shoes, and slipped gratefully into a pair of ripped shorts and an AIDS Ride sweatshirt, and tied my hair back with an elastic band. I spent the rest of the evening happily reunited with *Frasier* and a bowl of Häagen Dazs frozen yogurt, signed off at midnight, and went to bed.

The next night I found out why John was worth the extra twenty I'd decided to give him. Peach called around seven. "Work," she said, briefly, all business. I'd divided my day between sleeping in, working out at the gym, and thinking about my first lecture for the new class. Well, my second lecture. The first lecture was always housekeeping stuff—how you get graded, what I expect, what books you'll have to buy. The second lecture was when the relationship really began.

"Okay, what've you got?"

"Mark in Chelsea." My smile was immediate and spontaneous. Too cool, a regular client, one of *my* regulars in fact. The good thing about a regular is you don't have to play games . . . well, that's not quite true. You always play games. With a regular, at least you're familiar with the rules of the games you do have to play. It's the unknown element that's always unnerving.

Mark in Chelsea was pretty straightforward. I could run the program through in my head, even time it to the minute. We would sit and drink a really awful wine (my money was on it coming out of a box) and look at his view of Boston's skyline across the river (admittedly beautiful) for exactly fifteen minutes. While we were doing this, he would complain about his work and how everything and everyone conspired to keep him from the raises and advancement that were rightfully his. The fact that he was a whining weasel who, by his own admission, would sell out his mother if the price were right apparently didn't enter into it. It didn't matter. I would make dutiful and sympathetic noises at appropriate places in the monologue and think about my grocery list, or whether it was time to change Scuzzy's litter.

He would then kiss me, passionately and a little clumsily, and we would pretend that we suddenly couldn't bear to wait another moment, and mutually undress each other quickly in the darkened living room. We would have sex on the carpet, the only dialogue here being his grunt, "You got it?" as I handed over the condom. He would last as long as he could, he'd come, roll off me, and head off to take a shower. Premature ejaculation may be distressing in a husband or boyfriend; but, believe me, callgirls love it. The other extreme—and we see a lot of that—is tedious beyond belief. I would dress and be back on the balcony with the rest of my glass of wine by the time he reappeared. "Great view, huh?" he'd ask. "The whole evening was lovely," I'd assure him. He'd say, "Whenever you're finished . . ." and I'd say, "Oh, I really shouldn't have any more . . ." and he'd pay me and I'd leave. Thirty-five minutes, start to finish. Consistently. Yes: Mark was one of the good ones.

"You know I need a driver?" I asked Peach that Sunday.

"Oh, sure, no problem. I've got Ben coming by. Tell me your address, again."

I gave it to her, and she said, "Okay, I'll have him call you when he's downstairs."

"Okay, and Peach, remember Mark doesn't go the full hour."

"Yeah, no problem. Just tell Ben when to come back. He's thirty-five dollars."

Rapid calculations. Mark paid $180. "Peach, that leaves me making eighty-five for the call."

"Oh." I could hear her running the figures. "Okay, why don't you call Mark and tell him you have to get a driver, so it'll be an extra twenty-five."

No, Peach. That's why you get $60 a call, no matter what I make: so I don't have to say things like that to a client. Many—if not most—of the services in Boston charge by the event, so to speak. Say it's $60 for the girl to walk in. Then you and she negotiate the rest of the evening, a little like an à la carte menu. A blowjob adds $50 to the base price. Fucking adds $100 to the base. And so on through the more exotic options, with prices that are set both by the agency (general guidelines) and by the callgirl (specific to the situation). It is assumed that the client will have one orgasm. If he wants a second one, it gets negotiated. Nothing is left to chance, and nothing is given away.

If I had worked for one of those services, I'd have starved within the first week. There's something really Rabelaisian to me about arguing prices with a guy in an obviously stressful and adversarial way, and then opening your legs for him two minutes later.

One of the things I liked about Peach is that she took care of all that. If the client complained, I could purr, "Oh, baby, you know that if it were me setting your rates I'd help you out, but I can't help it, you have to talk to Peach." So at least there's a pretense that he and I have a little respect for each other, that we're in this together. It helps the fantasy.

Well, it does for me, anyway. Maybe it's just my issue. It's been my experience that men have never had problems fucking women they hate or with whom they're angry. Sometimes they even prefer it that way. Another difference between the genders that I will never understand. Besides, I liked Peach's premise. The client isn't paying for sex, for specific acts or games or behaviors. He is paying for an hour of the callgirl's time. He can come as many times as he is able or wishes. He can talk, or request a fantasy, or fuck. He can play games, he can maintain at some level the illusion that the girl is there because she likes him. It's a valuable commodity. Clients went to those other services—clients were consistent only in their fickleness when it came to escort agencies—and most of them returned to Peach in the end. She gave them what the others couldn't. Validation.

Dreams. Fantasies. Illusions.

In any case. I wasn't about to forego this benefit of working for Peach. I cleared my throat.

"No, Peach, I can't call him, I have to get dressed."

A loud sigh. I was supposed to feel sorry for putting her out. "All right, Jen, I'll take care of it, just be ready for Ben, okay?"

"You've got it, Peach."

The other great thing about Mark in Chelsea was that he didn't care what you wore, as long as he could take it off in a hurry when it came time to tussle on the living room carpet. Lots of buttons were out. Comfort, happily, was in. I put on a pair of sandals and a light summer dress with a zipper down the front for easy access. It was, in addition, the coolest thing I owned. Mascara. A hint of perfume. Here endeth the preparations.

Ben called about a half an hour later. "I'm downstairs."

"Be right there."

I grabbed my keys and the purse I used for work—no money, no ID, just lipstick and mascara, a couple of tissues, and three or four condoms. Just in case. Ben was in a large old American car of some sort. The first thing I noticed was that all the windows were rolled down. The second thing I noticed was that there were already three women in the car. Neither of these observations was exactly rocking my world.

"Get in, get in." A bit on the impatient side, our Ben. Not sure exactly where he meant, I opened the back door and joined the girls already sitting there. "All right." He had a list in his hand. "Tracy first, Brookline, right?"

The red-haired woman sitting next to the far window in the backseat drawled, "Yes. Coolidge Corner."

Ben pulled aggressively away from the curb, swerved to barely avoid an ancient couple attempting (the nerve of them!) to cross on the crosswalk, and hit the radio. Rap. Loud, pulsing rap.

Curiously enough, there was a time when I liked listening to this. The anthropologist in me, no doubt. The message, then, seemed more sincere, more raw and more real. That was before it started talking about getting bitches pregnant and blowing people away, back in the days when it was a snapshot, a message, a story of lives conceived and endured in poverty and hopelessness. When it reflected a lived experience, rather than a celebration of the worst consequences of the life it had previously witnessed. I even remembered, unexpectedly, some of the words that had been an influence in my life and thought. "Rats in the front room, roaches in the back, I can't take the smell, I can't take the noise . . ." Who was it? An odd name . . . right: Grandmaster Flash and the Furious Five. Back in the eighties, back when it was communication rather than posturing, before the gangsta rap, the denigration of women, the celebration of testosterone. I must be getting old, I thought—I was about to say: back when the world was innocent. My grandmother always said that the world lost its innocence with World War I. She hadn't seen nothing yet.

Back to the present, which was difficult to ignore. Just breathing was a bit of a challenge, even with all the windows down. Shalimar and Obsession were battling for precedence in the back seat. They didn't blend well, and I began thinking fond thoughts of John and his air-conditioning and his alternative rock.

By the time we made it to my stop ("Yo, Tia, Chelsea, right?") we had gone from Brookline to Newbury Street with a brief detour allowing the blonde in the front seat to alight in front of a wrought-iron gate on Beacon Hill. Ben kept bending over something next to him in the front and I had a sneaking suspicion that all his subsequent sniffling wasn't the harbinger of a bad cold. I paused as I got out and leaned in through the open front window. "I'll be ready in thirty-five minutes."

"No can do, babe." I could see him better now, and unless I was paranoid *and* delusional, he was snorting coke out of an issue of *People* magazine that was on the seat next to him. The requisite credit card and rolled-up bill were in plain view. I was taken aback for a moment with the enormity of what I had just seen.

Heaven help us if we were pulled over. Heaven help *me* if we were pulled over. Good-bye, job. Good-bye, future. I was seriously pissed off.

I jerked my attention back to what he had just said. "What do you mean, you can't do it?" My voice was sharp.

He sniffed. "Got a schedule to keep. Tracey's two hours over in Brookline, but Tiffany's hour's almost up and then Lisa's time's gonna be coming up. Be back in an hour." He gunned the engine to impress me with the importance of his schedule.

I held on to the door. "The client doesn't want me to stay an hour," I said. "He's a regular, I'd like to keep him happy."

"Hell, just give him another blowjob, that's what'll keep him happy."

Had he been standing in front of me, my response would have been immediate, physical, and temporarily disabling. As it was, there was only one obvious course of action. "Oh, okay, you're right," I said brightly. "Oh, wow, you've got *People*? That's cool, it'll give me something to read while I'm waiting for you to come pick me up."

Before he could react, I grabbed the magazine and stepped back from the open window, fanning myself with it as I did so, opening all the pages, practically in his face. Who knows how much coke fell out of its pages into the car, onto the street? I didn't care.

There are people who think that men don't say things like that anymore. I know better—most women know better—but here at least I didn't have to just take it.

I paid the price, needless to say. Ben never returned. Try finding a taxi in Chelsea on a hot summer night. Now try being an attractive woman finding a taxi in Chelsea on a hot summer night. You get my drift.

Peach was furious. "Ben's pissed at me now. What happened? You think drivers grow on trees?"

"No, apparently you get them out of cesspools!" I was just as mad. It was one in the morning, my easy call had turned into the Trek Home from Hell, there was obviously no chance of a second call, and now *she* wanted to yell at *me*?

"He told you to get an extra blowjob. So the man's a pig. You've got to be able to take a little misogyny," said Peach. "You get it from clients all the time."

"Yeah, and that's why I don't need it from somebody who's supposedly working for me. I get *paid* to take it from them, Peach. But let's not even go there, because that's not all. You know he had coke out in plain sight on the front seat?"

Silence. She hadn't known.

I pressed my advantage: "That's why he's pissed, Peach, I accidentally messed up his stash." Well, maybe not so accidentally. But she didn't need to know that. And he hadn't worked it into his tight little schedule to score some more. "You know what would happen to us if he got pulled over? With us in the car?"

What I really wanted to rant on about was the assembly-line approach to escort transportation, but I knew that this would get her where she lived. Peach prided herself on her record. Since she had been in business, none of her girls had gotten badly hurt, and no one had been arrested. This was risking the second alternative, big time. I pressed my advantage still more. "You've got a fucking time bomb there, Peach. He's not just using, he's using in public. He's using while he's driving your girls. He's a fucking disaster waiting to happen."

She believed me. That was one of the good things about Peach: once she had decided to trust you, she really trusted you. Peach knew me better a few weeks after we met each other than people who had been in my life for years knew me. . . . She knew I wouldn't lie about something like this. "I'll get back to you," said Peach, using her distant voice, the voice she used when her brain was in high gear.

"Just don't do it tonight," I snapped. "I'm signing off. I'm taking a long bubble bath and drinking a gallon of water. News flash, Peach: there aren't any taxis in Chelsea. And the bus is on hourly rotation. It was an education, truly. Good-night."

"Wait—" But I'd already hung up on her. I liked that. It wasn't often that you got to hang up on Peach: she usually did the hanging up.

I got my Civic back the next day and did everything but kiss its new tires. Since then, I learned that Ben was, comparatively speaking, mild.

Some of the other services *require* callgirls to use their drivers. They require it as a means of control, and they overwork the girls at the beginning, saying that there is a five call minimum per night, and then when the girl is falling asleep on her feet the driver offers her a line or two of coke. Just a little pick-me-up, on the house, just because he thinks she's nice and wants to help her out.

But the next time it's not on the house, and the girl is up to a six-call minimum, and the driver always has something on him. (Peach tries to get women drivers when she can, but with those other services, it's always a him.) Before long the girls can't function without doing lines first, and their money is all going into the driver's pocket.

So Ben wasn't too bad, I guess, when you consider the alternatives.

Cocaine was what everybody was doing then. Ecstasy hadn't yet made its comeback in the clubs, heroin had lost its chic, and thanks to a significant South American population in the Boston area with ties back home, cocaine was the drug *du jour*. It was impossible to avoid if you spent any amount of time out at night. Cab drivers made suggestive remarks concerning procurement. There were lines in the ladies' rooms in all of the clubs, girls waiting not for the toilets but for the counter space. Most of our clients got high. I did it, too, but for an entirely different set of reasons. I did it because No-Doz and espresso coffee just weren't cutting it with me anymore.

What I hadn't considered in my brilliant Master Plan, you see, was exactly how much I'd be burning the candle at both ends.

On Death and Dying was conveniently scheduled in the late afternoon. Most of the nurses taking it got off shift at 3:30, so the class started at four. Not so for Life in the Asylum, however. As a very junior faculty member, I was given the dreaded eight o'clock slot on Mondays, Wednesdays, and Fridays. I am convinced that A.M. stands for "(I) am miserable." I had never been one for early mornings to begin with; and my current moonlighting made the aversion even more pronounced.

Try getting home at two in the morning, still in work mode: nobody comes home from work and goes straight to bed, right? You have to unwind first, to decompress. So you have some wine or some herbal tea, maybe take a bath, maybe read a little or watch TV. I mostly read: late nights were the best time for the mystery authors I love, Michael Connelly and Kathy Reichs and Tony Hillerman. Eventually you fall asleep, and just as you're coming to the really good part in your dream, the alarm goes off. It's six-thirty in the morning, and in another hour and a half you will need to be bright, entertaining, and—most of all—awake. And you hit the snooze button one too many times to have the leisure to wrestle with the espresso maker in the kitchen.

It's bad on the other end, too. You decide that tonight you'll only do one call, an early one, and then get to bed because you only got four hours' sleep the night before. So you go on a call at eight o'clock, a perfectly reasonable time, but the client likes you and decides to extend . . . and extend . . . and extend. By eleven you've run out of witty and/or sexy things to say, you've run out of little games and trade secrets, you've run out of—well, energy. But you want him to call again, you want him to ask for you, so you need to recapture that *joie de vivre* that picked up and left about an hour ago.

The short-term solution for both, of course, was simple. A line of coke in the morning ("breakfast of champions," as one of Peach's other girls liked to call it) that at least clears away the cobwebs and gets you functional. Then, at night, you make a brief trip into the client's bathroom for a pee and another line, and suddenly you do get that second wind after all, and you leave with a great deal of money and the knowledge that he will indeed ask for you again.

Logical. Simple.

Not particularly healthy.

Even without unscrupulous drivers forcing drugs on the girls, it's easy to see why so many of them end up with problems. There's a lot of alcohol involved in this line of work, a lot of drugs. If one is at all susceptible, one is inviting the bogeyman to come right on in and take up residence.

It wasn't just us, either. It seemed for a few years there that everybody in town was doing coke anyway. That was in the days before so many of the cokeheads committed suburbicide—got married and had kids and bought SUVs and spent all their money on soccer camps and a new deck in the back of the house, and couldn't buy cocaine anymore. It seemed too bad: they were the ones who ended up looking so tired all the time. They probably could really have used it. I was lucky. That's all; it's not through some special skill or attitude that I survived my years working for an escort agency without developing serious problems with drugs or alcohol. There is, apparently, nothing addictive in my personality. I did way too much cocaine and drank way too much alcohol and didn't get caught in the bogeyman's lair. Pure dumb luck. Otherwise, if I had had the requisite addictive personality, if I had come to need the substances . . . well, if I were one of the fortunate ones, I'd be writing these lines from rehab. If I wasn't one of the fortunate ones, I would have given up teaching, given up my life, I'd be living in a crack house and exchanging blowjobs for rocks. I've seen it happen.

I got out. Not everybody did.

sex

The Invention of Patient Zero

How crystal-meth-fueled promiscuity, AIDS medical politics, and one very sick man combined to create a phantom superbug.

By David France
New York magazine / April 22, 2005

Maybe the forty-six-year-old New York man who had managed to avoid HIV for the life of the epidemic finally succumbed on Friday, October 22, 2004, when he failed to use even one condom during a weekend of crystal meth and multiple sexual encounters. Ordinarily, the New York man was sexually dominant, the penetrator. That changed on October 22. "Apparently he used Viagra, but when he didn't, he became a bottom," says Dennis deLeon, a grandee in AIDS politics who has been briefed on the case. "Crystal can make anybody a bottom. I've heard stories that even straight guys flip over on this stuff."

Maybe he was at the West Side Club that night, as one report says, and maybe out of the steamy recesses of the place came a man, as yet unidentified, who probably knew he was HIV-positive, who knew that his infection was defying treatment. Through the distorting lens of crystal, the New York man reportedly had hundreds of encounters around this time—and seven or eight that evening alone.

Let's say most of these strangers assumed the man was himself HIV-positive, which would account for why none of them insisted on a condom either. Many gay men practice this gambit, colloquially called "sero-sorting," based on the belief that having unprotected sex with somebody who shares your HIV status carries minimal risk. Most doctors believe otherwise, and point to the danger of reinfection. Studies show that in such encounters, those who are positive tend to assume their prospective partners are positive, and negatives make the opposite—and equally unspoken—assumption.

And maybe on that long night in Chelsea, the worst possible thing happened: This New York man contracted an extremely deadly "superbug" like nothing ever seen before. It appeared to carry a dreadful punch. While most people go a decade after infection before showing major symptoms, this man sank to a sickly shadow of himself by mid-November, and was an AIDS patient by December and a curiosity by January, when tests showed him resistant to most AIDS drugs. By February 11, when the New York City health commissioner, Dr. Thomas Frieden, called a press conference to alert the world to the case, the man had become a modern-day Typhoid Mary, Patient Zero in a foreboding new epidemic threatening New York City and the globe.

"We've identified this strain of HIV that is difficult or impossible to treat," Dr. Frieden announced ominously. "Potentially, no one is immune."

With those words, this man's misfortune became the biggest AIDS story of the twenty-first century, shouted in headlines as far away as India. The *New York Times* discussed the supervirus in twelve stories in the first week alone. The alarm about the drug-fueled, sexually irresponsible gay-male community has given new fodder to old anti-gay mouthpieces. "There's a new strain of HIV available in New York

City. It's because of gay men," the Catholic League's William Donohue said on MSNBC. "They're endangering the lives of everybody." Even William F. Buckley, who twenty years ago suggested the rumps of HIV carriers be branded with warnings, reentered the fray. "Murderers need to be stopped," he explained in *National Review*.

Panicking about the new pathogen, most gay men didn't race to denounce Buckley this time. Instead, they raced to their doctors. Physicians across the country reported a crush of visits from worried patients; the Gay Men's Health Crisis Web site experienced a 63 percent surge in hits. At two heated community meetings in Manhattan, gay men and AIDS service providers swapped accusations with rancorous outbursts reminiscent of early ACT UP meetings. Only this time, the anger was directed less at the health establishment than at the patient himself. "My first reaction was one of anger—that someone in his mid-forties, who had escaped the devastation and pain of the eighties and nineties, had seroconverted," Tokes Osubu, executive director of a Harlem-based group called Gay Men of African Descent, told more than three hundred people gathered at FIT in early March. "We have lost that sense of outrage. Many of our friends and lovers are dead, but we are not afraid anymore."

After the frenzy died down, however, the new epidemic began to look a lot less fearsome. In fact, on closer examination, almost everything about this case seems murky. An investigation by the Department of Health turned up no evidence that the New York man passed the virus to anybody. And on March 29, the department put out a press release saying that the patient was responding well to his medications.

"The virus that ate New York," as Richard Jefferys, basic-science project director for Treatment Action Group, put it, "is just one case."

The responsibility for this medical panic attack is spread widely: from the patient to the reporters who made him a caricature, to the city health commissioner for terrifying the city and the scientists who characterized the case, most notably Dr. David Ho, the top researcher at the world-renowned Aaron Diamond AIDS Research Center at Rockefeller University, and his deputy, Dr. Marty Markowitz, who warned of a "silent tsunami" of new infections spreading undetected across the land.

"There were all these signs that said, 'Slow down, take this with caution'—and they just weren't heeded," says Martin Delaney, the founding director of Project Inform, an AIDS-information clearinghouse. "Everyone down the line miscalculated. It was like a perfect storm; every element had to be in place for this to happen the way it did."

Let's go back to October 22, a warm and clear night in Chelsea. According to Dr. Larry Hitzeman, a colleague of the New York patient's doctor at Cabrini Medical Center, the man had by then negotiated a long courtship with crystal meth. "For five years, he took it one time a month on average," Hitzeman said at the FIT meeting on the case. "He was taking it every weekend for the past two years."

The drug has become endemic among gay and bisexual men in urban meccas. Some users, like a forty-two-year-old man I have known for more than twenty years, can snort a few bumps every few months without escalation. "In my world, it's an ordinary fixture," he told me recently. "If you go out to big dance parties, late at night, you're probably using a little crystal."

But crystal, for most, is one of the most dangerously addictive substances around. It is also a powerful disinhibitor, with a remarkable ability to concentrate the attention on sex for hours at a time.

Invitations to "party and play," or PNP, are often included in personal ads on sites like Manhunt and Craigslist. A recent survey showed that men taking crystal meth are twice as likely not to use condoms, and this man was no exception.

Among gay men, stories echoing the New York patient's headlong collapse into addiction are commonplace. "It's the most serious problem I'm dealing with," says Dr. Paul Bellman, an AIDS specialist in Manhattan. And with crystal-meth use comes a predictable upsurge in risky behavior—increasingly, people who have avoided HIV for decades are suddenly contracting the virus in middle age. "The way I look at it, Chelsea is like Iraq," says Bellman. "Every day, somebody gets blown up."

On October 22, the patient was still sinking into the drug's grip. He remembers staying up all night and through the next day, thanks to crystal. "He believes this was the night," Dr. Markowitz told a group of AIDS doctors in February. His last HIV test was on May 9, 2003—like four previous tests, it was negative and his immune system tested normal.

His doctors have tended to credit his own theory of when he contracted the virus, in part because two weeks later he suffered severe flulike symptoms, suggestive of what is called acute seroconversion illness. About half the people experience these symptoms following initial exposure to HIV. By mid-December, he was rapidly losing weight, and his fatigue kept him in bed. Concerned, on December 16, he saw his doctor. The news came back almost two weeks later, and it was bad: a massive viral load of 280,000 copies per milliliter, and a near total T-cell obliteration. A normal T-cell count is 700 to 1,200; he had just 80. It meant that just two months after his presumed exposure, he had developed full-blown AIDS.

"This was alarming to me," says Dr. Michael Mullen, the patient's longtime physician, speaking about his patient for the first time. "You wouldn't expect to see that sort of profile in early infection."

On December 29, just before Mullen gave him the terrible news, the patient, assuming he was still negative, picked up a young man in a bar and, according to Markowitz, had insertive anal sex with him, potentially infecting him as well.

Mullen referred his patient to doctors at Aaron Diamond AIDS Research Center, among the most highly regarded facilities in the field. Under the direction of Dr. David Ho, the center has scored some of the most spectacular advances of any AIDS research team. Ho discovered the triple-drug-cocktail approach to treating HIV, credited for turning AIDS from a fatal illness into a chronic disorder, saving tens of thousands of lives. In 1995, nearly 50,000 Americans died of the disease; in 2003, approximately 18,000 succumbed, a fraction of the approximately 850,000 living with HIV. For his efforts, Ho was named Man of the Year by *Time* in 1996, famously edging out the likes of Bill Clinton and Mother Teresa.

Since then, he has authored a number of important papers on viral replication that have helped shape the field. While there's broad consensus that different viral strains can produce different effects, Ho's focus on the virus as the most important factor in the progression of the disease strikes many as overly narrow. Some doctors say this approach deemphasizes the immunological issues involved, or whether environmental factors, like drug abuse, might be contributing. This has not always been a gentle dispute. A number of years ago, Ho courted fury in the tightly knit field by ordering up lapel pins for his staff that declared, IT'S THE VIRUS, STUPID!

Despite the tensions, Ho is still broadly respected as among the world's best AIDS minds. But more recently, the Aaron Diamond

Center has had trouble living up to its reputation. It has quietly changed focus from basic research to vaccine investigation, a field that has not produced promising news in two decades.

To some degree, Ho and his center are victims of their own success. At least among affluent Americans, AIDS is seen as a manageable condition rather than a death sentence. Perhaps as a consequence, funding sources have been going dry. In IRS filings, Aaron Diamond reported $9.4 million in donations and research grants in 2003, the last available year, down dramatically from $20 million in 2000. Ho's compensation package, meanwhile, has gone in the other direction—in the last reported year it was $518,000. With the stipends and consultancy fees from pharmaceutical firms, he is one of the highest-compensated medical researchers in the world.

An unusually large number of researchers have left over the years, many privately citing conflicts with Ho, whom they describe as a poisonous personality with little patience for dissent. In fact, many leading AIDS scientists, while giving him credit for leadership in the field, also criticize him for overplaying his king-of-the-hill standing.

Some wonder if he didn't see potential in the mysteries of this new case. "David Ho has a huge shop that he has to maintain," says Dr. Cecil Fox, an AIDS pathologist and veteran of many skirmishes, who owns a biotech company in Arkansas. "If he finds a new phenomenon, naturally he's going to jump on it with all four feet."

Ho denies he was under any particular pressure when the patient arrived at the center. "Think about this: We're doctors, scientists, doing research," he says. "Our mission is research."

On January 17, the patient was seen by Marty Markowitz, Ho's longtime research collaborator. Markowitz ordered more tests, which confirmed the dire clinical picture. The patient continued his precipitous decline, losing nine pounds in the next three weeks. His viral load rose to 650,000. Viral samples were sent to a San Francisco lab for resistance sequencing, tests that help determine which drugs are most likely to be effective.

Although Markowitz did not respond to interview requests, he has spoken often about the case in public. "Let me tell you, this guy told me he had four partners and no drug use," Markowitz said at a meeting of AIDS doctors at the Strata restaurant in New York on February 15. "And I am a very difficult guy to fool. But he's very charming, very handsome, very successful. You'd invite him to Christmas. You'd want your mother to meet him. He is not a demon. He's a great guy. But he has . . . he has a dark side."

Ultimately, he confided in Markowitz about how meth propelled him through the sexual underground. "This man," Markowitz told the meeting of doctors, "has had thousands of sexual contacts over the past three years. I said it right. Thousands."

In the weeks between his presumed exposure in late October and his diagnosis after Christmas, Markowitz learned, the man had swapped fluids with about ten other partners, unknowingly exposing them to his virus. This is one of the biggest problems with sero-sorting. People who don't know they're infected are responsible for more than 50 percent of all new infections.

This is why, despite all the internecine conflict, there's unanimity among doctors on the issue of safe sex. Still, some people have proposed population-based sero-sorting as a way to slow the epidemic. And one study has led researchers to speculate that if men born before 1980 never had sex with men born afterward, the epidemic would eventually die out in the gay community.

While the rate of HIV transmission seems to have dropped in each of the past three years, case reports of syphilis and drug-resistant gonorrhea are soaring among gay men, suggesting more people are having unprotected sex.

Though he felt ill, the New York patient assumed he was still negative and no risk to anybody else, his longtime physician says. Still, he's been vilified. "This guy is a total and utter asshole," Larry Kramer told the *New York Observer.* "What happens is, this is what people think gay people are like. Now we can't move forward, we can't get to our place in the sun, because of stupid assholes like this."

Michael Mullen emphatically defended his patient, who he says never engaged in unsafe sex after his diagnosis. "He's so beat up about this, he would never, ever do something like that. That's a total lie, a fabrication—it's just not true."

On January 22, a Saturday, an e-mail arrived on Markowitz's computer from the lab with resistance-test results showing the man's virus was extremely mutated, rendering it less likely to respond to nineteen of the twenty-one approved AIDS drugs. Markowitz had never seen a more resistant strain. The only thing that causes HIV to acquire resistance is sporadic exposure to anti-AIDS drugs—the virus, a clever foe, can seize the opportunity of poor drug adherence to change attributes and evade medication.

But that alone didn't cause Markowitz great concern. What worried him was the fact that this mutated virus seemed to cause disease so rapidly. On average, HIV needs about ten years to bring on full-blown AIDS, though in a small percentage of infected people—perhaps 45 in 10,000—it progresses in under a year. Ordinarily, rapid progression is more likely associated with viruses that have few or no mutations; the more changes a viral strain undergoes to evade medications, the less potent it becomes. But here was a mutated and fast-progressing virus, a frightening combination. In addition, when Markowitz cultured the virus, he found it was at least as contagious as non-mutated viruses. Markowitz has said he ordered the standard tests, which look for the nine markers that make some people genetically disposed to progress quickly to AIDS—all that came back were negative. Markowitz came to the frightening conclusion that he was looking at a deadly new viral subspecies. "If you can't see the horse and you want to see a zebra, that's your prerogative. But the data here is incontrovertible," Markowitz said.

Most leading researchers, however, were not so quickly convinced. Many viewed Markowitz's analysis as overly influenced by the Aaron Diamond Center's preconceptions. "It is fairly agreed upon that what produces rapid outcome is the host, not necessarily the virus," says Dr. Michael Ascher, an immunologist now working for the federal government. "We just don't know what all the factors might be yet."

Markowitz and Ho had some indication of resistance and doubt among their colleagues when they submitted their findings to the Retrovirus Conference in Boston. When it was decided, after a peer-review process, that the results were not significant enough to be discussed on a panel, but instead should be displayed on a large poster board in a room with other research posters, Markowitz reportedly became furious. "He began to argue with the organizers, saying the *poster* would present a danger to the public health—because so many people were going to crowd around it, someone would be injured," one attendee said. "People were scratching their heads."

Markowitz also began work on an emotional op-ed piece he hoped the *Times* would publish—and when the paper chose not to, he began to circulate it himself: "As I write, the extent of this potential, silent tsunami is being defined," he warned. "This untreatable virus with an aggressive clinical course can bring us back to the eighties and early nineties—the truly darkest years."

"It was of course a stressful, emotional moment for him," David Ho told me. "Marty saw that the man had a virus that was resistant to nearly all the drugs and he had a very aggressive course of disease, and that was sufficiently alarming to us to say, 'Wait a minute: Because of his active sexual history, are there more such cases out there?'" This was difficult to ascertain, because many of the patient's sexual contacts had been anonymous. Even those whose names he knew hesitated to come forward.

Lacking more evidence, many AIDS experts have questioned why news of this middle-aged man's declining health went any further than this. "This is an unusual virus in its resistance patterns. That's important," says Dr. Howard Grossman, executive director of the American Academy of HIV Medicine. "But there's nothing that suggests this is the beginning of an epidemic."

On the same Saturday Markowitz got the alarming lab results, he e-mailed the New York City Department of Health. The alert reached Dr. Susan Blank, the assistant commissioner for the Sexually Transmitted Diseases Control Program, on Monday, January 24. According to Markowitz's remarks in February, his dealings with them were heated. "The patient is sick in four months! He never got better really. Intractable pharyngitis, twenty-pound weight loss, bed-bound fatigue. These are bringing me back to the days of the eighties, and it frightened me so much that I stood on my soapbox and screamed and screamed and screamed until they listened."

The news reached Frieden within a week. Appointed by Mayor Bloomberg in 2002, Frieden is an activist commissioner widely respected for his medical instincts and his political courage—his steady hand guided the administration through its biggest medical crusade to date, the successful and politically risky campaign to ban smoking in public places. But before entering politics, Frieden was an infectious-disease doctor, specializing in drug-resistant tuberculosis. For much of the past eighteen months, AIDS has been his top priority, and he has earned high marks so far. As early as this month, he expects to announce a controversial new approach to the epidemic in the city, which is still the AIDS epicenter of America. Citywide, more than 110,000 are infected—and 20,000 of them don't know it. According to a draft of the report, which was leaked to me, he wants to change the state laws in order to streamline the consent process, making an AIDS test like other blood tests, while making AIDS testing much more widely available. "Knowledge is power," he told me in an interview in his Chambers Street office several weeks ago. "Most people who know their status . . . do the right thing. So increasing the proportion of people who know their status is probably the single most important thing we can do to reduce the spread of HIV."

Some activists are disturbed about this change. "It seems to me that's a slippery slope," says Tracy Welsh, the executive director of the HIV Law Project in New York. "Pretty soon we're looking at universal testing—i.e., mandatory testing. . . . And then what? Restrict their civil liberties? Criminalize their behavior?"

Frieden has been known to push the civil-liberties envelope in order to contain health risks. In New York in 1993, he helped establish detention centers for people with TB who refused to follow doctors' orders. But while the commissioner has expressed grave concerns about patients who are courting HIV mutation by not following their drug regimens, he's said he has no plans to make testing compulsory. Instead he wants to track patients' viral profiles case by case and help their doctors find a better regimen if their virus is mutating. For the most part, AIDS leaders take him at his word. In fact, he enjoys support from traditionally antagonistic groups like the National Black Leadership Commission on AIDS, GMHC, and the Harm Reduction Coalition.

At first, Frieden was skeptical of the supervirus case. "I asked both David and Marty, 'How do we know this isn't severe acute retroviral syndrome?' And I asked people from around the country, too. 'Could this be just a severe conversion reaction?' And they said, 'No.'" He also challenged the conclusion that the patient was newly infected. What if the patient's flu symptoms were caused by something else—something as simple as the flu?

For the next week or so, Frieden conferred with other experts, including AIDS specialists at the Centers for Disease Control and Prevention. Then, on January 31, Department of Health investigators interviewed the patient, hoping to develop a list of those he may have exposed. However, because a majority of the original patient's contacts were anonymous, Frieden says, "we started with less than a fifty-fifty chance." Those men whose names he recalled were invited to talk; many reportedly declined.

He also contacted three dozen blood laboratories in the U.S., Canada, and Europe and asked them to canvass their records for evidence of viruses that matched this patient's nucleotide sequences—potentially hundreds of thousands of samples.

Frieden then weighed various additional options, and sent out a blast-fax to a network of doctors. But he worried that some of these men weren't symptomatic yet or had mistaken their symptoms for something more benign. "You want to generate demand," he says. "You want people to think, Oh, I just had unsafe sex a couple of weeks ago, and I've got now what feels like a really bad viral syndrome. Maybe I should remind my doctor that they should test for

HIV now. It's important to do that, because the viral load and infectiousness of someone who's recently infected with HIV is astronomically high."

Ultimately, the decision to hold a press conference was Frieden's alone. He assembled some prominent community leaders to join him on February 11. The next day, the story dominated the covers of papers around the globe.

The announcement detonated a long-smoldering debate in the gay community over sexual responsibility. "We are murderers, we are murdering each other," says Larry Kramer, whose new book, *The Tragedy of Today's Gays,* was published this month. "If intelligent, smart people are unwilling to take responsibility 100 percent for their own dicks, I don't know how you stop the killing." Some, like the columnist Dan Savage, saw in the case a reason to bring on a new penalty phase for prevention activism. "There's a great deal of anger and frustration among gays and lesbians at the never-ending, nonstop coddling and compassion campaign that passes for HIV prevention," he says. "There will be no sympathy when this happens to us again. We are not going to be the baby harp seals the way we were in the eighties and nineties. We picked up the same gun and said, 'I hope it's not loaded this time,' and pulled the trigger again. And I'm gay—imagine how straight people feel."

But others took a more skeptical approach. "I thought this sounded familiar, so I Googled 'superbug' and 'AIDS,'" said GMHC's Gregg Gonsalves. He found two cases reported in 2001 by a noted Vancouver AIDS specialist, Dr. Julio Montaner. The *Vancouver Sun* quoted Montaner about the cases, but he could have been describing the newest Patient Zero: "In a matter of months, these people have gone from totally asymptomatic to very low immune systems."

Frieden says he was caught unawares by the Vancouver cases, and that he wishes he had known about them before deciding to hold his own press conference. Ho, who still maintains the uniqueness of the New York case, wasn't aware of the specifics of the Vancouver cases, and called Montaner the Monday following the press conference. "It was very cordial," Montaner says with a laugh. "He phoned me up to find out more about it." (Both Canadian patients, it turned out, have responded well to treatment and now have fully suppressed viral loads.)

Ho, meanwhile, was coming under heavy criticism. "When I first heard this, I said, *Holy shit—there is no evidence,*" says Dr. Robert Gallo, an eminent virologist. "Clearly, conclusively, scientifically, it was inappropriate to make that statement."

Gallo and other leading figures in the field—including Dr. Tony Fauci, director of the National Institute of Allergy and Infectious Diseases—believe the new case report, while unfortunate for the patient, is likely a statistically predictable outlier. Unfortunately, according to data generated by Ho's institute, drug-resistant HIV is now commonplace: Nearly 30 percent of newly diagnosed HIV cases are resistant to at least one AIDS drug, and 11 percent are resistant to drugs in two or more drug classes.

In much of the criticism, there was an undercurrent of resentment toward Ho. Many saw the announcement as grandstanding. Michael Petrelis, an AIDS activist and blogger from San Francisco, fanned the flames with revelations about Ho's links to Frieden (who sits on the Aaron Diamond Board of Directors) and the San Francisco laboratory that does the resistance testing, ViroLogic (as a scientific adviser, he receives a stipend and stock options). "I'm not saying any of that is wrong, or undermines the concern that Ho or others have about this mutant strain. I'm saying, we should know these things as we consider this case. That's all I'm asking for: Give us all of the facts." (In the interest of full disclosure, I should say that I also have some relevant history—I am a volunteer fund-raiser for Housing Works, the AIDS services agency that has been critical of Frieden, and I'm friendly with some of the players—including Frieden's press spokeswoman.)

"I think it is only a couple individuals working really hard to spread bad news about us," Ho says. "Whenever there is some news surrounding me or our institution, the usual suspects emerge—it's not surprising to me."

While Ho was contending with this backlash, his deputy Marty Markowitz surprised the February 15 New York meeting with a lecture stridently defending his superiority and referring to himself in the third person. "This is not for amateurs," he said at one point, in response to a question. "You are arguing the . . . you are taking the doubting-Thomas point of view. However, you must also yield to the expertise of people who do know better."

It was true that a kind of circuslike atmosphere was developing, with a laboratory in San Diego saying it had found a match there (not true, according to Frieden). *South Park* did an episode featuring a supervirus. And a doctor in Connecticut claimed he was treating the couple that infected Markowitz's patient in the first place. "My guys were at the West Side Club on the weekend in question," Dr. Gary Blick, a longtime AIDS practitioner based in Norwalk, told me. "The timing fits." Blick says Frieden tried to keep him from going public with his findings, but he sent out a press release anyway. "I felt obligated before the Black Party [a vast annual party, held this year at Roseland] to give a message about this transmission."

On March 29, Frieden announced the conclusion of the detective phase of his investigation. More than a dozen sexual contacts of the New York patient's have been interviewed, and thousands of blood samples have been retested. But the investigation failed to find an original source for this viral strain, nor did it locate anybody who might have contracted it from the New York patient. Frieden has ordered further tests on about ten additional mutated strains that surfaced in his investigation, but for now it seems his worst fears haven't come to pass. He hastens to say that he is relieved by this, not disappointed. And he has no second thoughts about going public. "The role of public health is to prevent outbreaks, not to describe them," he says.

The problem, however, is one of crying wolf—the alarm gets harder and harder to hear. Despite the spike in doctor visits, the gay community apparently hasn't changed course. Condoms are no more widely available at gay meeting places; drug use was just as prevalent at the Black Party as in previous years.

On one level, the case is a cautionary tale about the dangers of meth, unprotected sex, and complacency. And the mythological trappings surrounding the supervirus feed into that very sense of complacency. The introspection that rose up around the early epidemic has given way to what Dan Carlson, co-founder of the HIV Forum, calls a "culture of disease," in which HIV is now accepted as an intractable reality. "Whether there's a dangerous new virus among us or not, we need to talk about what HIV means to us," Carlson says. "Why are we so skittish or afraid to talk about the issues that lead us to have unsafe sex? Do we talk about the decisions we make that put us at risk? We have a lot of work to do."

And where does that leave Patient Zero? "It's not a walk in the park," Mullen says. "He's taking a lot of drugs"—his regimen involves two daily injections—"and there are toxicities. He was short of breath for some time. But he's responding to medications." And he's back at work.

If he continues his slow return to health, he may be allowed to fade into the ranks of the 110,000 New Yorkers who live every day with HIV without causing anybody alarm. But a thirty-nine-year-old veteran of AIDS scare stories named Hush McDowell wonders if that's possible. In 1998, McDowell made global news as the first known person to catch multiple-drug-resistant HIV—and the last one responsible for unleashing the phrase "superbug" in the press.

"I feel awful for him," says McDowell. "Maybe he's able to ignore the press and focus on his care, but I never was." These days, McDowell is doing well on medication, and he lives far from the media's glare, tending bees on a farm in Tennessee. "Best thing I ever did," he says.

Tahitillation

sex

By Nigel Planer
The Erotic Review / September 2004

When Herman Melville—later to be the author of *Moby Dick*—first arrived in NukuHiva in the Marquesas in his early twenties, he was surprised to see, in addition to the usual armada of canoes loaded with fruit for bartering, and the boat carrying the drunken English harbor pilot, a school of what appeared to be Mermaids swimming toward the ship, their long back tresses trailing behind them in the water. As they arrived at the side of the whaling ship *Dolly* and climbed the anchor ropes, clambering over the bulwarks and jumping aboard, he and his six-months-at-sea shipmates realized with glee that they were in fact being paid a visit by virtually the entire female population of the island of sexable age. These daunting visions of abundance then proceeded to rub themselves all over with coconut oil from the little jars some of them had carried over in their teeth. They swam because, unfathomably, it was considered taboo by nineteenth-century Marquesans for a girl to sit in a canoe—they were strictly reserved for the menfolk. The "swimming nymphs . . . dripping with brine and glowing with the bath" were to be a regular feature of the sailors' lives over the next few weeks, while refueling and mending the ship, and had a habit of "springing buoyantly in the air and revealing their naked forms to the waist."

Apart from bringing the obviously unwanted diseases to the Pacific islands, sailors, traders, whalers, and missionaries brought with them something else which was much prized by the islanders—iron. From the first cannon shot and pistol fire, the Polynesians were quick to realize its value. It became the chief sexual trading currency, and girls soon learned to ask for larger and larger nails in exchange for their services. In fact the ship's carpenter on Captain Cook's first voyage in 1769 complained that the *Endeavour* might disintegrate on departure from Tahiti since so many nails and cleats had been prized from its hull.

Later in Melville's account of his travels in the South Seas, he describes what became one of the most enduring erotic images of the nineteenth century. After obtaining permission from a high priest, Melville takes his special girl, "Fayaway" out to the middle of a lake in a forbidden canoe. A small breeze ruffles up and Fayaway whips off her "tapa"—a wrap-around sarong and of course the only thing she is wearing—and holds it high up in the wind like a sail, her graceful muscular arms and waist reflecting the gorgeous pellucid light of the southern hemisphere and her sturdy brown legs braced in the bow of the boat like the stout and slippery masts of a man 'o war, or the ripe muscular thighs of a thoroughbred race horse, and so on. In fact, Melville invented this episode, as indeed he did the existence of the lake itself, but the image lived on in the minds of most literate men between the ages of nine and ninety, making *Typee* a serious best-seller and Melville loads of money.

For some reason it was alright for writers and artists in the nineteenth century to get thoroughly sexed up when describing the females of the South Seas, though they would never have dreamed of describing their own womenfolk thusly. Even "New Man" Robert Louis Stevenson, who settled in Samoa in the 1890s with his (older) wife, his mother, and his stepchildren was to write lustfully in his diaries of his housemaid Java's legs as she dusted around his study, making it hard for him to concentrate on his next masterpiece: "the inside of Java's knees when she kilts her lavalava (frock) is a thing I never saw equalled in a statue." He seems to have spent quite a lot of precious writing time copping an eyeful of the delicious Java's "bread and butter beauty"—"I wait to look at her as she stoops for the pillows." He was at least aware that looking was all a man of his tubercular disposition was good for: "I am glad that I am elderly and sick and overworked."

Speaking as an elderly, sick, and overworked white male myself, I would say, that our lustful patriarchs were definitely on to something. This year, I went to Tahiti to find out if it really is as sexy a place as its legend would have it. I wanted to find out if the women there are as drenched in sensuality as writers, from Maugham to Michener to Melville would have liked us to believe. Do their cheeks glow with that luscious just-had-it-five-times lambency that Gauguin depicts, or was all of that merely the orientalist fantasizing of a load of sad old white blokes? (This doesn't mean that I actually went and had sex there; I think the days of the predatory sexual tourist are numbered.)

They didn't disappoint. The average Tahitian woman in the street was sexier than the perfectly proportioned American Barbies at my hotel, who jogged around in their string bikinis with bouncy tits like balloons strapped to their pecs; sexier than the chic Frenchwomen on the beach with their slim ankles and alluring spectacles; sexier even than the Italian Julia Roberts lookalike, who sat opposite me in the restaurant in Cook's Bay, with her carefully wild hair and her neurotic dark eyes and skin like brown velvet. Tahitian women don't tend to have good skin and their tummies tend to spill out a bit. Their calves are thick and their tits small. But they have got "it." Whatever "it" is. Gauguin may have been a bastard, but his paintings proclaim a glaring truth; these women wipe the floor with their occidental counterparts. Slouching out of the supermarkets, sitting smoking in their pick-up trucks, sitting on the beach with their red and white pareus wrapped round their sturdy backsides, they seem neither compliant nor dominant; but they would be worth giving up Paris for.

To understand why this is, it's worth looking back to before the fatal impact of the Americans and Europeans. Sexuality had been as tightly woven into Tahitian culture and religion as its repression was into those of the North and West. It would not be unusual for a Tahitian wife to take lovers or to move on to another husband if the first one got a bit boring or was sexually inadequate. Many had three or four husbands. And sex was never something hidden: quite the opposite.

The "Aiori," a Tahitian high-caste religious sect, performed ritual group sex ceremonies and it seems that in general, flaunting it was fairly acceptable and not something merely for narcissists. The traditional Tahitian welcome was sexual and when the French explorer Bougainville arrived in what is now Papeete in 1768 he observed, "the bare skinned women offered themselves enticingly." Pressed to "choose a woman" from those who had boarded the ship, one of the crew was very excited to be approached by three gorgeous topless girls and taken ashore to a secluded glade where they made it clear they would all be up for it. Only problem was all their boyfriends and other family members who were sitting on the grass to watch and applaud any particularly deft moves. The Frenchman fled back to the ship and barricaded himself in for the rest of their stay.

So there is not much chance, thankfully, of a Bangkok-style sex industry starting up in modern Tahiti. These women did not act like victim material. There has been no tradition of female circumcision, no tight corsetry, no foot-binding, to cow them. If I can be forgiven this last fantasy, it seems that in Tahiti, the women own their sexuality. They are not afraid of their own pleasure; with their taut buttresslike calves and their large, firm bottoms and their Rubenesque thighs, gripping and holding and . . .

sex

XXXchurch Wants No More XXX

By Julia Scheeres
Wired News / May 20, 2004

"Rick," a 20-year-old Krispy Kreme employee from Washington, says he has a serious problem: He masturbates.

He recently befriended several other Christian men who share his belief that masturbation is sinful, and together they've pledged not to "defile themselves" for forty days—the same amount of time the Bible says Satan tempted Jesus in the desert. They encourage each other to remain steadfast by e-mail and instant messages.

"I'm only a few days into it, but I'm really seeing how used to it that my body really is, and how I am addicted to it," Rick writes in a blog chronicling his quest. "As difficult as it is, I'm contending not only for myself, but the men that are on this fast with me, to be strong, and beat this addiction. Let's do it guys! We can be holy."

The men were inspired by XXXchurch whose mission is to help people overcome the twin temptations of pornography and onanism and bring them to God.

Started by two young pastors from the porn capital of the world—Southern California—the ministry is aggressively fighting carnal sin on the porn medium of choice, the Internet. It's an uphill battle. There are millions of XXX sites, but only one XXXchurch.

"(We) saw the church really doing nothing about the issue of porn, so we decided to step up and do something," said Craig Gross, twenty-eight, who started the XXXchurch with Mike Foster, thirty-two, in 2002. "We wanted to do it outside the context of a normal church so we could attract both secular and church people."

The site—which advertises itself as the No. 1 Christian porn site—features downloadable bible studies, a virtual prayer wall and free software that records sites visited by Internet users and sends the log to a third party. There is also plenty of practical advice. Here's what the pastors recommend instead of self-gratification:

"Remain calm and tell yourself, 'You don't own me, masturbation! I'm taking my life back!' (or something of that nature). If that doesn't work, you can pursue alternatives like chewing gum, blasting John Lennon's song 'Cold Turkey,' eating chocolate or whatever helps you best (not masturbation)."

The ministry is based on Matthew 5:27–30, which condemns lust and recommends amputating body parts that cause a believer to sin, "for it is better that you lose one of your members than that your whole body go into hell."

First they capitalized on an existing spoof—the "Save the Kittens" e-mail campaign—which featured a photoshopped picture of a kitten being chased by two snarling red monsters and the phrase "Every time you masturbate . . . God kills a kitten." Gross said the euphemism "killing kittens" made it easier for people to talk about masturbation. Although the e-mail was widely disseminated, some people were offended by a video spin-off of the campaign, which showed a cat being thrown across a room.

Next there was a television commercial featuring a dwarf and the tag line, "Porn stunts your growth." The ad ran on MTV and on television shows targeting young people, but was pulled after a dwarf-empowerment group called Little People of America found it offensive.

The XXXchurch recently wrapped its second commercial, which has been no less controversial. It was shot by veteran porn director James DiGiorgio, whose filmography includes *Nutjob Nurses* and *The Anal Life*. "Jimmy D," as he's known in the porn biz, met the two pastors during their yearly trek to the *Adult Video News* Adult Entertainment Expo in Las Vegas, where the duo open a booth and hand out Bibles and "Jesus loves porn stars" stickers.

DiGiorgio offered to direct the new commercial—which features simulated puppet sex and an admonition to keep porn away from children—for free after hearing about the dwarf debacle. He has not publicly stated his motivations for shooting the antiporn ad, and did not respond to an interview request.

The pastors have raised the hackles of conservative Christians, who accuse them of fraternizing with pornographers and find their irreverent style unbecoming to ministers.

"The main reason we do not support them is because their method is not biblical, nor are they fruitful as a ministry," wrote Mike Cleveland, the founder of a competing antiporn group in a letter found in the site's hate mail section. When contacted for an interview, Cleveland refused to elaborate on this criticism.

But others have praised the duo's approach, including Steve Gallagher, the president of Pure Life Ministries, which operates a treatment center for Christian sex addicts in Kentucky. Gallagher said he was skeptical of the ministry when he heard it was called XXXchurch, but changed his mind after the pastors flew out to visit him.

"Their simple message, 'There's something better than porn, and His name is Jesus,' delivered nonjudgmentally with an edge, and a witty sense of humor, is building a bridge into a subculture that will someday be crossed by those who find themselves at the end of their rope, discarded by an industry that they thought was their friend," Gallagher said.

Gross said he could care less what people think of his ministry.

"Jesus was a controversial figure so (we) are fine if people don't like us," he said. "The sad thing is that most of the hate comes from Christians, same as in Jesus's day. The so-called religious people were always pissed at him."

Meanwhile, the pastors are busy with speaking tours and developing an Internet reality show that will document their "adventures in the world of porn," and will feature a real-life porn star and a young man recovering from porn addiction. The name of the show? *Missionary Positions.*

sex

The Battle Over Birth Control

The right has moved its war on abortion from the clinic to the pharmacy, where it now seeks to cripple the sale of contraceptives.

By Gretchen Cook
Salon.com / April 27, 2005

Some names have been changed.

One controversy over the morning-after pill is whether it prevents pregnancy or terminates it. Opponents equate the use of "Plan B," as the emergency contraceptive is called, to a chemical abortion. Supporters—and most physicians—counter that it does not destroy the embryo but blocks a fertilized egg from becoming implanted in the uterus. But in one sense, contraception may indeed be the new abortion—that is, the next battleground for reproductive rights.

From conservative pharmacists refusing to dispense birth control pills to abstinence-only programs and anticondom campaigns, access to contraception is facing tough challenges from the right. The strategy is similar to one that conservatives have used for abortion: Since overturning *Roe vs. Wade* looks unlikely in the near term, opponents have turned their sights on limiting access to the procedure. Now members of the religious and political right—including the Bush administration—are focusing on contraception, raising concern that they will succeed in curbing women's birth control choices and the ability to prevent unwanted pregnancies.

"I am deeply concerned that they have gone further than I have ever seen them. This is far past a woman's right to make decisions regarding abortion to the point now that it's about their right to make decisions on contraception," Sen. Patty Murray (D-Wash.) told *Salon.* Murray and her Senate colleague Hillary Clinton have blocked President Bush's nominee to head the FDA, Lester Crawford, over his inaction as acting director of the agency to approve the morning-after pill for over-the-counter sale. An FDA advisory committee has given the drug overwhelming support as safe and effective, and Canada approved its nonprescription status last week. Publicly, Crawford says his indecision on the drug has nothing to do with ideology, but privately he told Murray it raises his concerns about "behavior," apparently alluding to arguments that the pill will encourage promiscuity.

There are also indications Crawford sides with those that equate Plan B with "chemical abortion." During his confirmation hearing two weeks ago, Clinton asked Crawford: "Would you clarify for the committee that emergency contraception is a method for prevention of pregnancy, not the termination of pregnancy?" Crawford responded: "I may need to confer with the experts in the FDA about exactly what the physiology of it is." Labels on Plan B, the name that its maker, Barr Laboratories, has given it, say "for the prevention of pregnancy."

Crawford's remarks troubled Murray. "We need to have confidence as consumers that the FDA approves drugs based on science and efficacy and not on ideology," she said. Murray added that Crawford's views suggest trouble for reproductive rights advocates if he is confirmed. "New contraceptives have been going on the market in the last few years and they would all be jeopardized by an FDA using ideology instead of science."

So far, Crawford's confirmation vote has not been rescheduled and his appointment has been held up on a different issue—albeit a "moral" one. The Republican chair of the Senate Committee on Health, Education, Labor and Pensions, Michael Enzi of Wyoming, is calling for a probe into charges Crawford had a "personal relationship" with a female FDA staff member that may have led to her receiving "significant promotions." White House spokesman David Almacy would only say that Bush still backs Crawford and that "we are hopeful they will approve the nomination so he can receive a full Senate vote and ultimately confirmation."

Opposition to Plan B is just the latest and most visible drive by conservatives to curtail contraception, according to Heather Boonstra of the Alan Guttmacher Institute, a nonprofit research group for reproductive issues. "There's a constituency out there that equates all contraception with abortion, and they're organizing in concerted ways to denigrate it," she says. That constituency includes a number of social and religious groups, but the one that takes the abortion-contraception connection perhaps the most literally is the American Life League (ALL), one of the largest antiabortion lobbyists. Founded twenty-five years ago, it claims 300,000 families as members.

"Many forms of so-called contraception work by preventing the implantation of an already created human being, and that kills a baby in the womb, and we consider that to be an early abortion," says ALL's vice president, Jim Sedlak. He says ALL's main mission is to inform women that all hormonal birth control methods and the IUD "are actually causing abortions themselves" and to force manufacturers to put that description prominently on contraceptive labels.

ALL's STOPP International campaign also seeks to cut government funding for Planned Parenthood, which it believes misinforms women about how contraception works. Sedlak says STOPP has been successful at the city level—closing over one hundred clinics around the country in the last ten years—and is now targeting state funding. He pointed to the Texas Legislature's recent decision to cut Planned Parenthood's state funding as one of ALL's biggest victories. "It's not as fast as we would like, but we'll take it, and we believe it will have a snowball effect and that when people understand what they're doing we'll be closing clinics even faster."

ALL is not the only threat to Planned Parenthood's funding. In every one of his budgets, Bush has frozen funds for Title X, the thirty-year-old program that pays for family-planning services for low-income women. Susanne Martinez, Planned Parenthood's vice president for public policy, says that although Congress has restored some of that money, this "assault on family planning" has crippled Planned Parenthood's contraceptive distribution—about 95 percent of the Title X funds it receives go directly to that service. She is also concerned Bush has appointed to agencies like the FDA and Health and Human Services "people who have very publicly said they opposed the use of birth control for the unmarried. It's something [Bush] has been doing in a very strategic way."

Several other groups support ALL's views and its mission. The Family Research Council joined Republican leaders last Sunday on a national telecast blasting the Democrats for blocking appointments of conservative judges who could decide key reproductive-rights issues. And while the conservative Concerned Women for America (CFA) says it does not take a position on contraception, it does oppose abortion and has been vigorously defending the recent drive by antichoice pharmacists to stop distributing emergency contraception, which CFA considers an "abortion pill."

One of the social conservatives' biggest victories has been the "abstinence-only until marriage" sex education programs in the public schools, according to Boonstra, of the Alan Guttmacher Institute. Those federally funded programs prohibit any discussion of contraception except in the context of failure rates—which Boonstra says are inaccurate. An AGI survey of teachers found one in fifty schools taught abstinence-only in 1988; the number increased to one in four in 1999. That is the most recent accounting period, but the movement has clearly snowballed. The federal government has spent more than $1 billion since 1982 on those programs—of that, $620 million has been spent in the past seven years, and President Bush is seeking an all-time high of $206 million for the 2006 budget. Some states are also moving the programs into elementary schools.

The abstinence-only programs—which have largely replaced safe-sex education—have not only curbed the distribution of condoms and birth control pills in school health clinics, but have entirely banned information about contraceptives and sexual health. The nonprofit Abstinence Clearinghouse, which promotes such programs, says few could argue that refraining from sex is the only surefire way to prevent pregnancy and sexually transmitted diseases. And it dismisses repeated studies finding that abstinence-only programs are ineffective in either delaying sexual experience among teens or protecting them from disease. So does Alma Golden, Bush's pick to head the Population Affairs department, which runs the programs. "One thing is very clear for our children, abstaining from sex is the most effective means of preventing the sexual transmission of HIV, STDs, and preventing pregnancy and the emotional, social, and educational consequences of teen sexual activity," she says on the Clearinghouse's Web site.

Recently, pharmacies have provided another avenue for restricting access to contraception. At least twelve states have introduced "conscience clause" laws that would allow pharmacists to refuse to fill contraceptive prescriptions on moral or religious grounds. Four states, Arkansas, Georgia, Mississippi, and South Dakota, already have such laws on the books. The flap over Plan B and RU-486, which results in an abortion within seven weeks, have intensified this drive, but some pharmacists are refusing to dispense any form of birth control. The American Pharmacists Association, which represents about 52,000 pharmacists, supports a compromise that would allow pharmacists to "step away" from dispensing drugs they oppose as long as another pharmacist is on hand to fill the prescription.

Meanwhile, condoms remain on most drugstore shelves, but Boonstra says conservatives have made significant inroads on those as well. "There's been a campaign against the condom since the late 1990s to say condoms don't prevent disease," Boonstra says. She points to a chart on the government's www.4parents.gov Web site that shows that condoms are only 50 percent effective in preventing chlamydia, gonorrhea, and syphilis. "There's no scientific evidence for this, and in fact, the National Institutes of Health says condoms provide an 'impermeable barrier [to disease].' Social conservatives are trying to use science to say condoms don't work, and they do work." Fewer clinics, like college health and AIDS-prevention centers, are distributing condoms now thanks to things like budget cuts. Human Rights Watch, a gay-rights advocacy group, has also charged that police have confiscated condoms from AIDS outreach programs in some areas for use as evidence of prostitution or sodomy.

Today, nine in ten insurance plans cover contraceptive prescriptions, a considerable climb from just a few years ago, but that number could slide again. Twenty-one states mandate contraception coverage in insurance policies, stemming in part from a push by women's groups outraged that insurers covered Viagra for men but excluded birth control for women. However, about half of all Americans with workplace insurance are covered by employers who self-insure (rather than buy an insurance company plan), and the self-insured are exempt from state requirements.

Conservative groups like the Heritage Foundation and some Catholics are lobbying for plans that can also sidestep state rules. Bush backs such proposals and has made his own moves against contraceptive coverage. His 2002 budget dropped funding for contraceptive benefits in federal-employee insurance plans. Congress restored that funding—though lawmakers have rejected a federal mandate to require contraception benefits as the states do—and the president has since dropped the effort. But last year Illinois became the first state to allow federal employees an insurance plan that does not cover contraceptives, fertility treatment, or abortions. Adam Sonfield, of the Alan Guttmacher Institute, is not surprised that the Republican-led Congress and businesses—including conservative ones—are unenthusiastic about such plans; they realize that pregnancy prevention is cost-effective. "There's only so far the congressional conservatives are willing to go," he says, "but sometimes they get pretty extreme."

So how far will this anticontraception campaign go? As usual, both sides are looking to the polls and public opinion to support their cause. Sen. Murray welcomes the Plan B debate and insists that as the conservatives' contraception agenda is exposed, they'll lose ground. "I think the American public is basically outraged. People just cannot believe that access to birth control is in jeopardy. So the more they're aware, the more they'll act," she says. Murray believes she is backed by the polls, which show most Americans still support abortion rights. A *New York Times*/CBS News poll late last year also found 78 percent of Americans favor requiring pharmacists to fill prescriptions for birth control despite religious objections.

ALL's Sedlak agrees exposure is key—and that his side will ultimately win over the public. He points to a survey showing that 78.6 percent of Americans believe using birth control will reduce the number of abortions. However, he says that if the public is informed of his position that most contraception actually constitutes abortion, that same majority will then oppose such birth control methods.

"We've found that once the women understand that, their whole attitude really changes," Sedlak says. Bush may also be counting on support for his anticonception agenda from all those "moral values" voters who turned out overwhelmingly for the Republicans in the last election. A new Belcher poll commissioned by the Democratic National Committee found that in eight battleground states—Ohio, Iowa, Virginia, North Carolina, Georgia, Wisconsin, New Mexico, and Nevada—47 percent of the voters and 51 percent of white women said religious faith influenced their votes as much as traditional political issues.

SEX

Now I Feel Whole Again

By Christine Aziz
The Independent (London) / February 15, 2005

Some names have been changed.

Eight months ago, Fatoumata al-Hussein boarded the Eurostar at Waterloo station. The thirty-two-year-old Sudanese nurse was heading to Paris, but she wasn't going as a tourist—instead she was going for pioneering surgery with the surgeon and urologist Dr. Pierre Foldes.

Fatoumata grew up in Khartoum, Sudan, and at the age of six became a victim of female genital mutilation (FGM). After reading about a unique surgical technique performed by Dr. Foldes which restores the clitoris, she immediately decided to make the journey to France. Every year Dr. Foldes—who has become a savior to thousands of women—operates on two hundred genitally mutilated women at the Louis XIV hospital in Saint-Germain-en-Laye outside Paris. Fatoumata's operation took two hours, and she says that she feels she has finally been transformed into a "complete woman."

Dr. Foldes, father of five children and married to a fellow doctor, Beatrice, performs the operations in addition to his full-time hospital work. He refuses to charge for the surgery because he considers his patients to be victims of one of the biggest crimes against humanity. "Victims shouldn't pay for the crimes against them. These women have already paid a huge price," he says. "It is like a violent rape which has involved family members."

Fatoumata lives in west London with her husband, Faroud, a doctor, and her two daughters, aged six and three. She was the same age as her eldest daughter when her mother and grandmother took her to local clinic where a medically trained midwife excised her clitoris, labia majora, and labia minora with the use of a local analgesic. What was left of the outer skin was then sewn together, leaving a pinhole opening. This is the most severe form of genital mutilation, and it is estimated that 15 percent of the two million girls and women who are genitally mutilated each year undergo this procedure. In other cases, the clitoris only is removed, or the clitoris and the inner labia are removed.

"I can't remember much about it. It was just an explosion of pain," Fatoumata says. "The onset of menstruation was terrible. I had terrible stomach cramps because the blood couldn't flow as normal." When she married at eighteen, it was more than a year before she managed to have sex with her husband. "Some women have to go with their husbands to midwives to get help. My husband was very patient and loving but intercourse for me was about pain not pleasure. Other couples use little knives to make the opening a bit bigger each time but we couldn't stand the idea of that."

It was not until Fatoumata arrived in London ten years ago that she realized the extent of her mutilation and how much it affected her psychologically and sexually. "I talked to my husband about it and he never liked the way I suffered, especially after I had our two children. He doesn't agree with the custom, and will never allow our daughters to have it. I am so happy it is illegal here. In Sudan if you don't have it done no one wants to marry you, and you're considered dirty. Even the educated people think this. When I was nursing here and saw the genitals of an English woman for the first time I was very shocked and wanted to cry. 'Is this what has been taken away from me?' I screamed inside."

Dr. Foldes was working as a humanitarian doctor in Burkina Faso in West Africa, twenty-five years ago, when he first encountered the traumatic effects of excision. "Some women came to me complaining of scarring which was very painful to them every time they moved," he recalls. "A special type of scar tissue called a keloid can develop on black skin, and in these cases it grows hard and thick and attaches itself to the pubic bone. The women asked me if I could do something about it. While I was operating, I began to do some reconstruction surgery on the vagina and labia as well as clearing scar tissue." The surgery, he says, was carried out in secret because of death threats from community members supporting the practice.

"The African women whose scar tissue I operated on in France were asking me if I could do more to help them. They wanted to feel like 'proper' women," he says. When Dr. Foldes continued his surgery on African women back in France, the death threats continued. "The police take them very seriously but I don't," he says, and points to a photograph in his office of a bullet hole in a wall in Cambodia. "If I can survive that and keep on working, why should I be scared of threatening phone calls and letters?"

Dr. Foldes's crusade to restore the clitoris to women who have been mutilated began fifteen years ago. He began to research the subject but was shocked to find that the only organ in the human body devoted solely to pleasure had been metaphorically excised by the male-dominated medical fraternity. "It was invisible," he says indignantly. "It was shocking for me to discover in my research that there was nothing, absolutely nothing, on this organ, although there are hundreds of books on the penis, and several surgical techniques to lengthen it, enlarge it, or repair it. Nobody was studying the clitoris because it is associated with female pleasure. There was very little anatomical detail on it. Let's say I had to start from scratch."

It is now known that the clitoris is much larger than was originally thought, with nerves surrounding the vagina and extending down the thighs. "It's about ten or eleven centimeters long, like a penis, and changes shape when erect," Dr. Foldes explains.

To reconstruct a clitoris, Dr. Foldes removes all scar tissue that has grown over the excised tip and snips the supporting ligaments, allowing more of the clitoral body to be exposed. The ligaments are then repaired and tissue removed from the thighs to create the labia. According to Dr. Foldes, the area begins to look normal after six weeks, but it takes four to six months for his patients to feel any sensation.

More than 130 million women worldwide are estimated to have undergone FGM. According to Comfort Momoh, a midwife at the African Well Woman Clinic at Guy's and St. Thomas's hospitals in London, approximately 15,000 of them are living in the UK. Every week she refers three or four women to British doctors for what are termed "reversals" of FGM, but these operations do not involve restoring the clitoris. "I don't know of anyone else, apart from Dr. Foldes, who does this work. But I have my reservations," Momoh says. "The effects of the technique have not been fully researched, and doctors here don't know much about his work, although I think they should. I've discussed the effects of surgery with some of the women here, and while some believe it can be great mentally and psychologically, some women say it could be traumatic and bring back memories." Momoh also points out that, "Just because women have FGM, it doesn't mean they don't enjoy sex. Some women argue that they do, and that other parts of their bodies become very sensitive, such the breasts, nipples, and belly. Some insist that they do orgasm."

Dr. Foldes agrees that the results of his surgical techniques have yet to be fully researched. "Women tell me they have sexual feelings they didn't have before, but if you've been excised at birth how can you know what an orgasm feels like? It does need to be researched scientifically and moves are afoot for that."

In the meantime, Fatoumata cannot find words to express her gratitude. "Yes, I was in pain after the operation, and yes, it reminded me of that dreadful time, but I feel so happy now. I can be with my husband like all women are with their men. I feel things I never felt before, and I am not in pain. I am feeling like a real woman."

sex

from *Blue Days, Black Nights: A Memoir*

By Ron Nyswaner

STONE
Dominant Master
6'4", 230 lbs.
Dominant Verbal Top into all aspects
of Safe Dominant Fantasies.
Water Sports, Boxing, Martial Arts,
Wrestling Scenes, 24/7.

—*classified "model" advertisement*

Johann placed his lips over the opening of the soda can, gesturing for me to light the crack, which nested in steel wool over a second hole freshly punctured with my manicure scissors. The rock sizzled in the flame, and Johann drew a deep breath; the smoke that escaped his lips smelled like singed hair. His facility with the crack belied his claim made earlier in the evening that he didn't do drugs, but I decided to let the discrepancy pass without comment. I was anxious for my turn at the improvised aluminum crack pipe, and had no wish to start an argument with the storm trooper who was holding it.

Whenever I traveled to Los Angeles, I lived in the guest wing of my agent's house, purchased from the estate of Vincent Price. Years ago, someone had painted every room a deep orange. "Coral," my agent explained, "for Vincent's wife, Coral Browne." The walls had been painted over, but my agent kept the original color inside the guest room closet, enjoying the effect on guests when he flung open the closet door and announced, "Imagine every wall of this house in *that* color! *Every wall!*"

Johann's eyes were closed after he inhaled the crack; he sat composed, as if meditating. I wanted his attention, so I opened the closet door and proclaimed, "Imagine every wall in this house painted *that* color!"

"You." He offered the can.

This was new for me. I had snorted my share of cocaine, but smoking crack seemed different, tawdry, and desperate, conjuring TV news images of ravaged urban neighborhoods and bullet-ridden victims of gang wars. I supported a foster home in the Bronx for orphans of crack addicts; I pictured the wide, frightened eyes of the babies on the brochure.

"Sure," I said, swallowing a familiar feeling of disgust.

Johann arranged a waxy rock of crack in the metal nest and placed the can against my lips. He held the lighter and commanded me to inhale. I obeyed. As my body left the ground I heard him say, "Very good, Ronnie. Someday you will be a professional crackhead."

He removed his shirt and took a bodybuilder's stance in front of a mirror. "Not bad, hey, Ronnie?" His torso was muscled, nearly hairless, freckled along the shoulders. His biceps protruded like baseballs. "I go to Sports Connection gym four times a week. I never pay. I run to the place, I get all sweaty. I don't carry a bag. I walk past the desk, no problem. So, Ronnie, you could say I have a free lifetime membership to Sports Connection."

He sat on the edge of the bed and spread his knees. The pose seemed staged, professional. I knew my role; I fell between his legs and opened his pants. Pulling down his jeans, I wondered if *all* the gestures of the evening had been part of a performance: the quips, the accent, placing his hand on my thigh. Was he keeping me on the hook with hopes for a generous tip, running out the meter, like a New York cabbie delivering a tourist from midtown to the Village via the Brooklyn Bridge?

Johann wore no underwear, and his crotch smelled of cologne; I imagined him dabbing himself as he dressed for work. He made no sound as I stroked his pale, lightly haired legs. He looked past me. I followed his gaze to a mirror and caught him staring at our reflection.

I became lost in the feel of him inside my mouth and the salty, sour taste on my tongue. I began to hallucinate. The floor and the ceiling of the room stretched away; we hurtled through the atmosphere in a spaceship deriving its power from the movement of my head bobbing up and down. I heard the Scottish guy from *Star Trek* calling from the engine room, demanding "More power!" and I moved my head faster. The ceiling disappeared and the floor fell away. I held tight to Johann's legs. I had no idea what he was doing above me; I lost awareness of anything above his waist and below his knees. I was afraid to look up, in case Johann's upper half had disappeared. Then, as if I'd been thrown into a tub of cold water, the hallucination vanished. I felt Johann's boots poke my legs and my knees burn against the scratchy carpet.

Johann offered a compliment. "You know what you are doing."

"I've been schooled by professionals."

He settled onto the pillows, arms above his head. "This crack is not so good. I will give Fred a hard time."

I curled against him. "You can always cut his heart out with a shiv."

Johann hummed a few measures of "Happy Birthday." "This is relaxing," he sighed, and began to tell me of his career at the "office," his name for Numbers.

"Usually they hire me as a master. I order them around. I beat them. It makes me tired. I wear a leather mask. It gets sweaty. The next day my face is dry and full of pimples."

I remembered the shame I felt after my own tentative excursions into domination: a spanking on my birthday by a prostitute named Rex; a dog collar placed around my neck by a bodybuilding porn star who asked me to lick his feet, which turned out to be, mercifully, spotless and professionally pedicured ("I take care of my feet," he claimed, in response to a compliment). These episodes had left me bewildered; I didn't understand the pleasure I derived from being subjugated.

"It feels good for these people to let go, to lose control," I ventured, keeping the conversation at a general level, in case Johann viewed his submissive clients with contempt.

"No, Ronnie. These people are lonely."

"How does getting beaten make you feel less lonely?"

Johann shrugged. "Some things happen to these people when they are children. Someone beats them, and they think, *Oh, this is great, this is love.* So I beat them, and they think they get more love. In my profession you cannot be judgmental." Johann turned toward me. "Ronnie? You want me to be the master with *you?*" He posed the question with a complete lack of investment in the answer, the way a waiter inquires if you'd like regular or decaf.

"I'm perfectly satisfied with what we're doing right now." It was true. I liked this man, this nonjudgmental storm trooper, who was slightly above it all yet touched by the complexities and loneliness of his clients. I didn't want him to disappear into some role. And I wasn't afraid of him or nervous about my body or self-conscious; in the light of Johann's aura, I had no need to disappear. I ran a hand along the inside of his thigh, the gesture of a lover, not a slave or a trick or a john.

"Ah, I see. Gentle type, likes to cuddle," he said, placing me in the appropriate category in his mental Rolodex.

Johann described his customers. There was the guy who kept a suitcase of different-size dildos and paid Johann to insert them (into the client), from smallest to largest. "Boring," Johann said. "Who wants to look at someone's asshole for two hours?" Then there was the guy from Pasadena, a postal worker named Howard who lived with his parents. When Howard's parents were away, Johann received a call and a request to meet Howard in a particular Bob's Big Boy.

"Ronnie. This guy makes me eat everything on the menu while he watches. I eat pancakes and eggs and ham and toast and a turkey sandwich and french fries and a big piece of apple pie with ice cream. He drinks coffee. We go to his house and he takes off all his clothes. Now, Ronnie, you have to understand, this is the ugliest man God ever created. He is seven feet tall. His nose, Ronnie . . . no man ever had a bigger nose than this. You look at him and you think a big crow has landed on his face. His ears are tiny. They stick out sideways. Ronnie, no one can love this man. Maybe his mother. But he has the biggest dick you ever saw. Twelve, thirteen inches. No one in a porn movie has a bigger dick than this. So he takes off his clothes. I stay dressed, in my boots, my leather jacket. He watches me. He jerks off harder. He says, 'Johann. Did you weigh yourself this morning?' I say, 'Yes, Howard. Right after you called me.' He says, 'How much did you weigh?' I say, 'One hundred fifty-two pounds.' He starts jerking off harder. He shows me a scale, in the bathroom. I step on the scale. Now Howard is all covered with sweat. His hand is pumping his dick a hundred miles an hour. He says, 'Johann. How much do you weigh now?' I say, 'Now I weigh one hundred and fifty-*four* pounds.' He jerks harder. He can barely talk. He says, 'You gained *two pounds* at Bob's Big Boy!' And then he comes all over the place."

"How much do you charge him?"

"Four hundred dollars. I could charge more. I go the whole day without eating. But Howard works in a post office. I can't take all his money. You see, this is my problem. I'm compassionate."

Johann rolled toward me. He wrapped his hands around my penis, which had deflated. "I like talking to you. You're a nice guy. I wish I could stay here all night."

"Well. You could." Johann seemed to consider the offer. I added, "If you need to charge extra . . ."

His eyes narrowed, calculating—I imagined—hours and dollars. I expected him to name a price for the service known as an "overnight."

"No, Ronnie," he said. "You need to sleep, and why should you spend so much money when I am tired?" He kissed me on the forehead. Perhaps it was the crack, but I recalled my childhood, a winter night in a small town with a clear sky, the warmth of my moonlit bedroom, overheated by a coal furnace, the consoling voice of my mother bidding me to say my prayers, and her lips on my forehead.

I counted money as Johann pulled on his black jeans. There's something about a stack of twenties on a bedsheet that sucks the romance out of a room. Johann folded the bills into his pocket without verifying the amount, giving the wad of cash no more significance than his keys and some change. I watched as he finished dressing, his gestures precise: running two fingers of each hand through his hair, pressing it behind his ears.

I stood to say goodbye, wanting to kiss him on the lips, but did not dare. Experience had taught me that the only taboo between prostitutes and johns is a kiss on the mouth.

"Are you going back to the office?"

"No way. I see one customer a night. I am not an ATM machine."

We hugged, and my lips brushed his neck. "Call me," he said. "I gave you my pager number." He smiled. "But don't use 911."

The next day I was thickheaded and impatient. A script meeting seemed to go on for hours. I was trapped in a plush office with seven well-groomed colleagues drinking Evian, debating a single line of dialogue: "You shouldn't have left us, Mama." A vice president of production, in a Laura Ashley dress and cowboy boots, had proposed another version: "Mama, it was wrong for you to leave us."

I said nothing. My head was pounding, and I was nauseous. Familiar feelings, after a night of martinis. But there was another feeling under the normal hangover feelings, a dryness in my throat and a jittery, recurring tingle in my extremities: the residue, I surmised, of crack working its way through my system. Across from me, a bespectacled, chubby senior executive peeled a banana. Her brow scrunched, she pondered the competing lines of dialogue. The problem confounded her, the way some people are confounded by the question of God's existence. As she placed the banana in her mouth, I thought of sex with Johann and the feeling of hurtling through space.

I covered my face with my hands so no one could see me laugh. They did see, however, that I had covered my face with my hands. Someone asked if anything was wrong. I kept my hands on my face, enjoying the warmth of my own recycled breath. The room fell silent. I realized I had reached a potential turning point. I might remain as I was, keeping my hands on my face, until someone had the presence of mind to call 911 and summon a team of paramedics. They will whisk me to an emergency room and then to a psych ward and possibly a rehab. It will be dramatic. And it will be over: the searching for drugs, the hangovers, the hours in hotel rooms crashing from speedy coke, the degrading moments with prostitutes who declare their heterosexuality the moment you try to kiss them, the promises to God never to do it again. I thought, *If I keep my hands on my face, I will be saved.* People forgive these minor breakdowns. In show business they admire them.

I remembered Johann, his freckled shoulders, and the smell of cologne in his crotch. He said he hoped to see me again. He wanted to show me his master's leather mask. I remembered how he'd held my flaccid penis while humming "Happy Birthday." I had his pager number in my wallet. They will make me throw it away, the people in the psych ward and the rehab. Certainly, that's the kind of thing they make you do, throw away the pager numbers of prostitutes with good drug connections. Johann promised the next time we got together he would come prepared, with powdered cocaine. "More sophisticated," he had said. "Like you, Ronnie." I imagined making love to Johann with my heart surging after two thick lines of coke. *I will kiss him deeply and for a long time. I will somehow come to possess him or convince him that he ought to possess me.*

I dropped my hands from my face and delivered a revised line of dialogue: "Mama, you shouldn't have left us. It was wrong!"

Relief flickered over the faces of my colleagues. I wasn't going mad. I was being *creative.* The chubby senior executive swallowed a chunk of banana and declared, "It's a compromise. But it works."

Faces of Ecstasy

By David Steinberg
Sexuality.org / May 21, 2004

Masturbation is usually a private thing.

And orgasm, that moment when everything spins so delightfully and totally out of control—your mind, your body, your face—well, that's private, too, something you only want the most intimate and trusted of other people to see.

Usually.

But now, on a sunny Sunday morning, I'm driving to San Francisco for the purpose of masturbating in front of three other people and having my orgasm recorded on videotape for (potentially) all the world to see.

Part of my orgasm, that is. The plan is to videotape my face, only my face, close up and personal, as they say—all the way through arousal and climax.

It was all Joani Blank's idea. Joani is the marvelously creative, innovative founder of San Francisco's famous Good Vibrations sex emporium. She had decided to make a video—*Orgasm! The Faces of*

Ecstasy—that would show a wide variety of people having orgasms. What Joani wanted to record was not people's bodies, not their genitals, but just their faces. We concentrate too much on genitals and intercourse when we think of sex, Joani has long complained. Pornography, she notes, is positively obsessed with genitals, much to its detriment.

She wanted to offer an alternative—an alternative sex video, an alternative sex vision, an alternative attitude about sex altogether. In 1996 she had made a nine-minute video of people's faces during orgasm, which was received with great enthusiasm by friends and professional colleagues alike. Now she wanted to expand that pilot, with proper video equipment and lighting, and with people talking about how they felt about sex, orgasm, and masturbation, in addition to the footage of their sexual excitement and release.

She had called one day to ask if I wanted to be part of her project—to be interviewed and videotaped by herself, and by Jack Hafferkamp and Marianna Beck, the editors of recently deceased *Libido* magazine, while I masturbated until I came. After about a quarter-second of careful thought, I jumped on board.

I completely agree with Joani about the general sexual obsession with genitals and intercourse, as if there were nothing else that matters about sex, that counts as real sex. I mean, genitals are important, of course, and intercourse, too. But so much of what I value most about sex gets lost if genitals and intercourse are all you think about.

And faces! There is so much going on, so much to see, in people's faces during sex. I have, for the last four years, made a project of taking fine art photographs of couples being sexual. I photograph plenty of genitals and plenty of p-v penetration, but I find that I focus most on people's faces and hands. So much of what is going on in sex gets expressed in faces and hands—the subtleties as well as the more obvious heat and passion.

The idea of a video that showed nothing more than the ecstatic, twisted, confused, amazed, nervous, vulnerable faces of people at the height of sexual excitement was intriguing to me. And, yes, I'm something of an exhibitionist too, so I was delighted to sign up as one of what would become twenty-two subjects, aged 22–68.

Unfortunately, all that interest and conceptual excitement feels like something from the very distant past as I negotiate traffic on Interstate 280 at 9:30 in the morning and wonder what in the world I've gotten myself into. I've dutifully refrained from sex for a couple of days, but I'm not feeling the least bit sexy or sexual. Whatever prompted me to agree to a 10 A.M. time slot? And how am I going to get myself out of an utterly mundane frame of mind so I can jack off with proper enthusiasm and offer the cameras a wonderfully passionate picture of my self-induced sexual excitement?

It helps to remember that Joani, Jack, and Marianna are all close and longtime friends, serious documentarians who, I know, will not portray my sexuality in some stupid, trivial, or sensational way. It helps to remember—as I emphasize so strongly to the couples I photograph—that this isn't some kind of grand performance, that I don't have to produce some preordained image of sexual heat, that I don't have to prove anything to anyone.

It does not help that the place Joani, Jack, and Marianna have chosen for their videotaping is a huge, empty, art gallery space sans art, totally devoid of human presence, visual aesthetics, or even any soft surfaces except for a forlorn-looking bed set under two spotlights in the middle of the vast floorspace, looking more like an interrogation site than an invitation to erotic pleasure.

Fortunately, before jumping into any kind of sex, I am going to be interviewed, which just might give me a chance to get used to the physical space, to the cameras, to Joani, Jack, and Marianna, and to being out of the car. I'm placed on a stool against a blank white wall, and Joani asks me a series of questions while Jack and Marianna film my responses, peering out from behind big cameras on tripods.

Why do I want to be in this video? What do I think the significance of this video will be? Who do I especially hope will see this video? Who do I especially hope will *not* see this video? Is there something political about making this video?

When Joani asks me to fake an orgasm for the cameras, it brings me up short. I've never faked an orgasm in my life and don't have the slightest idea where to begin. I try to make some appropriate faces and sounds but feel so utterly ridiculous that I have to stop.

"I really don't think I can do this," I say, finally, embarrassed at my embarrassment.

"That's ok, you don't have to," Joani offers quickly, to my tremendous relief.

Then it's time to go over to the interrogation bed. I take off my clothes and lie down, a little colder than comfortable. I'll warm up soon enough, I tell myself hopefully. Jack and Marianna position their cameras around me. Marianna is to my right, a few feet away. Jack is on my left, much closer, the camera practically on top of my face.

"The one thing we ask," he says in his soft, comforting voice, "is that you keep your eyes open as much as possible and look directly at the camera." I nod. When I look directly at the camera I see a miniature of myself reflected in the lens. Not helpful.

Someone asks if I want lube. I decline. The cameras go on. "Whenever you're ready," Jack suggests.

"Ok," I say.

There's no music, no incense, no sexual or sensual input coming from the outside. It all has to come from me. Just what *is* the sexual desire I'm expressing here? The only desire I feel is the desire to produce something useful for the video. That and the desire not to make a fool of myself. What does that mean? I want to be genuine, but I also seem to want something more—to be seen as sexy, attractive, desirable. I want the picture of my desire to itself be desirable. Interesting, but not helpful.

Too much thinking, I realize.

I start to touch myself. Fortunately, touch has its own way of generating desire and of getting my mind to shut up. Out of the desire void I begin to feel genuinely aroused, in waves that come and go. I still feel pretty distracted and self-conscious. With my eyes open I don't have the option of getting lost in an appealing fantasy. This is going to be about me, Joani, Jack, and Marianna making a video in a big empty room at 848 Divisadero. Reality video.

"This may take a while," I announce, apologetically.

"That's fine," says Jack. "Take your time."

I feel myself working, trying to accomplish the task of turning myself on. I imagine, with some dismay, how that must look to the camera. Indeed, I can see, in miniature, how I look in my camera lens reflection. I look like I'm working much too hard. I breathe deeper, encourage myself to relax, to really take my time. Gradually the pleasurable feelings take over from the need to deliver a product. I get more and more deeply turned on. Jack reminds me to keep my eyes open, to look directly at his camera, at my little face staring back at me from his lens. When I come I'm aware that my head is jerking around a lot, through the big release and a series of aftershocks, all of which sweep remarkably strongly through my body. I manage to keep my eyes open through all of it, I think. And then I burst out laughing at the whole thing—the absurdity of the situation, the build up and release of tension, the ego confusions, the simplicity and the complexity of physical sexual pleasure.

Something like a year goes by. Occasionally I hear from Joani or Jack or Marianna about how the editing is going. They have over forty hours of tape to edit down to less than an hour. They are blown away with what they've gotten on tape and working hard to create a video that does justice to the heart and soul of what these twenty-two people have given them. There are the usual hundreds of unforeseen production problems, crises, and delays—and then some.

Eventually I get an email from Joani that it's all done—edited, remixed, boxed, and ready to go. There will be a release party at Club Mighty in San Francisco. I invite everyone I know and make my way to the city for the big event.

Some 250 people show up, far exceeding anyone's expectations. The mood is joyous, celebratory, friendly, congratulatory—sexy in the understated, somewhat-overly-conscious way of the Bay Area's unique pan-sex-exploration/writers/artists/photographers/publishers/activists subculture.

I feel excited, and surprisingly nervous. It's not as if I haven't had my sexuality out in public before, but there's something about this particular situation that makes me feel particularly vulnerable, particularly exposed. Something about the combination of orgasm and masturbation. I'm glad Susie is there to hold my hand, and glad when I run into more than a few close and more distant friends.

The room quiets down. Joani, Jack, and Marianna offer thanks and introductions, and then the video comes on—projected in triplicate on huge scrims above everyone's heads. The talk and the ecstatic faces have been interwoven into a powerful flow. The orgasm sequences, in particular, are collectively amazing. As viewers, we're inches away from each person's face as they go through arousal and dissolution. It's a physical closeness usually reserved for lovers, so we all become, in a sense, each subject's lover for a minute or two, participating in their sexual excitement and culmination. The eye contact that was so difficult to maintain makes the intimate connection between subject and viewer unmistakable and inescapable. I am deeply moved by this recurring intimacy, by how beautiful each person is in this state of vulnerability, and by the honor of being permitted to witness such unfiltered, soulful, revealing pictures of one person after another.

Then it's my turn on the screen. I relive the embarrassing tension, the softening, the release, the manic head twitching, all redeemed by the final laughter which, even in my state of nervous self-criticism, I can see in a positive way. Some people laugh at my laughter; a few applaud. I feel seen and validated. I've just had sex with all these people, I think to myself. I smile and relax.

There's something to be said for telling the truth about who we are sexually, and a lot to be said for letting other people see our more vulnerable sexual sides. Maybe truthfulness, pleasure, and joy can win out over anger, fear, and guilt—even in these strange and confusing times.

Violence in the Garden

By Polly Peachum
Submissive Women Speak.net / September 2004

> *"The locus of fantasy of a lucky man holds no robots; of a lucky woman, no predators; they reach adulthood with no violence in the garden."*
>
> —*Naomi Wolf*[1]

We have an indoor cat, and so each morning, as a special treat, I carry our little gray tiger in my arms as I walk through the wildly disorganized jungle that my neighbors mistakenly call their garden. As I take my tom along paths lined with flowers almost a foot taller than I am, beside a dark stand of pines, and back around the magnolia tree and through the weedy grass to the struggling tomato patch, I often find myself daydreaming about who or what might be hidden in the vegetation, watching me with hungry eyes. In my "unlucky" imagination, the dark, fertile garden is populated with predators. Behind every bush, lurking just out of sight within the shadows, is someone stronger and more brutal than I, someone who will overpower me and bend me to his will, someone who will cruelly torture or humiliate me just to see me blush, whimper, or scream with pain.

It is a wonderful, thrilling daydream, and I live a less feral version of it in my daily life. I spend my life as a full-time slave within a heterosexual sadomasochistic relationship. To many, I know that this must make me seem to be a self-destructive, abuse-loving victim. That view is neither right nor fair. My jungle daydreams (and my hardcore reality) represent the living out of sexual desires that are for me far more positive than—albeit radically different from—what most people consider to be healthy or even sane.

I am not alone in having these kinds of dreams. According to a study mentioned by Naomi Wolf in *The Beauty Myth*[2], Dr. E. Hariton finds that 49 percent of American women studied have submissive fantasies. Like me, they have dreams of being captured, spanked and whipped, controlled, used like a toy. But because sexual dominance, submission, and sadomasochism in general are looked upon with horror and distaste in mainstream society, most people with submissive sexual fantasies, women or men, stop at the level of fantasy. I have chosen, however, to turn my fantasies into reality, and in doing so, I have made my most cherished dreams come true. I believe myself to be the happiest and most fulfilled person I know. I am certain that I owe my happiness to one simple fact: I have pursued and embraced my deepest desires instead of ignoring them. I have become the person whom I feel I was always meant to be, the person I needed to be. I am reasonably unconflicted, reasonably at peace with myself, and vibrantly alive. I have accepted my passion for submission absolutely as the healthy, life-affirming, and wondrous choice that it is for me. In the six years during which I have been living the dream, I have never once regretted my choice or cursed my perverse desires. In fact, I consider myself to be one of the luckiest people alive.

I suspect that many women must see me as a downtrodden tool, duped by a man into doing what women have done for men in most cultures from time immemorial: serving, obeying, and sexually servicing them. I see myself, in contrast, as a conscious, intelligent, and intrepid individual who has dared to do what few women attempt: I have taken an enormous risk, rejected almost everything that the organs of society have told me should make me happy, and deliberately pursued that which I knew inside would actually make me most happy. And I have succeeded.

My success was hard won and all the more dear to me for that. No one in this culture grows up being told that being a slave is a good thing. No one is encouraged to become a servant or praised for her subservience. If you are a child with such desires, you learn to keep them from your parents. As you grow older, you hide them from your playmates. And if you, like me, reached puberty in a time of growing feminist consciousness, you may even have learned to keep them from yourself. But in the end, hiding your true sexual desires from yourself never works. Like the proverbial bad penny, one's sexuality always comes back from whatever faraway land it's been banished to and must, sooner or later, be consciously dealt with, even if the conscious decision that results is to be aware of but to ignore one's urges.

Many of the women who, like myself, have gone beyond the fantasies and are active submissives struggle with the apparent contradiction of these desires with what society at large—and some doctrinaire feminists—tells us is good for our mental and emotional health. Resolving this contradiction is central to our sense of self-worth and humanity. Is what sadomasochists do, think, or desire wrong, as so many would certainly demand? If so, why do we want it so badly?

The emotional and intellectual conflicts that a submissive must resolve while learning to accept herself involve a wide range of issues beyond the core question of "Am I sick?" These are questions such as: Must I repress parts of my personality in order to be a submissive? Can I ever get angry? How can I take pride in myself as a strong woman and as a feminist if I am always at my master's beck and call? In my selfish desire for sexual satisfaction, am I perpetuating violence against women? What happens if I am ordered to do something I really fear or hate and I am incapable of doing it? I may believe that my desires are okay, but how can I live with other women's hatred of what I represent and—even worse—their pity for me?

The reality of my life is deeply shocking to most people. Among active submissives, I belong to the rare subset that lives the dream twenty-four hours a day, absolutely and completely, without breaks, time-outs, or respites. In the sadomasochistic subculture, this is referred to as life-style submission. Since the moment I gave myself away to another, I have taken my slavery very seriously. It is as real to me as if it were legally sanctioned, perhaps more real, as many legal slaves refused to consider themselves as owned chattel. Although no court would uphold my master's ownership of me, I consider our master-slave relationship to be far more binding than any legal document, because we decided together that we would both make it so. When I gave myself away to my master, it was with the explicit understanding that I would not be able to leave the relationship no matter how much I might later want to. In our arrangement, only he has the power to dissolve the bond of ownership, and this will remain true no matter how unhappy I might become. I have not once in six years become so miserable that I have wanted to leave. If I should feel that way at some point in the future, however, my master has promised me that he will carefully observe me and our relationship and try to resolve its difficulties for a long period in order to determine if leaving is really the best thing for me. If, after many months of careful observation, he believes that my unhappiness with him or with the relationship is a permanent condition that could not be fixed by either of us, he will release me. But he will not release me from slavery to him immediately if I should express such a desire. I cannot just walk out of the relationship. If I did, he and I both know he would have every right to get me back by whatever means he could, as I really belong to him absolutely, and not just when it is convenient for me to belong to him.

Although relationships like mine are not unique, in many other power relationships that I have observed, the couple does not take this aspect of ownership to the extreme that we have. The concept in these relationships is that the slave is continually giving her slavery to her master. That "gift" is constantly renewed with every moment and can be taken back by her whenever she wishes. Doing this would probably end the relationship, but ultimately both partners want the slave to have the final say, the final veto, and ultimately, absolute power. To me, such a relationship would be a sham, much as a child's "let's play house" game is an inconsequential and unreal imitation of an actual family, with all of its moral responsibilities and legal obligations. I would never have consented to such a sham slavery. Yes, certainly, I could gather up our little cat and then drive off in the car, never to return voluntarily, but the truth is that I will not, ever, do this. I have committed myself to being this man's slave for as long as he should want me to be, and that commitment, that decision to give myself away, is sacred to me. In a culture where marriages, the priesthood, and other commitments that are supposed to be permanent and sacred are broken as easily as we change our minds about what to wear to work, many people find this concept of absolute dedication difficult to understand or to credit; they don't believe that it really works. But I know myself to be a person capable of keeping such a commitment, and so does my master, and that's all that matters. The opinions of others on the actuality of my slavery have about as much effect on it as a swarm of suicidal moths has on the ability of a campfire to stay lit. The moths' effect, if any, is—in a very small way—to feed the flames of my dedication.

My life with my master is very tightly controlled. I must try to obey every order given to me, and on the few occasions when I disobey, I am severely punished. My actions are not my own, except during those limited times when my owner allows me to act freely (for example, he has given me permission to write for this publication; had he refused me permission, you would not now be reading this). My dreams are not my own, nor are my thoughts: I must reveal them to my master upon demand.

All the money I make is immediately turned over to my master, and he decides how or when it is spent. Likewise, all my former personal property, everything I used to call my own, now belongs to him. I must get permission for all major actions and for many trivial ones. For example, if I want to buy a new suit or take a new work contract (as a high-tech consultant, I do projects for a variety of clients), I have to get his permission. At home and often when I am away, if I want to use the bathroom, I must again get permission. I am not allowed to leave the bed at night without permission; in fact, I am tied each evening to the bed by a rope attached to a collar. If I am invited out for drinks or dinner by someone I work with, I must get permission, and often orders are given about the quantity and kinds of food and drink that I may consume. My owner requires me to do most of the housework, to exercise regularly, and to come immediately when he commands, no matter what else I might be involved with. Spankings, whippings, and other physical "abuse" are a recurring part of my life.

Although I am bound by the many rules that control my behavior, my everyday life, on the surface, resembles most people's. I keep my sexuality absolutely hidden at work, and while the occasional perceptive coworker will guess that my partner is "controlling," that's as far as it ever goes. We are "out" as master and slave only to other sadomasochists and to those very few of our straight friends and acquaintances whom we trust. Although this is not so for my master, I have discovered that the only people I really want to become good friends with these days are people who share my sexual practices. Submission is such a big part of my life that friendships in which that aspect of myself must be hidden feel incomplete, almost dishonest. My master is out to the immediate members of his family; I am not out to mine, primarily because I am estranged from them and cannot trust them. I left my family and my friends behind when I moved across the country to live with my master, and since the move, sadly, I have acquired many acquaintances but no close friends (it is difficult enough to find good friends when you have all of humanity to choose from; when you limit your selection pool to a small fraction of that, the search for simpatico people takes much longer). Although I am actively searching for new friends, I have resigned myself to the idea that this search may very well take years, if not decades.

Despite the fact that I am searching for my friends among other sadomasochists, I have a suspicion that the friendships I do form someday will probably be with sexually conventional people who have the understanding and compassion necessary to accept me as I am. The other kinky people that I meet are often disappointing because it so often turns out that the only thing we have in common is what we do for erotic excitement, and that is never enough to base a friendship on.

My relationship with my master is able in many ways to compensate for my lack of close friends. Unlike the cold and forbidding routines which are so often the lot of fantasy slaves in erotic literature, our everyday life is full of intimate, loving rituals, combined with a dash of sadism to keep things interesting. On an average morning, I am awakened by my master at the time he decides I should get up, usually between 5:30 and 6:30 A.M., even on weekends. I tell him my dreams from the night before, and, as I am usually still half-asleep after this recital, he lets me "float" for a few minutes before untying me from the bed and sending me off to use the bathroom. Our morning wake-up routine includes a number of other activities which we do purely for fun: an in-bed wrestling match, a morning song, a wake-up spanking, and a head over heels "airplane ride." I then go to make breakfast, collect the newspapers, and take my little cat for his garden walk. After a leisurely breakfast, I clean up the dishes and do some other morning chores. With those out of the way, my master has a brief planning conference with me to discuss what I must accomplish that day. During these conferences with my master, as with all our conversations, I am allowed—in fact, encouraged—to make any comments or suggestions that I wish, but the final decision on what I actually do that day rests with him. If I am working on contract, I either dress and go to the client's or go into our home office to begin my work. If I am not working that day, what I do depends upon what my master wants to get done and also on what I would like to do. I may run errands, I may clean house, I may write email to my electronic pen pals, or I may simply settle down in an easy chair with a good novel. Like conventional couples, we take vacations to the mountains or the shore. The crucial difference between what I do on an average day and what a person living a conventional life does is not in the kinds of things that I do but in the fact that whatever the activity, I must first get my master's okay. Another difference is that, when I am at home, whether working or playing, my master will interrupt my activities many times during the day with orders for me: to get him lunch, to fetch him something from another room, to listen to him read me a news story, to have another planning conference, to bend over and be caned, and so on. It could be anything. At night, after dinner is cleaned up and all my evening chores are finished, we will often do something together before bedtime, such as watch a TV show or play a game of cribbage or backgammon—or something more intensely sadomasochistic. When it is time for bed, I participate in another set of playful rituals. Just before lights out, I am tied to the bed and blindfolded. I am usually sound asleep within ten minutes.

My tightly structured life with its heavy workload and the never-ending requirement to obey may seem intolerable to most people, but I reap many rewards from it. I am madly in love with my master and he with me: he understands my special needs and complements them perfectly. Within this relationship exists a level of intimacy that I haven't experienced anywhere else. It is so comforting to be able to tell—in fact, to be required to tell—one's darkest secrets to someone else: someone else knows all of this; I am not alone. My master is a gentle and compassionate dominant, and there is a strong healing aspect to our relationship. He supports me, builds me up, makes me feel good about myself, but never lies to me. I have absolute trust in him. I find that the longer I live with him and the better I know him, the more time I want to spend with him.

No matter how benign the rule, no matter how eroticized the

physical pain, the question remains, however, of why anyone would subject herself to outrageous violations of her personal freedom. Part of the explanation is purely sexual: giving away control, having no say in the major or trivial decisions that affect me, provides me with a continuous low level of erotic excitement. I am always slightly turned on. Beyond that, most life-style submissives, including myself, include something that I think of as a "service ethic" in their personalities. I long to serve. I love to bring my master pleasure by doing his bidding. At no time in my life have I been unaware of that service ethic.

As important for most of us female submissives as the joy of service is intimacy: experiencing extremes of pain and humiliation at the hands of one's dominant creates an intensely intimate bond. This person can do anything to me. I have absolutely no defenses against him. My soul is stripped bare and on display before him. This intimacy is frightening in its intensity. The trust required to experience it is prodigious. But submissives who have felt it within the context of total powerlessness describe it in ecstatic, almost mystical, terms. For us, the admission price of fear and vulnerability is well worth paying for a ticket to heaven on Earth.

These are some of the general features of submission valued by myself and other submissives. But just what a submissive feels, what turns her on, surprises many people. The tediously conventional answer, often said with a snicker in the voice, is "whips and chains," but for me, the richly idiosyncratic sensations, fantasies, and impressions that excite my erotic imagination and bring my submissiveness to the fore are practically endless in their variety. They include the intoxicating smell of new leather; the sight of someone dressed entirely in black; the thrilling touch of cold steel restraints against my skin; watching a pair of gloves being slowly drawn on; the pungent and humiliating taste of my own juices on a pair of fingers being forced into my mouth; hard, sharp sounds, such as a club coming in contact with a golf ball, which remind me of wood or leather being brought sharply to bear against flesh; the terrifying sensation of blood trickling down the back of my leg; the vision of someone slapping a riding crop rhythmically against his hand; the acidic taste of fear accompanied by a crazy leaping sensation in the stomach; the intent eaglelike expression found in the eyes of certain dominants; a slap on the face; a hand at my throat, gently squeezing, threatening; the sight of a needle as it passes through skin; the unique sensation of lying on the floor with a boot pressing down on my head; an intense, embarrassing, goose-bumpy awareness of one's nakedness in front of a group of fully clothed people; being forced to kneel, crawl, or grovel; being forced to assume the classic slave position of head to the floor, bottom raised to expose the buttocks and genitals for my dominant's amusement; an inability to catch my breath and an aching pain in my mouth that come from giving forced oral pleasure; the sound of my beloved's laughter in response to my screams of agony; the close embrace of a locking steel collar around my neck; the taste of a leather whip that is shoved against my lips to be kissed or licked. The life of a life-style submissive at its best is a low-level—and often not so low-level—phantasmagoria of erotic stimulation, profound intimacy, and intense awareness of specialness.

Such a life, obviously, is not lived unexamined. The questions that submissive women ask themselves, the internal colloquies which they engage in, arise from the cultural sea which surrounds them: the submissive's questions are the inverted accusations of society. But are these accusations fair, or do they embody myths that most people believe simply because it seems the right or obvious thing to do? The myths themselves must be examined. Do the assumptions made by conventional society about submissives match the submissives' personal experiences? The motives of those who publicize myths and negative attitudes about submissive sexuality must also be examined by the female submissive in search of her own acceptance of her needs.

The mythic female submissive is weak, unable or unwilling to make decisions, because she does not want to bear the normal burdens and responsibilities that other adults bear, or because of a pathological need to be dependent upon the dominant. She and her dominant are said to form a particularly violent and sickly codependent relationship.

As is often the case with popular beliefs about people or things we are uncomfortable with, the belief in the weak female submissive is often the exact opposite of the reality. In fact, most people would be incapable of full-time, life-style submission no matter how much they might desire it, because they simply don't have the strength of personality required. Most people, when they think of a submissive, picture a rubber-willed, weak little doormat whom everyone, not just a particular dominant, can walk all over. The truth is that while there are certainly some weak submissives who fit the rubber-mat profile, there are also many weak people involved in conventional, nonkinky relationships. Self-destructive people exist—period. Some are drawn to sadomasochism, most not, but they will go wherever they must to find affirmation of their worthlessness.

Weak individuals are a minority among conscious female submissives and are especially rare in life-style, permanent relationships, for a number of interrelated reasons. Most important among them is that people involved in life-style submission tend to take their sexuality and their potential partners very seriously. A lot of careful evaluation goes on, both by the submissive and by the dominant, before a union, especially a permanent union, is formed. It would be awfully hard for a weak or self-destructive individual to hide such tendencies from an experienced dominant, as signs of pathologically low self-esteem are one of the primary traits that an experienced dominant looks for—in order to avoid—when getting to know a submissive woman (healthy male dominants avoid self-destructive submissives because dominants are interested only in an actual exchange of power, and power is not something that a self-destructive submissive has much of to exchange). Successful life-style relationships require a measure of strength and unselfish giving that a person obsessed with getting her negative sense of herself confirmed has no energy for nor interest in. Absolutely sincere obedience, the kind that resonates in the soul as the required action is performed, is rare and, even if you have a knack for it, is extremely difficult to cultivate. Only an individual with a good grasp of her own strengths and a positive opinion of her abilities is capable of learning obedience in the form required in an absolute master-slave sadomasochistic relationship. Only a very strong and stubborn personality will have the ability to stick with it when the going gets rough: when she doesn't want to obey or when orders are given in a humiliating fashion, perhaps in front of others whom she wishes to impress with her independence.

Another feature of the weak-submissive stereotype is that submissives "escape" into a life-style relationship in order to avoid adult responsibilities and decision-making. I can't speak for all life-style submissives, but I certainly didn't volunteer for a lifetime of slavery out of a need to have my decision-making taken away from me. I was thirty years old, had been living on my own and making decisions for over twelve years, and was having not the slightest trouble fending for myself before I became involved with my master. In fact, giving up decision-making was particularly difficult for me. I was used to making decisions in my personal relationships. I was used to being among people who liked me to make the decisions, and I had grown to trust my own judgment. Trusting someone else to make decisions about the relationship, let alone about me, that are as good as or better than my own was very difficult to do, and only lengthy experience with someone who actually is as competent as myself has eased my mind in this area.

(Closely connected with the stereotype of a submissive as a weak doormat is the image of the dominant as a manipulative, selfish, and immoral predator on weak people: a person who cannot form a relationship with someone his equal. While some people are attracted to the dominant role out of personal insecurity, out of the belief that the only way they can attract and hold a woman is by dominating her, successful life-style dominants do what they do out of a deep wellspring of confidence which tells them that what they do is profoundly right: that this is what they were meant to do. It is a mirror image of the submissive's feeling of being "home." Experienced members of the S&M communities know how to differentiate between a wannabe dominant doing it for all the wrong reasons and the real McCoy. Insecure people who are not really dominant show numerous clues, and these traits can be spotted by experienced submissives, just as experienced dominants can spot individuals with severe self-esteem problems posing as submissives.)

A crucial question about ourselves that most female submissives must contend with, and a particularly important one for feminists, is whether we, in our selfish desire for bizarre sexual satisfaction, are perpetuating violence against women. Sadomasochistic sex is commonly seen as ritualized violence: impersonal, brutal, dehumanizing, and objectifying. It is said to perpetuate hostility toward women and to turn the paradigm of loving, intimate relationships on its head. It is seen by many as amplifying power inequalities between men and women and promoting a form of sex that is cold and emotionally distant. These ideas are multifarious and must be looked at piece by piece.

Does conscious submissiveness have anything to do with cultural inequality between the sexes? It doesn't seem so to me. On the Internet is a section where people can post personal ads for those interested in sadomasochistic sex. Typically, the posters of such ads reveal their dominant or submissive orientations. Most messages posted here are from submissive men looking for dominant women. (This is not definitive information, of course. Many factors affect the willingness to search publicly for sexual partners. But the reality as represented on the Internet does not support the idea that the roles played in sadomasochistic sex reinforce sexual stereotypes—nor does any other available information.)

According to *Different Loving: The World of Sexual Dominance and Submission*[3], "Sexuality theorists traditionally have held that men are more likely than women to have sadistic sexual fantasies . . . that women are more likely than men to have masochistic fantasies. No evidence, anecdotal or otherwise, supports these conjectures. Indeed, submissive men are the single largest component of the [sadomasochistic] communities, and widespread male interest in submission is an observable phenomenon." Some of the belief that female submissiveness perpetuates stereotyped sex roles and violence against women is no doubt rooted in confusion about violence. Those who believe in the perpetuation myth assert that when one person hits another person hard enough to cause pain, this physical act, irrespective of whether the person being hit has asked the hitter to do so and is taking great pleasure and satisfaction from it, is violence in the same sense as a rape or mugging or spousal abuse. Neither the intent of the person being "abused" nor that of the "abuser" matters at all. But what about the submissive woman who eroticizes pain and force? If these are things that she wants, that affirm her from day to day and raise her to ecstasy at times, can they in any way be compared to the brutal violence forced on a desperate and unintentionally helpless victim?

The belief that female submissives take part in relationships that are impersonal and dehumanizing is particularly appalling. Those who so believe tend to be individuals who have no experience with female submissives or with sadomasochistic relationships. Some experience with such people and relationships would teach them that the people in long-term sadomasochistic relationships tend to be those with considerable conventional sexual experience who find it lacking in intimacy and intense personal communication (for example, I had a small number of short relationships, one twelve-year relationship with a man, and one relationship of two years with a woman before I became an active sadomasochist). Submissive women generally find that sadomasochistic sex allows a deeply felt intimacy and closeness that conventional sex doesn't approach. The "consensual nonconsensuality" that is central to conscious sadomasochistic relationships requires a profound and even radical level of honesty and communication between dominant and submissive if it is to function successfully. Successful sadomasochists have learned to practice this hothouse honesty as a matter of course. Submissives who are unwilling to share what they really feel or who are actively dishonest as the whip falls or as the humiliation commences are avoided by experienced dominants and, in any event, generally fail as submissives (similarly, dominants who are dishonest and uncommunicative are dangerous and tend to fail as active dominants). Trust and honesty, the cornerstones of intimacy, may exist in a conventional sexual relationship, but nothing within the dynamics of such a relationship requires them in any high degree of either individual. Because these qualities are mandatory among successful practitioners in conscious sadomasochistic relationships, impersonality in such relations is simply impossible. Similarly, dehumanization, although it is often used by dominants as a technique to produce erotic fervor in a submissive during sex, dooms a life-style sadomasochistic relationship to an early end if it is a reflection of the actual attitude of either partner.

Yet despite the reality of being a female submissive, so much warmer and fuzzier than suspected by the unknowing, requiring such self-confidence and emotional strength, so exquisitely fulfilling, virtually every female submissive struggles, sometimes recurringly, with the question of whether her sexual and social tastes reflect serious pathology, perhaps involved with early physical or sexual abuse. I have certainly struggled with that idea.

Someone who knows my tastes and attitudes very well once gave me a little button that reads, "I've been reduced to THIS!" I like it very much, but I'd like to modify the button a little to make it read: "I've always wanted to be reduced to THIS!" as this wording aptly describes the story of my life.

I don't know if I was always submissive, but some of my first memories, beginning at age five, involve submissive acts and thoughts. I was the little girl who always wanted to serve the other kids I played with. I remember games in which I pushed my sisters around in a little toy wagon to the point of my own exhaustion, while thinking all the time of how comfortable they were and how much fun they were having thanks to my toils. I loved being able to be of service to them. With my parents I felt similarly but much more strongly. I glowed when they gave me things to do to help them around the house, and I accepted most punishments, when they came, with unquestioning obedience. Punishment held, even at that age, a distinctly erotic thrill. I was being physically corrected by someone stronger and wiser than myself, and that was not only just and right but also terribly exciting.

As I grew, I started to have explicitly erotic submissive fantasies: I'd make up stories about being a captive or a servant, forced to do extremely embarrassing things and endure painful punishment from those older and stronger than myself. These fantasies always excited me: they never made me feel evil or guilty. I think I assumed that all little kids dreamed of being chased naked in a circus arena by a swarm of bees trying to fly up their bottoms as the crowd laughed uproariously at such a shameful and painful predicament.

Around the age of nine, I tried consciously to engage the children I played with in master-slave games in which I, naturally, was always the slave. But while most kids loved the novelty of being the master, of being in charge of someone for a change, I seldom found any playmates who liked the game after the first few times we played it. I, of course, could play it all day if they cooperated, and I felt titillated while obeying my Lord or Lady's increasingly outrageous demands. Paradoxically, when I actually learned some facts about sex in my early teens, the constant and powerful sadomasochistic themes that had pervaded my childhood faded into the background. Perhaps this was because I was too busy trying to learn what to do on a date; perhaps it had something to do with the fact that I, a voracious reader, had discovered feminist literature at the tender age of thirteen, literature which strongly suggested that fantasies along these lines were not appropriate. Whatever the reason, my submissive urges became, at puberty, much less conscious than before, only emerging at night, as an accompaniment to masturbation. But even at those times, I did not associate these fantasies with myself or my needs; they were just something I did while jerking off.

For years my sexual fantasies and inclinations went consciously unexamined, at least by myself. At age seventeen, an older acquaintance gave me a copy of *Story of O*[4], the classic sadomasochistic novel of the twentieth century, to read, saying simply, "I think you'll find this interesting." I devoured the book, and it formed the basis for my fantasies for years to come, but I smothered any speculation about why she might have given me that book. I simply did not want to think about it. In retrospect, my denial seems amusing and also understandable. Try to imagine a precocious teenager taking community college classes and living with two male graduate students ten years her senior. A true child of the '70s, her curriculum includes a women's-studies class taught by a lesbian and a touchy-feelie human-sexuality class, in which sadomasochism is mentioned briefly in a five-minute talk about variations and fetishes and then never brought up again. Yet she comes home each night and spends forty to sixty minutes kneeling on a hardwood floor at the foot of a bed, massaging her politically correct, ecologically conscious, and sex-role-sensitive roommate's feet, until he falls asleep! And the time she spends doing this is the most thrilling, exciting, and intimate part of her day. Once again, in a limited and socially acceptable way, I got to relive those thrilling times in childhood when serving gave me such pleasure. But sexual submission was just not something related to me. I did not reject it; I simply did not think about it—except as a nighttime fantasy.

I did nothing more about my fantasies until six years later, when, at the age of twenty-three, I tried to spice up a five-year relationship by telling my boyfriend incidents from *Story of O* while straddling him during our lovemaking. He became so turned on by my stories that, to my great delight, he surprised me one day by tying my arms to a hook in our dorm-room ceiling. He then beat the living daylights out of me with a switch he had cut outdoors, degraded me, and attempted anal sex with me. This first genuine experience with forced submission thrilled me to my core, but the next morning, when my boyfriend saw the bruises on my hips and buttocks, he was absolutely appalled. His guilt at having caused these marks to appear on his lover's flesh prevented him from ever doing anything that "sick" with me again, despite my assertions that I had loved it.

Once again, my awareness of my submissive desires seemed to go underground, but they never were quite as buried as before. During the six years that I spent with my boyfriend after that one submissive experience, I'd listen to music by Frankie Goes to Hollywood and the Eurythmics and actively fantasize about being captured, beaten and abused, and made into someone's masochistic plaything. But I took no action.

An awareness of my relationship to submissiveness may have been slowly moving toward consciousness during those years, but it took a catalytic experience, an epiphany of sorts, to bring home to me the fact that I am a submissive. I was almost thirty years old and had been seeing LuAnn, a woman I had worked with for nine months. She was an avid reader of popular fiction and had made me aware of Anne Rice's Vampire books[5]. While reading them I was strongly affected by and attracted to the power relationships between a vampire and his chosen victims—really, between a centuries-old, experienced vampire and a young, recently human protégé. In my usual steamroller reading style, I went on to read everything Rice had ever written, and I eventually stumbled upon her erotic novels, written under the pen name of A. N. Roquelaure[6]. It was then, as I began to read about the erotic fairy-tale adventures of Beauty, wakened from a deep slumber by a rape and a spanking, that I was suddenly roused from my personal slumber to make the essential connection: this is me. I am like this fairy-tale character. I am a submissive, and I want nothing more than to be someone's slave! Bingo. The penny dropped. The trumpets blared. I went directly to "Go" and collected two hundred dollars. There I was. But where was I? Was I nuts and just didn't know it? It didn't feel nuts. It felt right.

At that time I had no idea of how few people viewed sadomasochistic relationships as acceptable for others, let alone for themselves. It really hurt to learn, as I quickly did, that LuAnn was utterly unprepared to accept my self-discovery. I was suddenly isolated, had no idea of where to turn to meet people who shared my new interests, even to talk to someone who would not be repelled by my feelings. Like many people in my lonely circumstance—until later I had no idea how many—I turned to the computer nets for relief. Alone in my apartment, I learned how to attach a modem to a computer and discovered the world of online communications. I also quickly found, thanks to some surprising assistance from my ex-boyfriend, the kinky areas on the BBSes and the commercial online services that I subscribed to. Here I began to meet other submissives and dominants. I left long, probing messages about my sexuality and within hours received numerous replies and private electronic letters. I got to know a number of people, even "played" with a few over the computer. I learned that the kind of total-immersion, or life-style, submission that I craved was not what everyone involved in sadomasochistic sex wanted. In fact, most people I met online seemed satisfied with doing a little S&M with their partners in the bedroom or over a weekend and then returning to a conventional relationship of equals after these relatively brief "scenes." I, on the other hand, was certain that I wanted nothing less than absolute, neverending slavery.

I searched among the people I was meeting online for my dominant counterpart: someone who wanted to dominate and control as much as I wanted to submit and be controlled. Eventually I found him—actually, he found me. After a long correspondence, numerous phone calls, and several meetings lasting many days, I was thrilled to be given the opportunity to give myself to him in slavery. Although he could have ordered me to become his slave, and I would have obeyed instantly, he wanted this to be my choice—and my final free decision. I thought very carefully about it for several weeks, and up to the second when he told me it was time to decide, I consciously considered the idea that I had a choice, that I could back out. Even though I didn't want to back out and all of me was screaming for the experience of slavery, I was still very aware that up until the second I gave myself to him, I had the power to remain free. I wasn't brainwashed; he hadn't talked me into anything. On the contrary, I had been actively and aggressively searching for him, or someone like him. It was my decision, and it's been the best (and last) serious decision I've made.

When I first met my master online, I expected to be manipulated. I expected bravado and show, masking a bottomlessly insecure ego, just as I had found in so many men whom I had met or had had relationships with. He had told me in one of his first electronic letters to me that he was a healer, someone who helped unhappy people to get better emotionally. In fact, when we first began to talk, he made it clear that although he was attracted to me, he saw me as someone he could help rather than as a potential lifemate. At the time, he had a slave whom he was happy with, and although that relationship later ended (he had chosen to end several earlier life-style dominant-submissive relationships which he had found to be unsatisfactory for various reasons), he was not "trolling for slaves," or trying to add me to some sort of sadomasochistic harem. He healed on an informal basis, he said, not charging the people he helped for his services, because he had a passion for it, a vocation. This all sounded so vague and New-Ageish to me. I felt the same suspicion I would feel for someone who announced that he was a witch or that he could communicate with the dead. I assumed that this so-called healing was probably his ego outlet. And so I tested him.

Not really believing he could help me emotionally (no one in my life had been able to help me—any accomplishments or growth I had achieved had been in spite of the people around me, not because of them), I issued to him, without fully realizing that this was what I was doing, a challenge. In response to his healer message, I said in effect, and rather cynically, "Sure, Mr. Healer, you're welcome to do your thing all you want, but don't expect any fancy results from me." Much later, my master told me how he had chuckled over this "uppity" statement of mine and how he knew, even before we began, how quickly I'd change my mind. How did he know this about me? Having read my public messages carefully, and having a wide range of experience with people, he already knew that I was bright, motivated, and very sincere about my desires for submission. He also knew by then a lot about my personal problems and hang-ups: the things I wasn't facing, the assumptions about life that weren't working for me, my fears and sensitivities.

Realizing, as I soon did, that he knew so much about me was only the first of many extraordinary realizations I was to make about him over the years. As the master-lover-slave dynamic was slowly added to the healer-patient dynamic, I began to realize that everything he had said about himself, even those things that sounded as if they had to be idle boasting because they were too good to be true, was accurate and genuine. He really did have an immense confidence in himself and a positive attitude toward undertakings, which he was able to convey or project to people he was trying to help. He really did take responsibility for everything he did, and he always kept his word. If he said he was going to call me at 7 P.M. on Tuesday, he did. He had an absolutely steady personality which was unafflicted with mood swings and invulnerable to conversion syndrome. (After reading this last sentence, my master said with his usual sardonic humor—he fancies himself a latter-day Oscar Levant—"Another way to say that is that I'm a fanatic.") He had enormous emotional strength and maturity and a baffling lack of emotional hot buttons. He was not overcome when terrible things happened in his life, nor was he strongly angered or upset by anything I did. Most refreshingly, he did not take either himself or anything in his life too seriously, and he constantly poked fun at both—something that an egotist posing as Lord Sir Omnipotent Dominant of the Universe is incapable of. These strong personal traits have allowed my master to be reasonably successful, and sometimes very successful, in almost everything he has undertaken. In five decades of living he has been a writer and an editor of newspapers and magazines; a writer of books; a photographer, actor, and musician; a small business owner; and a labor organizer and civil-rights worker. In addition to all of these paid occupations, he has always found time to counsel people who come to him for help and, more often than not, to help them to effect in themselves profound personal change. Finally, he has been a staunch feminist for decades and was fighting for the rights of women long before they became fashionable things for men to pay lip-service to.

Six long and wonderful years have gone by, and I am extraordinarily happy with the choice I have made and the course my life has taken as a result. Were I given the opportunity to decide about becoming a slave again knowing everything I know now, I would choose identically. Looking carefully at myself as I am now and at the person I was before I became a life-style submissive, I can say that my experiences as a submissive have enormously enhanced my life and in some ways completely turned it around. Without my master's experienced guidance, I don't believe that any of this would have been possible. Six years ago I was incapable of pulling myself out of my self-made quagmire. I was very overweight and steadily gaining. Although I had a moderately interesting job, my own apartment, and a lover, I was at loose ends. I was deeply dissatisfied with myself and felt impotent, powerless to change a life that was perfectly functional but stuck in emotional neutral. I had my little satisfactions, things that made me happy, but most of these had become vices. I drank almost a six-pack of beer every evening while eating my enormous dinners. After months of this bodily self-abuse, I could barely drag myself out of bed each morning and into work. I often called in sick and felt tremendously guilty for doing so. I liked to correspond with people over the computer, but this, too, quickly became an addiction. I bought every beauty and fashion magazine as soon as it came out and spent hours enviously gazing at the beautiful models and dreaming of looking like one of them. Like eating and drinking, trying to match society's ideal of beauty was one of the ways I avoided confronting the real problem: the barren, unfulfilling aspects of my life. Oddly, I considered myself to be happy.

Now all of that has changed. I lost the weight I needed to lose on a slow and healthy eating and exercise plan (I wouldn't even call it a diet—it was so moderate and inclusive). For the most part, I no longer have a compulsion to overeat. I no longer drink heavily, nor crave drinking as an escape. I rarely read a fashion magazine these days, as the women in them no longer strike me as that attractive or desirable to emulate—in fact, I sometimes find myself thinking, when staring at one of those grotesque, heavily made-up bags of bones that these magazines so love to promote as the pinnacle of attractiveness, that it's a pity that poor scaggy model can't look more like me! I am no longer dissatisfied with my career: I make things happen. Unexpected results of my own unconscious making rarely sneak up on me, as they once regularly did. I'm not avoiding the knowledge of the effect that my actions have on my social and work environments any more. My subterranean efforts to sabotage my life have ceased. I don't believe that I am trying to escape or avoid any aspect of my life. Most importantly, who and what I am is no longer a dark mystery to me. I've discovered who I am, what I want from life, and am learning more each day about how to get it. I no longer let people walk all over me, and I can do things—like express anger to strangers—that were inconceivable to me six years ago. My low-level, ongoing emotion has changed from one of mild depression to one of happiness and peace with myself. I am no longer searching for a place in life; I have come home.

As much as my master has helped me to heal and grow, I have done most of the hard work myself. But what has allowed me to develop the power to change my life in such important and positive ways, when people can spend decades in formal therapy without getting these sorts of spectacular results, is that I am finally doing what I was meant to do, doing what I need to do in my life. I am living and experiencing, in a positive, sane, and unharmful way, the fantasies I've had for years of ravishment, violation, loss of control, erotic suffering, and degradation. After years of trying to understand just why I have been able to achieve all I have, I have concluded that when a person finds where she belongs or finds something she really loves to do, a lot of negative behaviors, including entrenched habits, may fall by the wayside, the superficial symptoms of a deep dissatisfaction with life.

I believe that I became a submissive in spite of my environment and experiences, not because of them. I have the kind of background that turns people into emotional basket cases, not sexual submissives. My father was an alcoholic who died before I reached puberty. While he was alive, he alternately abused me physically and emotionally and spoiled me with love and attention. After he died, I spent months crying myself to sleep with loneliness. Bad as he was, he was the one in the family who had given me a sense of myself as someone special and loved. (I am aware that my life as an adult in some ways is an acting out of my relationship with my father. I am also aware that for me it is a healthy one and that much more is involved in my sexuality than childlike re-enactment.)

Shortly after Dad's death, my mother dragged me out of the public-school system and sent me to Catholic school. The effect of our family constantly moving around and my going to a new school each year, in addition to the recent shock of losing my father had had its effect on me by then, and I was a pathetically shy, insecure child. I stood against the wall of the playground, watching the other children play, and made up hurtful fantasies about why I was never asked to join in the fun. I was too stupid; I was awkward; my family was too poor; I was a stranger; I was not as good as they were.

And then there were the nuns. Take an already insecure child with a very poor sense of herself and set a vicious and embittered pack of half-crazed emotional abusers loose on her, and watch the blood fly!

During those tortured years, my mother worked at a low-paying teacher's job to try to support a family of six. Her exhaustion and disappointment in her life left her emotionally distant and entirely oblivious to my misery. Although I was an intellectually and creatively gifted child, I developed a sense of myself which contained almost overwhelming elements of inferiority and defeat. I felt helpless, that almost everyone else around me was more powerful or more intelligent than I, that I could not do anything, and that I was incompetent to handle life in many ways simply because I was a woman like my mother. While I knew deep inside that my male classmates were not, in almost every case, more intelligent than I, I discounted my ideas and opinions as worthless next to theirs, abetted by my teachers. My large creative resources were put to heavy use inventing reasons for why the boys' thoughts were always better than mine.

My emergence from Catholic school, terribly wounded, left me facing puberty and my first genuine sexual experience, a rape at age fourteen, unarmed. And with this marvelous introduction to the wonderful world of sex under my belt, I passed through my teens and most of my twenties as frigid as the North Pole. The feminist literature which I began reading at that time gave me idealistic hopes about how things should be—how I, as a strong young woman, should act and feel—but I was in no position to put such ideals into practice. I had no experiences of success on which to build. But I was still alive deep down there, with an unshakable core of optimism, a stupid, unflinching hope that things would work out for the best. It's as if I had and have a metaphorical core of steel in me, raw and unforged, but nevertheless unwilling to give way. I know that I managed to keep a place in me safe from the awful things that life threw in my way, safe from the cruelties of the world. In that place I was happy, in that place I had hope for a better life, and in that place I lived my fondest and most intimate sexual fantasies.

My history is difficult but far less difficult than some and in no way different from the backgrounds of millions of women whose submissive feelings, if they have them, are unimportant in their lives.

Yet many of these women, in a nearly infinite variety of circumstances, are unhappy, confused, at a loss—and I am not. Paradoxically, I have discovered how to act on my feminist convictions, how finally to make them a real and practical element in my life, during the last few years, which I have spent in slavery to a man. The basic theoretical premises of feminism, as I have seen them, are that women are as capable as men; that women ought to have as many rights, options, and responsibilities as do men; and that it is deeply wrong that anything should or should not happen to a woman simply because she is female. Feminism, as I have been living it during the last six years, has been bound up with the parts of my personality that were affected by sexist cultural attitudes. My becoming a practicing feminist (as opposed simply to believing in feminist ideals) has involved learning to believe that the lessons I learned as a child—that I was inferior, incapable of accomplishing anything important, that my opinions weren't valuable or important, especially when compared to a man's—are not true and acting as if they aren't true.

I work as a contractor in the field of high technology: an extremely risky and competitive career. I have no job security, I don't know where the next assignment or project will come from, and yet I am very successful at what I do. Part of the reason I get the jobs is that I have confidence that I will get them. Although I work in a technical field in which men predominate, I don't believe that the men who compete with me for contracts are any better than I am. I don't believe they'll get the jobs instead of me. And they usually don't. My confidence in my own abilities allows me to persevere in an environment where many people give up in despair due to the large number of rejections inherent in this kind of work. This confidence comes not entirely from my feminist reading, which, although it laid the groundwork, could not, given my background and expectation of failure, be put into practice, but also from the support and nurture that my master has given me. He believed from the beginning that I could do exceptional things. He knew that what was holding me back was not any lack of ability but my own lousy expectations. He helped me to see myself as a strong and competent woman. He also taught me how to succeed and how not to ignore and brush aside as meaningless past successes. I now feel ever stronger, more competent, and just better about myself than I ever have, and I expect these feelings to grow for a long time to come.

My experience of living within a power-exchange relationship and my acquaintance with other sadomasochists have also provided me with an important skill which gives me an increased sense of mastery over my life and environment. I have acquired a deep insight into the fact that power is a part of all relationships, whether professional, political, or personal, and I use that insight on a daily basis to satisfy more fully my personal and professional feminist ideals.

Most people are unconscious of the primary role that power transactions play in their lives. They don't realize when they are giving power away or when it is cleverly wrested from their grasp. They don't always know when they are taking it from someone else. Being oblivious to the power exchanges that occur in everyday life, people often base their actions and decisions upon false assumptions which ignore an important part of reality. Because dominants and submissives are constantly dealing with power directly and consciously in their primary relationships, it can sometimes be shocking to them that other people don't see this dynamic as clearly as they do. This awareness of interpersonal power dynamics has changed my life profoundly: I know how to handle most people. I can sense how situations are going to develop and therefore can predict when it is realistic to give up and when it is realistic to push on through.

These developing skills have come to my aid often. Once, for example, a manager I did a project for clearly appreciated my skills and experience but occasionally would insist that I had made some obvious mistake when I had not. I realized from the way this drama played itself out (he insisted he was right and at first refused to look at clear evidence showing that his assumptions were incorrect) that I was doing too good a job for his comfort and that he needed to perform this correcting every once in a while to reassure himself that he was still in charge of the project. Understanding this underlying power dynamic allowed me to do two things. I offered minimum resistance and backed down in those cases where his thinking that he was right would not adversely affect our work; this allowed him to feel in charge of the project again. But when the error he was making would have had a strong impact on the success of the project, I calmly stood my ground in spite of his escalating anger and accusations that I had "lost it," and I continued to point out the facts to him until he eventually saw what I was getting at. At heart, this man was rational, and, knowing this, I had the perseverance to wait out the emotional storm until his rationality returned.

Had I been unconscious of the ways in which people use power without knowing what they are doing or why they do it, the kind of behavior exhibited by this manager might have pushed my personal-integrity button (How dare he mistrust me; how dare he doubt my word about this issue!), and I might have walked off the contract and, master permitting, never returned. Knowing what was going on inside his head, however, made my personal indulgence in indignation unnecessary. Thus, oddly, my submissive sexuality has helped me to overcome emotional limitations that were once imposed by my history.

The relationship of my history to my sexuality is mostly obscure.

It must be understood that, although theories—many of them preposterous—abound about the reasons for an individual's unique sexual needs, none of these theories has proven to be generally valid. And so, inevitably, it is futile to try to measure a woman's sexual needs against an arbitrary and unproved standard of psychological "normalcy." Even worse, less humane, is to imagine that an individual's sexual needs have some general political meaning. Dr. Ronald Moglia, the director of the graduate human sexuality program at New York University, says in an interview in *Different Loving: The World of Sexual Dominance and Submission*[7], "There's so much we don't know about how our sexual desires are formed. People often perceive sexual behaviors in a political manner. A lot of our behaviors are as a result of our social-cultural leaning and influences, and certainly, in women, that's a great force. But to then take that and apply it to people who act in a masochistic way—or in any other particular kind of way—makes me question how scientific the observations are, how politically biased the observations are, and what [such people] would say about the sadistic female that's appropriate and the masochistic female that's inappropriate." Nevertheless, the hostility of mainstream society, and of many feminists, to sadomasochists, and particularly to submissive women, is overwhelming.

That's one of the painful ironies of being a female submissive. Even after struggling with all the emotional confusion and political ambiguity engendered in one with strong submissive desires and finally reaching some level of internal resolution, she faces hatred and dismissal coming from most of the people among whom she must live and function. Hostility seems inevitable from an unthinking mainstream that regularly lumps sadomasochism with pederasty and bestiality as utterly beyond the pale—after all, this is the same mainstream that bathes in racism and sexism while denying both and which is rapidly and mindlessly destroying our planet. The hostility of a majority of high-profile feminists, however, is much more difficult to stomach.

Why are so many doctrinaire feminists, including some with high public profiles, so hostile to submissive women?[8] Their explanations, as noted above, center around the idea that the relationships that submissive women enter promote male cultural dominance and that images of submissive women, in sadomasochistic erotica and elsewhere, promote violence toward women. In *Powers of Desire: the Politics of Sexuality*[9], essayist Jessica Benjamin says, "The danger has always been that women and other victims of violence will be blamed or will blame themselves for 'provoking' it. This has led to an attitude of counter-blame: the discussion of erotic domination or rational violence in which participation is voluntary or fantasized seems to some an apology for male violence in general." But the first objection—that dominant-submissive relationships promote male dominance—even if it were true (and I do not believe that it is) denies the importance of the positive experiences of submissive women like myself as we live with and live out our sexual identities. And the second objection—like similar ones raised by censors and reactionaries of many stripes and over many centuries—is unsupported by honest data and is discredited.

I suspect that a low, vile hunger for power masquerades behind all of this righteous concern over the political meaning of my or my submissive sisters' activities and for our personal welfare. There is something incredibly arrogant and frighteningly Third-Reichish about a reasoning that goes "Because my own personal opinion of this form of sexuality is that it is terribly wrong and causes harm, it is therefore terribly wrong for everyone else and should be attacked and repressed."

Feminism, for me, has always been at its core about giving women freedom to make choices for themselves, not about taking that freedom away for their own good. I've had enough of patriarchal society doing that for me; the victim theorists and antipornography feminists of the world trying to deprive me of my right to choose freely the kind of sexuality and lifestyle that will make me happiest are no better. In fact, because they have in a sense hijacked feminism, they are worse. Such people, in their attempts to define and control people like myself who don't fit into their mold of the healthy heterosexual, are, in their need to control and shape others' destinies, simply following in the patriarchy's footsteps, and I will certainly not exchange my hard-won freedom from institutional male power for slavery to an equally odious and jarringly wrong—for me—female power. I want feminism to help me achieve my goals of freedom to choose and freedom to pursue happiness—not deny me them.

In the final analysis, I believe that the pressure that female submissives feel from some feminists stems from a fundamental misunderstanding of the fleeting nature of their political power by those feminists. Barely twenty-five years ago, discussions of feminism and its practical meanings were mostly academic. Today, however, through ideological agitation in academe and a newfound skill at influencing the media and some elected officials by addressing them with the hot-button shorthand that impresses them, feminists have been able to exert a certain effect on practical political dialogue and even to wield some political power. Some of them have quickly begun to use this power to repress, as in the campaigns, successful in some places, to ban erotic and pornographic materials because they are asserted to promote violence toward women. In these campaigns they happily unite on this single issue with the Christian right and other hard-core reactionaries, who have a repressive agenda far more substantial than that of a few self-important feminist ideologues.

What such feminists do not understand is that when their momentary vogue is past, when academe and politicians have lost interest in them and have moved on to the next fascination, the Christian right will still be there, the more powerful for having duped and been supported by some feminists. It is from that Christian right, and not from sadomasochists, that the long-term threat to the emancipation of women really comes. If they have their way, then all of us women, including their current feminist allies, will find ourselves or our daughters returned to an entirely involuntary slavery.

I take my little male cat out each morning to the jungle-garden cradled safely in my arms because outdoors, once the natural paradise for a cat, has become, with the epidemic spread of feline leukemia and feline AIDS, a deadly environment. Likewise, I fear that the lush sadomasochistic jungle in which I am so at home is rapidly becoming too perilous to roam. Currently, my beloved could be prosecuted for what he does to me in almost any jurisdiction in this country without my even bringing a complaint to the authorities. If I were to protest and say that I love and encourage what he does to me, that protest could be ignored, and this utterly unfair prosecution would continue. And the current rapid rightward motion of American politics and its concomitant pressure for ever more draconian punishments—combined with the attention being given to crimes of violence toward women—is darkly foreboding. Thus we submissive women are much less equal than others and have fewer rights under the law, like homosexuals in many jurisdictions. Unlike women satisfied with a conventional sex life, a submissive's body is not her own, and she cannot choose what happens to it; nor is it fully her master's: instead, it belongs to the state, which dictates what can and cannot be done to it, according to political definitions of violence influenced by those who, as women, should be supporting and helping us, not trying to repress us! If we submissives don't replace our rich, wonderful, violent gardens with what would be, for us, the sexual equivalent of a Putt-Putt golf course, we are threatened, should this choice be discovered, with punitive measures taken against the ones we love. And the efforts of certain of those who dare to call themselves feminists are making this condition even more intolerable. What choice have I and submissive women like myself but to reject utterly that which demands our loyalty but betrays our trust and ignores our appeals for open-minded tolerance and support? Although I will always be a woman who supports the causes of women everywhere, there may soon come a time, sadly enough, when I will be too ashamed to call myself a feminist, especially if that term continues to grow synonymous, for women like myself, with "oppressor."

1. Naomi Wolf, *The Beauty Myth* (New York: Doubleday, 1992), 140.
2. Naomi Wolf, *The Beauty Myth* (New York: Doubleday, 1992), 141.
3. Gloria G. Brame, William D. Brame, and Jon Jacobs, *Different Loving: An Exploration of the World of Sexual Dominance and Submission* (New York: Villard, 1993), 10.
4. Pauline Reage, *Story of O*, trans. Sabine d'Estree (New York: Ballantine, 1980).
5. Anne Rice, *Interview With a Vampire* (New York: Ballantine, 1989).
———, *The Vampire Lestat* (New York: Ballantine, 1985).
6. A. N. Roquelaure [Anne Rice], *The Claiming of Sleeping Beauty* (New York: Dutton, 1983).
———, *Beauty's Punishment* (New York: Dutton, 1984).
———, *Beauty's Release* (New York: Dutton, 1985).
7. Gloria G. Brame, William D. Brame, and Jon Jacobs, *Different Loving: An Exploration of the World of Sexual Dominance and Submission* (New York: Villard, 1993), 15.
8. A notable exception to the almost overwhelming feminist response of condemnation of sadomasochism is Jessica Benjamin, whose sympathetic, though flawed, Freudian analysis of the motivations of dominants and submissives (Jessica Benjamin, "Master and Slave: The Fantasy of Erotic Domination" in *Powers of Desire: the Politics of Sexuality*, ed. Ann Snitow, Christine Stansell, & Sharon Thompson [New York: Monthly

Review Press, 1983]) appeared in print over a decade ago. Her analysis of why people choose erotic domination and submission is flawed because it is based entirely on a fictional account of sadomasochism, *Story of O*, which real life-style dominants and submissives often laugh at as being a patently false and misleading, albeit erotically exciting, representation of the complex emotional realities of their relationships. What I find most interesting about Benjamin's analysis is that the environment of feminist hostility that she described so clearly in 1983 is still with us, virtually unchanged except for the fact that some reactionary feminists are now, terrifyingly enough, in a much better political position to act on this irrational hostility.

9. Jessica Benjamin, "Master and Slave: The Fantasy of Erotic Domination" in Powers of Desire: *the Politics of Sexuality*, ed. Ann Snitow, Christine Stansell, & Sharon Thompson (New York: Monthly Review Press, 1983), 282.

sex

Last Rites

This was the last time we had sex. But it was the only time we ever made love.

By Augusten Burroughs
Salon.com / June 28, 2004

I was exhausted. Which isn't even the word for it, really. I was in the midst of my last month with Pighead, only I didn't know it. I was giving him daily injections, flushing his I.V. line, cleaning diarrhea off his legs, counting endless pills and sorting them into the plastic pill box. I was drinking, but not for pleasure. I was drinking at night alone, just because it was my comfort. I knew it was a lousy comfort. But my life was about triage, and drinking was my consistency, dependability, slight warmth. And I knew I'd fucked up everything. Gone through rehab, become clean, now become filthy again. But it didn't matter, because Pighead was sick. And I just had to get through this. Which is what I called it to myself, *this*.

Pighead was dying. And I just wanted to sleep for a very long time.

We were in his bedroom on Perry Street. It was midafternoon, spring, and his mother was in the next room, crammed onto the tiny bench that was built into the wall next to the fireplace. She was sleeping, the Windex bottle tucked under her arm, a roll of paper towels as a pillow. She was snoring. And I was certain she wasn't dreaming. I slept the same way in those days: hard, dreamless. It was efficient sleep, nearly German. It was diesel Mercedes truck sleep—there to get the job done, not to be luxurious. From my position on the bed, I could just see her feet.

Pighead was sleeping, too. Finally. He'd been awake the previous night, awake coughing and bleeding out of his holes and finally, now, he was napping. I wasn't napping. But I was beside him, his I.V. line stretched across my chest. The I.V. pump was on my side of the bed because I knew he might knock it over, by accident. His coordination was gone now, along with much of his mass. Only a gaunt face, protruding lips, enormous teeth, and sticklike arms and legs remained. He looked famished, and was. But not for food.

I was next to him because I needed to listen to him breathe. Sometimes, mucus lodged in his throat and his breathing stopped; then he choked. So I was there, listening.

It was my way of controlling the situation. It was my way of insisting that he continue to live.

He woke up after an hour. "Was I asleep?" I told him yes. "For a little while. Do you feel better?" I sat up, leaned on my elbow.

He swallowed, frowned slightly. "I don't know. I don't think so." He spoke slowly, which had the effect of making him sound less intelligent than he actually was. And I wondered, has it damaged his brain forever?

Because I was still thinking things like "forever." I was unaware of where, exactly, I was in time.

"Oh, God," he sighed.

And the way he said this, the way the words—so trite—contained so much weight and fatigue and crushing sadness and exhaustion. I knew what he meant. He meant, "Nothing has gone according to plan. How did I get here? When will it end? Why isn't there something to cure this?" He was saying something that could never be said in two words.

I reached over and I put my hand on his crotch. This move startled me. I hadn't known I'd do this. I'd only been aware of a certain longing, of a pit I wanted only to cover. I put my hand on his crotch as though it was a time capsule and could take me back.

You'd think I slapped him hard across the face. He turned fast to look at me, his eyes large with the surprise of it. And something else. Confusion? I wasn't sure. And then I was sure. I massaged what I felt under my hand. The look in his eyes was just exactly this: disbelief.

He got hard.

It had been almost a year since we'd had sex. This, for us, was quite a record. Our other record was twelve times in twenty-four hours. That was on Christmas 1993.

He grinned a little. "The bruised banana still works," he said, somewhat marveling at the fact. Everything else was broken. But this still worked. "It hasn't done that for a while." He looked at my fingers working his zipper. Then he glanced at me and I saw something that made me feel just tiny with sadness: He was grateful.

He closed his eyes. He fell asleep so quickly I thought he'd simply died.

I moved my hand up to his forehead and I traced his eyebrows with my finger. "My Pighead," I whispered.

This was the last time we had sex. But it was the only time we ever made love. Only I didn't know the difference at the time.

About the Contributors

Jeannette Angell is a novelist and writer who currently lives in New England. She is the author of *Légende,* which has been described as a lesbian fairy tale, *Wings, Flight,* and *The Illusionist.* She has also written two memoirs: *Callgirl* and *Madam.* More information is available at www.JeannetteAngell.com.

Christine Aziz has spent most of her working life as a freelance journalist for both British and international publications, focusing on gender and humanitarian issues and has reported from around the world, including Iraq, Afghanistan, India, Africa, and Europe. She graduate with a degree in homeopathy in 2003, and now works as a homeopath in Dorset, England, but makes the occasional foray into journalism. Her first novel, *The Olive Readers,* is to be published in the UK by Pan Macmillan in November 2005. Christine remains a Londoner at heart and has two grown-up children and is a grandmother.

Dave Barry is a humor columnist for the *Miami Herald.* His column appears in more than five hundred newspapers in the United States and abroad. In 1988 he won the Pulitzer Prize for Commentary. Many people are still trying to figure out how this happened. Dave has also written a total of twenty-five books, two of which were used as the basis for the CBS TV sitcom *Dave's World,* in which Harry Anderson played a much taller version of Dave. Dave plays lead guitar in a literary rock band called the Rock Bottom Remainders, whose other members include Stephen King, Amy Tan, Ridley Pearson, and Mitch Albom. They are not musically skilled, but they are extremely loud. Dave has also made many TV appearances, including one on the David Letterman show where he proved that it is possible to set fire to a pair of men's underpants with a Barbie doll. He lives in Miami, Florida, with his wife, Michelle, a sportswriter. He has a son, Rob, and a daughter, Sophie, neither of whom thinks he's funny.

Toni Bentley danced with George Balanchine's New York City Ballet for ten years. She is the author of *Winter Season: A Dancer's Journal, Holding On to the Air: The Autobiography of Suzanne Farrell* (by Suzanne Farrell with Toni Bentley), *Costumes by Karinska,* and *Sisters of Salome*—all *New York Times* Notable Books. She has also written articles for numerous publications including the *New York Times, Los Angeles Times, Rolling Stone,* the *New Republic,* and the *New York Review of Books.* Her most recent book *The Surrender: An Erotic Memoir* was named one of the 100 Notable Books of 2004 by the *New York Times.*

Augusten Burroughs is the #1 best-selling author of *Magical Thinking, Dry, Running with Scissors,* and *Sellevision.* His books have been published in fifteen countries and both *Sellevision* and *Running with Scissors* are in production for film. His writing has appeared in newspapers and magazines around the world. In addition, he writes a monthly column for *Details* magazine and is a regular contributor to National Public Radio's *Morning Edition.* He lives in New York City and Western Massachusetts.

Sherry F. Colb is a professor at Rutgers Law School in Newark, New Jersey. Colb has taught courses in criminal procedure, evidence, mental health law, and feminist legal studies. She has published articles in a variety of law reviews, including Stanford, Columbia, and Georgetown, in areas such as Fourth Amendment privacy, Fourteenth Amendment liberty from physical confinement, and the role of personal character in criminal culpability. She has been a law professor since 1993, prior to which she worked for two years as a law clerk, first to Judge Wilfred Feinberg of the United States Court of Appeals for the Second Circuit (1991–1992), and then to Associate Justice Harry A. Blackmun of the United States Supreme Court (1992–1993). In 1991, Colb received her JD magna cum laude from Harvard Law School. In 1988, Colb graduated from the second co-ed class at Columbia College, valedictorian, summa cum laude and junior Phi Beta Kappa.

Gretchen Cook is a freelance writer and radio reporter in Washington, D.C. The former White House correspondent's work has appeared in the *New York Times,* the *Washington Post,* and on National Public Radio.

Ben Ehrenreich's work has appeared in *LA Weekly,* the *Village Voice, McSweeney's,* the *New York Times,* and many other publications. His first novel *The Suitors,* will be published in the spring of 2006. He lives in Los Angeles.

Born in Sydney, Australia, **Paul Fischer** has been a film journalist for over twenty years. Beginning his journalistic career at the University of new South Wales, Paul has edited Australian magazines such as *Preview,* and has contributed to many daily national and regional newspapers. At the end of 1999, Paul relocated to Los Angeles, to be with his then fiancée, an L.A. local. He has contributed interviews with Hollywood's elites to some of America's most significant movie Web sites, including the hugely successful *Dark Horizons.* Still married, Paul and his wife live in the San Fernando Valley, not far from Universal Studios

David France was senior investigative editor at *Newsweek* until 2003. He has written two books, most recently *Our Fathers,* an investigation into the Catholic Church sexual abuse crisis that was published in 2004 to critical acclaim. Several films have developed from his work, including the landmark *Thanks of a Grateful Nation,* a controversial Showtime miniseries about the first Gulf War, the Peabody Award winner *Soldier's Girl,* about a private's murder, and this year's *Our Fathers.* Originally from Kalamazoo, Michigan, France now lives in New York City and the Catskills, in upstate New York.

Rabbi Marc Gellman holds a BA from the University of Wisconsin and a PhD in philosophy from Northwestern University. He was ordained by the Hebrew Union College-Jewish Institute of Religion in 1972 and has served Temple Beth Torah in Melville, New York, as its senior rabbi since 1981. Rabbi Gellman is a past president of the New York Board of Rabbis. He also writes a weekly opinion column, "The Spiritual State" for *Newsweek.com.* With his friend Monsignor Thomas Hartman he writes a nationally syndicated newspaper column called "The God Squad." Rabbi Gellman has written several award-winning children's books: *Does God Have a Big Toe?*, *God's Mailbox*, and *Always Wear Clean Underwear.* With Monsignor Hartman, he published *Where Does God Live?* (which won a Christopher Award) *Lost and Found*, *Bad Stuff in the News*, *Religion for Dummies*, and *How Do You Spell God?* Their HBO animated special of the same name received a Peabody Award. Gellman and Hartman host a cable television program called *The God Squad* and appear regularly on many TV news programs and on *Imus in the Morning*.

Sebastian Horsley is an artist, writer, and failed suicide. He lives in Soho, London. (Editor's note: Horsley achieved notoriety by having himself crucified "for his art" in the Philippines in 2000.)

Sarah Klein couldn't figure out what the hell she wanted to do in life, so she decided she might as well become a writer. She first came to *Metro Times*, Detroit's largest alternative newsweekly, as a gossip columnist. Five years later, she is the culture editor. In 2004, she won first place in the features category of the Michigan Press Association awards. She lives in Detroit with a cat with no tail.

Steven Kurutz was born and raised in central Pennsylvania and educated at Pennsylvania State University. As a writer, he is often drawn to topics and themes that fall into the loose category of "Americana," and his work has appeared in such publications as *Details*, *Spin*, and *Playboy*. He is a regular contributor to the *New York Times*. He lives in Brooklyn, New York.

Jonathan Margolis is the author of the 2004 book O: *The Intimate History of the Orgasm* (Grove Atlantic) and lives in London, where in addition to writing books, he is a feature writer for the *Independent* and the *Financial Times* magazine, and a contributor to *Time* magazine. His 2001 book on futurology, *A Brief History of Tomorrow,* was published in the U.S. by Bloomsbury USA. He is currently working on a history of persuasion and mind control—including plenty on the secrets of seduction.

Ron Nyswaner has written many films including the award-winning and groundbreaking *Soldier's Girl* and *Philadelphia.* His screenplay for *The Painted Veil* has gone into production starring Naomi Watts and Edward Norton. *Blue Days, Black Nights: A Memoir,* his first book, has been nominated for a Lambda Literary Award. He lives in Woodstock, New York.

Alasdair Palmer is public policy editor of the *Sunday Telegraph.* He is also a consultant for HBO Films in Los Angeles. He won the Charles Douglas Home Essay Prize in 2002. He is married with two children and lives in London.

Polly Peachum is a pervert living in Atlanta, Georgia. She has no professional publications other than her Web site http://www.submissivewomenspeak.net, but she publishes erotic fiction on the Web under the name Unda. Cruica. Eximius. Her stories are currently showcased at http://www.sandm.com. Polly's recently deceased husband, Jon E. Jacobs, coauthored *Different Loving: The World of Sexual Dominance and Submission* (Random House/Villard, 1994).

Nigel Planer has written two novels: *The Right Man* and *Faking It;* the nonfiction *A Good Enough Dad;* and the spoof theatrical biography *I, An Actor* (with Christopher Douglas). He was a cofounder of

London's Comedy Store and Comic Strip clubs and went on to star in the classic TV shows *The Young Ones* and *The Comic Strip Presents.* He starred in the original London production of Queen's *We Will Rock You* at the Dominion theater and the original casts of *Evita* and *Chicago,* the smash hit political satire *Feelgood,* and the takeover cast of Ayckbourn's *Man of the Moment* where he replaced Michael Gambon. In the guise of Neil the Hippy, Nigel has twice topped the British pop charts, receiving silver and gold records and winning a Brit Award in 1985. *On the Ceiling,* his first play, opened at Birmingham Rep in May 2005. He lives in central London.

Katha Pollitt is a poet, essayist, and columnist for the *Nation.* Her work has appeared in many magazines, including the *New Yorker,* the *Atlantic,* the *New York Times,* and the *Guardian.* Her most recent books are *Reasonable Creatures* and *Subject to Debate.* She has won many prizes and awards for her writing, including two National Magazine Awards, a National Book Critics Circle Award, and a Guggenheim fellowship. She lives in New York City.

Harry Reems achieved legendary status with his appearance in the classic porn film *Deep Throat.* Succumbing to alcoholism, he eventually cleaned up his act, found God, and moved to Park City, Utah, where he now has a successful career in real estate.

Steven Rinella lives in Miles City, Montana. His writing has appeared in many publications, including *Outside, Nerve, DoubleTake,* the *New Yorker, Playboy Germany, American Heritage,* and *The Best American Travel Writing 2003.* His first book *A Scavenger's Guide to Haute Cuisine,* will be published by Miramax Books in March 2006.

Julia Scheeres has an MA in journalism from USC and has written for the *Los Angeles Times, LA Weekly,* the *San Francisco Chronicle,* and *Wired News,* among other outlets. Her memoir *Jesus Land,* will be published by Counterpoint Press in October. She lives in San Francisco.

Amy Sohn is the author of two novels: *My Old Man,* which was optioned for the screen by Focus Features, and *Run Catch Kiss,* which was published in five languages. She is a contributing editor at *New York* magazine, where she writes the "Mating" column. She is also the author of the *New York Times* best-selling *Sex and the City: Kiss and Tell,* the companion guide to the hit television show. She created the Oxygen television show *Avenue Amy* and has written two screenplays, *Spin the Bottle* and *Pagans.* She was raised in Brooklyn, where she still lives today.

David Steinberg writes a monthly column, "Comes Naturally," focusing on the culture and politics of sex. Since 1999, he has also been taking fine art photographs of couples of all ages, genders, and sexual orientations, engaged in sex. His books include *Photo Sex, The Erotic Impulse,* and *Erotic by Nature.* He lives in Santa Cruz, California.

Barry Yeoman is a freelance journalist based in Durham, North Carolina, and is a frequent contributor to *Discover, Mother Jones, AARP: The Magazine,* and *Attaché.* In 2001, *Columbia Journalism Review* named him one of "the best unsung investigative journalists working in print in the United States." His work is available at barryyeoman.com.

sex

About the Editor

Mitzi Szereto is the author of *Erotic Fairy Tales: A Romp through the Classics, highway,* and the M. S. Valentine erotic novels; and editor of *Wicked: Sexy Tales of Legendary Lovers* and the Erotic Travel Tales anthology series. She's the pioneer of the erotic writing workshop in the UK and Europe, conducting them from the prestigious Cheltenham Festival of Literature to the Greek islands and Big Sur, California. She has been featured in publications ranging from the *Sunday Telegraph* (London), the *Independent* (London), *Family Circle, Writing* magazine, and *Forum* to Bravo UK Television, Telecinco TV 5 (Madrid), and BBC Radio. Her work as an anthology editor has earned her the American Society of Authors and Writers' Meritorious Achievement Award. Her fiction and nonfiction have appeared in publications worldwide. Originally from the U.S., she now lives in England. Her next book *Dying for It: Tales of Sex and Death,* will be out in Spring 2006.

Permissions

"The Big Ooooooohh!" by Jonathan Margolis. © Jonathan Margolis, 2004. • "Andrea Dworkin 1946-2005" by Katha Pollitt. © Katha Pollitt. • "The Sex Files" by Ben Ehrenreich. © 2004 by Ben Ehrenreich; originally published by *LA Weekly*, Dec. 10, 2004. • "The Brothel Creeper" by Sebastian Horsley. © Sebastian Horsley. • "Performance Anxiety" by Steven Rinella. Originally published on *Nerve.com.* Reprinted with permission. © Steven Rinella and *Nerve.com.* • "Focus 19" by Alasdair Palmer. © *Sunday Telegraph*, 2004. • "Forbidden Science" by Barry Yeoman. © 2004 by Barry Yeoman. Originally published in *Discover*, Aug. 2004. • "Head Case" by Amy Sohn. © 2004, Amy Sohn. • "Building the Better Vagina: Does This Make My Labia Look Fat?" by Sarah Klein. © Sarah Klein and *Metro Times*, Detroit, MI; www.metrotimes.com, 2005. • Excerpt from *The Surrender: An Erotic Memoir* by Toni Bentley. © 2004 by Toni Bentley. Reprinted with permission of HarperCollins Publishers. • "Exclusive Interview: Harry Reems" by Paul Fischer. © Paul Fischer, 2005. • "Sex, Guys, and Fruit Flies" by Dave Barry. © Dave Barry, 2004. • "When Oral Sex Results in a Pregnancy" by Sherry F. Colb. This column originally appeared on *Findlaw.com.* © Sherry F. Colb. • "Toy Story" by Steven Kurutz. Originally published on *Nerve.com.* Reprinted with permission. © 2004 Steven

Kurutz and Nerve.com. • "Deep Gidget" by Rabbi Marc Gellman. © Marc Gellman. • "Callgirl" by Jeannette Angell © The Permanent Press, Sag Harbor, NY. • "The Invention of Patient Zero" by David France, *New York Magazine,* May 2, 2005. • "Tahitillation" by Nigel Planer. © Nigel Planer, 2004. • "XXXchurch Wants No More XXX" by Julia Scheeres. Reprinted from *Wired News,* www.wired.com. © 2005, Lycos, Inc. All rights reserved. • "The Battle Over Birth Control" by Gretchen Cook. This article first appeared in *Salon.com,* at http://www.Salon.com. An online version remains in the *Salon* archives. Reprinted with permission. • "Now I Feel Whole Again" by Christine Aziz. First published in *The Independent* February 15, 2005, © *The Independent.* • Excerpt from *Blue Days, Black Nights* by Ron Nyswaner. © 2004 by Ron Nyswaner. Reprint by permission. • "Faces of Ecstasy" by David Steinberg. © 2004, David Steinberg. • "Violence in the Garden" by Polly Peachum. © Polly Peachum, 1995–2005. • "Last Rites" by Augusten Burroughs. This article first appeared in *Salon.com,* at http://www.Salon.com. An online version remains in the *Salon* archives. Reprinted with permission.